Deepti Priya Mehrotra graduated from St. Stephen's College, and has a doctorate in political science from Delhi University. She carried out independent research supported by fellowships awarded by India Foundation for the Arts, the MacArthur Foundation, and the Indian Council for Philosophical Research. Her interests include feminist thought, people's movements, education and theatre. She works with several civil society organizations as an activist and researcher.

Deepti coordinated Charkha, a developmental communication network, for some years, and currently teaches Developmental Communication and Traditional Media as well as Gender and Schooling at Lady Shri Ram College, Delhi University.

She writes in English and Hindi. Her publications include *Home Truths: Stories of Single Mothers* (Penguin, 2003), *Ekal Maa* (Books for Change, 2002), *Bharatiya Mahila Andolan* (BFC, 2001), *Western Philosophy and Indian Feminism* (1998) and *A Passion for Freedom: Kisanin Jaggi Devi* (Indira Gandhi National Centre for the Arts, 2005).

She lives in New Delhi with her daughter.

Gulab Bai
The Queen of Nautanki Theatre

DEEPTI PRIYA MEHROTRA

PENGUIN BOOKS

PENGUIN BOOKS
Published by the Penguin Group
Penguin Books India Pvt. Ltd, 11 Community Centre, Panchsheel Park, New Delhi 110 017, India
Penguin Group (USA) Inc., 375 Hudson Street, New York, New York 10014, USA
Penguin Group (Canada), 90 Eglinton Avenue East, Suite 700, Toronto, Ontario, M4P 2Y3, Canada (a division of Pearson Penguin Canada Inc.)
Penguin Books Ltd, 80 Strand, London WC2R 0RL, England
Penguin Ireland, 25 St Stephen's Green, Dublin 2, Ireland (a division of Penguin Books Ltd)
Penguin Group (Australia), 250 Camberwell Road, Camberwell, Victoria 3124, Australia (a division of Pearson Australia Group Pty Ltd)
Penguin Group (NZ), cnr Airborne and Rosedale Roads, Albany, Auckland 1310, New Zealand (a division of Pearson New Zealand Ltd)
Penguin Group (South Africa) (Pty) Ltd, 24 Sturdee Avenue, Rosebank, Johannesburg 2196, South Africa

Penguin Books Ltd, Registered Offices: 80 Strand, London WC2R 0RL, England

First published by Penguin Books India 2006

Copyright © Deepti Priya Mehrotra 2006
India Foundation for the Arts supported the research for this book.

All rights reserved
10 9 8 7 6 5 4 3 2 1

For sale in the Indian Subcontinent and Singapore only

ISBN-13: 978-0-14310-043-0   ISBN-10: 0-14310-043-2

Typeset in AGaramond by S.R. Enterprises, New Delhi
Printed at DeUnique Printers, New Delhi

This book is sold subject to the condition that it shall not, by way of trade or otherwise, be lent, resold, hired out, or otherwise circulated without the publisher's prior written consent in any form of binding or cover other than that in which it is published and without a similar condition including this condition being imposed on the subsequent purchaser and without limiting the rights under copyright reserved above, no part of this publication may be reproduced, stored in or introduced into a retrieval system, or transmitted in any form or by any means (electronic, mechanical, photocopying, recording or otherwise), without the prior written permission of both the copyright owner and the above-mentioned publisher of this book.

Contents

ACKNOWLEDGEMENTS vii

PART I: SETTING THE STAGE

1. THE LEGEND 3
2. THROUGH OTHERS' EYES 15

PART II: GULAB'S STORY

3. NOMADIC PAST 35
4. GULAB IS BORN 51
5. MUSIC IN THE AIR 57
6. VILLAGE DEITY 63
7. GOING TO THE FAIR 68
8. IN A MALE BASTION 77
9. THE WORLD OF TRAVELLING THEATRE 88
10. KINGS, QUEENS AND BANDITS 97
11. A NATIONALISTIC STREAK 105
12. RISING PROSPERITY 113
13. ONE MAN'S OBSESSION 124
14. BACK ON STAGE 134
15. FINE-TUNING 144
16. A RARE BALANCE 158

17. THE GREAT GULAB THEATRE COMPANY **173**
18. SWITCHING ROLES: QUEEN NO MORE **181**
19. THE SHOW MUST GO ON **190**
20. COEXISTING WITH CINEMA **198**
21. LIFE CYCLE OF A BUTTERFLY **208**
22. A CULTURAL ICON **220**
23. INTO OTHER WORLDS **233**

PART III: NAUTANKI TODAY

24. UNEMPLOYED HEROES AND MUSICIANS **243**
25. SIDE-HEROINES AND BAR-GIRLS **264**
26. DHRUPAD TO DISCO **288**

LIST OF INTERVIEWS **304**
NOTES **306**
REFERENCES **311**

Acknowledgements

India Foundation for the Arts provided a fellowship that enabled me to carry out intensive research for writing this book. I must thank everybody at IFA, in particular Anjum Hasan and Anmol Vellani, for their unwavering support and enthusiasm for the project.

I am grateful to the editors who have contributed to the book: especially Ravi Singh and Manjula Lal.

Veteran theatre-person Rati Bartholomew encouraged me to pen the proposal—she thought it was important to write such a story. The organization Alaripu first exposed me to the Nautanki form; I take this opportunity to thank Tripurari Sharma, Shivji and Bhurji (late Bhanwar Gopal) for all I learnt from, and because of, them.

A warm thank you to Rashmi, of the NGO Sanskara, Kanpur, for her invaluable assistance in research during 2002-03. This work has been immeasurably enriched by her keen involvement. Mukesh, Rashmi's husband and colleague, offered ready support for my project, as did Neelam Chaturvedi, director of Mahila Manch, Kanpur.

I am indebted to Gulab's daughters Madhu and Asha for their generous and frank sharing. Gulab's sisters Paati Kali and Sukhbadan added to the treasures steadily building up in my notebooks and audio-cassettes. Gulab's niece Munni Bai gave a great deal of her time, escorting us to the family villages Balpurva and Tera Mallu. In Balpurva,

Shaila provided access to priceless family lore. Assorted relatives, Nautanki artistes and musicians gifted me with bits and pieces of memory—anecdotes, fragments, nostalgic descriptions and thoughts. What they shared has been absorbed into the fabric of Gulab's story, as related here.

The Sangeet Natak Akademi, New Delhi, allowed access to its photographs, audio-visual archives and the books in its library. Shrabani Mukherji, head of the music section, and Prithpal Singh of the photo-documentation centre were particularly helpful. The Sangeet Natak Akademi, Uttar Pradesh, provided access to literature and recordings. Tabla maestro Kamal Kant Sharma, Shah Music Centre in Chandni Chowk, New Delhi, and music aficionado Jyoti Swaroop Pandey helped locate sixteen songs sung by Gulab Bai. I have listened to those songs often during the course of writing this book.

I'd like to thank my daughter, my parents, the rest of my family, and all the friends who have heard endless tales of Gulab Bai and my adventures while excavating her life. Special thanks to cultural-anthropologist Kirin Narayan and film-maker Sehjo Singh, both of whom read an early draft and provided useful feedback for the socio-historical and storytelling dimensions of this work.

I hope the book lives up to the expectations of all those who have contributed to its making. The flaws and shortcomings that remain are, of course, entirely mine.

PART 1
SETTING THE STAGE

1

The Legend

Imagine a village near Kannauj in the mid-1930s: a Nautanki performance of *Raja Harishchandra* is on. The stage is a waist-high wooden platform set amid open fields. Villagers huddle on the ground, eyes glued to the makeshift stage. The entire village has turned out—women, men and children, rich and poor, upper-caste and Dalit.

The play begins with a flourish of drums: the beat of nagaras. The cast of five or six gathers on stage, their ghungroos making a *chham-chham* sound, and sing an invocation to devi Saraswati. The Ranga sings a dramatic synopsis of the story and introduces the characters. Each actor performs multiple roles. Gulab Bai—then fifteen years old—the only woman in the company, is the star attraction. She enacts the heroine's role. When, as Rani Taramati, she sings a plaintive song, the audience is sad. When she cries over the dead body of her son Rohtas, everybody is in tears.

Two petromax lamps, pumped from time to time, provide the only artificial lighting. A fire, lit near the stage, keeps the nagaras warm. From time to time both nagaras—one kettledrum large, the other small—have to be moistened, to preserve sound quality.

Dialogue delivery is crisp. The actors, trained in classical music, can hold a note for three or four minutes at a stretch.

The unbroken *taan* seems like an eternity to enthralled listeners. There is no microphone, yet the voices carry clear and loud. The audience is mesmerized by the events unfolding on stage, as scene melts into scene. Nobody leaves for home until the show is over, even as the rising sun sends a shaft of light over the tired actors.

*

Nautanki drama was larger than life. The precursor to Bollywood extravaganzas, it was a world of glamour, glitz and pure fantasy. Its tales towered above the workaday lives of people who gazed, wonderstruck, at the spectacles unfolding before their eyes. Song, dance, romance and melodrama wove many a magic spell.

Popular dramas performed in this genre were peopled with historical figures like Raja Harishchandra, who gave up wealth, kingdom, wife and child for the sake of keeping his word; Majnu, who went crazy for love; Rani Taramati, who too became crazy, but for her child; Laila, who was torn between loyalty and love; and Sultana Daku who robbed the rich and gave to the poor.

A folk form of entertainment among the Dalit classes, Nautanki rose to prominence during the latter half of the nineteenth century. Endless upheavals including wars, intrigues, exploitation and resistance were the order of the day in north India. Small peasants were increasingly impoverished by the excesses of zamindars and talukdars under the overarching tyranny of the British Raj. The region boasts a rich history of subaltern struggles; yet conditions altered only for the worse.

Within this melee, fantasy held a place of honour. People were exhausted by their daily lives. Fantasy provided a means of escape. Ordinary people often got

A typical Nautanki performance, with the musicians in an enclosure just in front of the stage

together and put up Nautanki troupes in their humble homes, providing simple food and warm hospitality in return for a night's entertainment.

Traders, zamindars and petty British officials also provided patronage to maintain performers and put up shows. They saw it as a narcotic for the masses. It would entertain and distract, help release frustrations and soften the edge of untold miseries.

Nautanki dramas were fine-tuned, its protagonists highly skilled. Few props were used, yet actors created forests, rivers, battles and royal courts by the sorcery of their art. The same spot would be transformed into a different place by a word or a gesture. The Ranga or Sutradhar built up a montage of varied dramatic episodes and threaded them together like fine beads in a storyline.

As the years went by, Nautankis became increasingly elaborate with ornate sets, sophisticated props and gaudy costumes. Drop curtains and painted sceneries were used. These dramas continued to draw crowds through the 1940s and the 1950s.

In the free space of unfettered imagination, Nautankis presented dilemmas people could relate to. They found some of their own concerns mirrored on stage. The dramas were like a distorting mirror—stretching figures, exaggerating details, making everyday concerns look bizarre, funny, grand and interesting.

The dramas worked at several levels. Some encouraged a sense of high moral duty, true love and loyalty. At the same time tensions, conflicts and varied points of view were communicated. Through play the audience could begin debating deeper social, political and ethical questions, bringing these out from subliminal spaces into the light of day.

For nearly a century Nautanki reigned as north India's most popular form of entertainment. Gulab Bai shone as its brightest star, its foremost exponent.

*

Gulab Bai began acting in Nautankis in the early 1930s and rose to dizzy heights within a few years. By the time she died in 1996, she was widely acknowledged as the uncrowned queen of Nautanki. She was a celebrity, a rags-to-riches story who had won some of the highest honours awarded to artistes by the government.

Exploring Gulab's life means seeking to understand the person she was as well as the legend built around her. No doubt Gulab Bai was exceptional. She acted well, sang even better, and proved successful. A woman born in a poor household, she earned widespread fame and glory.

People speak of her in tones of awe. She commanded respect within the cultural enclaves of north India's artists and musicians. Beloved of her audiences, she was feted and celebrated by the cultural elite. Later in her life, she became a cultural icon in twentieth-century India.

I unravel her story not only for its intrinsic charm but also for what it tells us about the complex dynamics of popular culture. Stars are made and unmade in a world of tinsel, paint and make-believe. Gulab was a real person surrounded by a world of shadows and appearances.

Gulab Bai won recognition for her talents as a singer. No doubt she sang beautifully. Her voice had a unique timbre—yet she was not unqualifiedly the 'best'. Her long-time accompanist, tabla and nagara player Rashid Khan, once confessed, 'Bai never understood ragas. She thought Nautanki ragas are different from other ragas!'[1]

Gulab was a talented actress, but not necessarily more talented than all others. As a company owner Gulab Bai was competent, but, again, not always the most competent. Barely literate, she was ill-informed about many aspects of life and the world. She was often frazzled and self-absorbed. A knowledgeable insider in the Nautanki world alleged, 'Gulab Bai never helped other artistes. She only looked after her own interests.'[2]

On the other hand family and fellow artistes hold on to her image as a fixed pole in the midst of choppy seas. Saajan, an actor who worked in Gulab's company, poignantly remarked, 'After Bai we have nobody. We have lost the one who rowed our boat.'[3]

Cultural mandarins zeroed in on Gulab Bai as one fixed point they could focus attention on. They offered her awards and accolades and paid lip service to 'the greatest folk art of Uttar Pradesh', but did little to ensure its survival.

Somewhere along the way, Gulab Bai came to symbolise Nautanki. The roots of this identification lie in humble village fairs where people flocked to see her on stage. Much later the government recognized her as representing the lok-kala Nautanki. In a grudging, guilty way, the elite have tried to pay homage to a people's art form. At the same time the form has been reduced to an image, and relegated to the hoary past. One figure was picked out, a halo arranged around her head, and she was installed as a symbol that dazzles even while the art itself is dying.

In this sense Gulab Bai became part of the problem, even as she sought to be part of the solution. Her image was manipulated so that she seemed to be under the patronage of the state, whereas in fact the same state, occupied with other priorities, neglected and abandoned the Nautanki form.

The legend of Gulab Bai serves varied interests. Most Nautanki artistes today are impoverished and out of work. For them her towering figure has become a repository of hope, faith and a potential that, once realized, could perhaps be realized once again. Her memory is constantly refreshed and enlivened, the many strands washed, kept clean and glowing. The tapestry is ever woven anew, pulled by lingering fingers of affection, awe and nostalgia. Her people will not let her memory die or fade, for if it did, so would their last hope. So long as her image is alive and aglow, they feel Nautanki too may revive.

Swirling about in clouds of fantasy, these Nautanki artistes help me access Gulab's world. Part of what they tell me is definitely fantasy. Living between dream and reality, they conjure vivid images out of airy nothings. They have a way with words—after all, they have been adept at constructing entire worlds through dialogue and song, poetry and metre.

Having dwelt briefly in the limelight, they are condemned to long years in the dark. This darkness has provided fertile space for nurturing the memory of Gulab Bai.

*

In telling the story of Gulab and the story of Nautanki, it will be difficult—often impossible—to demarcate fact from fiction. Gulab Bai left no written record of her life and times. And even if she had, it would have presented only one person's point of view. Each person who spoke to me, or whose writings I read, revealed certain aspects of the truth. Often there were contradictory versions and conflicting accounts of the same incident or phenomenon.

In attempting to write the history of a legend, each version is significant. The truth may lie somewhere in the interstices of the various versions. For instance, Gulab Bai might have been a brilliant singer without strictly knowing what a raga is. An intuitive grasp of music might have sufficed.

We are privileged to look in from several levels, through different windows, gaining access to varied scenes in a colourful life. As I record a vanished past, we may perhaps salvage something that has meaning for us in the present, and future.

*

Year after year, decade after decade, *Raja Harishchandra* was played out on the Nautanki stage. *Raja Harishchandra*, by Dadasaheb Phalke, was the first silent film made entirely in India. Released in 1913 at the Coronation Theatre, Bombay, it 'built the Indian idiom for the new language of cinema'[4]. This language was close kin to the language of Nautanki theatre.

In select sites of north India, Nautanki troupes still stage *Raja Harishchandra* on special days, for a discerning audience of local aficionados. The Nautanki still flowers. It flowers in certain rustic enclaves, but also in wildly extravagant screen avatars. Its royal lineage has given birth to screen Lailas, Taramatis and several other heroines. Early Bollywood was critically influenced by Nautanki and related operatic forms. Films borrowed plot, storylines, music, lyrics, acting styles, local humour and idiom from folk theatre.

Today's sparkling item girls and beleaguered bar-girls have some history in common with Nautanki. In between scenes, the rustic audience would be regaled by special song-and-dance sequences. Some were romantic; all were erotic, many were salacious. Gulab was one of the first women to dance and sing thus, for public consumption.

Her ancestry lives on, taking fresh and fantastical shapes—on screen and stage, and in unknown hearts and minds.

*

On 8 March 1997 I saw a Nautanki performed by the Great Gulab Theatre Company. It was a new production called *Teen Betiyan urf Dehleez ke Paar*.[5] A few thousand women and a fair sprinkling of men and children gathered at the venue—an open ground in Garadiyapurva, Kanpur. A colourful shamiana sheltered the audience. The stage was an elevated platform with a red velvet draw-curtain and a few well-appointed stage props.

The drama began as a Nautanki must: with the mesmerizing beat of the nagara. The cast walked in gracefully, greeted the audience with a low bow and sang an invocation to Saraswati. Harmonium and tabla provided musical accompaniment. The Ranga—a tall, vivacious middle-aged woman with false eyelashes, long hair and a love-curl on her forehead—described the storyline and introduced the characters. The audience—largely from slums, working-class neighbourhoods and nearby villages—was absorbed in the events unfolding on stage. The play was action-packed, with quicksilver movements, lively acting and melodious singing.

The form unfolding on stage was aesthetically pleasing, energetic and enormously powerful. I was intimately familiar with street theatre and the sheer vitality of live performing. In 1988 I had helped Mahila Manch, Kanpur, put up a street play based on the recent joint suicide of three sisters in their city. The play evoked strong responses wherever it was performed. The Nautanki *Teen Betiyan urf Dehleez ke Paar* was based on the same tragic incident. Unlike the starkly realistic street play however, the Nautanki production was replete with dance, song, humour and melodrama. The story changed: one sister committed suicide, the second ran away from home to become a professional dancer, and the third married a man chosen by her parents. This man neglected her because of his ongoing liaison with a danseuse. This danseuse turned out to be the second sister. Eventually the two sisters met and decided to live together, abandoning the fickle man. The Nautanki music was mesmerizing, the acting polished. The sheer colour, vigour and artistry of the performance kept people glued to their seats, at the same time inducing them to question entrenched social practices.

During 1996 I'd spent some time with a Khayal group in Rajasthan, witnessing rehearsals and performances of *Meera Bai*. Khayal is a folk form strongly resembling

Nautanki. One striking difference is that there are no female Khayal performers. Umed Khan, a shy village lad, had acted as Meera Bai. Cross-gender acting added a special piquancy to the Khayal shows.

Nautanki and Khayal are earthy genres, though rooted in classical aesthetics. Plot and characters are exaggerated. There is an element of burlesque. They have a great deal of 'masala': romance, ribaldry, melodrama and passions running riot.

I found myself strangely fascinated by the Nautanki form. The beat of the nagara gripped me. The spectacle on stage had me in its thrall. That's when I began wondering about Gulab Bai, who had spent a lifetime doing Nautankis.

*

Whenever *Teen Betiyan urf Dehleez ke Paar* was performed by the Great Gulab Theatrical Company, a large framed photograph of a portly bespectacled woman was placed on stage prior to the show. A member of the company garlanded the photograph and made a brief speech dedicating the performance to her memory. This silent image was the legendary Gulab Bai.

Gulab Bai died in 1996. I could never meet her. I was scheduled to visit her in Kanpur in June of that year, but postponed my trip because she was ill. She never recovered from that illness.

*

Gulab Bai was a powerful figure, and this appealed to me. I was curious about her poor Dalit background, and her reputation as the first woman in Nautanki—a male-only domain before she entered it. In time she established her own Nautanki company and ran it with aplomb. Later in life she received a Padmashree award. All this teased my imagination. I sensed stories lurking in the shadows, waiting to be told.

Gulab interested me because of the differences between us as well as the commonalities. I imagined her living in her body, at ease with song, dance and movement from early childhood. I grew up tone-deaf and painfully shy, and spent much of my early adult life struggling to outgrow these attributes. I acted and learnt to sing—both uniquely satisfying experiences. I recall a family elder chastising me one day for acting in street plays—'like a Nautanki-wali,' she said, with deep disapproval.

Living in the thick of society, Gulab was different. Social norms were not exactly woman-friendly or nurturing of independent female identities. Evolving a distinctive identity was a definite challenge. Gulab emerged as a personage in her own right largely because of the determination to nurture her innate creative abilities. She was unlettered, while I work through the written word. I figured this difference could form a bridge between us, since it provided a formal rationale for exploring her life.

I decided to explore and write about the myriad facets of her public and private life. How did the personal and professional co-exist? She was a daughter, sister, lover, friend, mother and grandmother, all the while being deeply immersed in the world of Nautanki. Were there any tensions between these various roles? How did she reconcile and combine the creative with the mundane? How did she manage to concentrate on her art, achieve excellence and soar above the common lot?

*

I was interested in the various layers of identity inhabited by this complex persona. Gulab was in many ways a paradox, representing processes of transformation and subversion of received identities, yet caught within them. Even as she grew in power, she remained vulnerable. Her personal and professional lives co-existed in uneasy sympathy: there were sharp ruptures, with jagged edges and deep fault-lines. Gulab asserted her freedom, awakened to her own vital sources of energy, yet remained trapped in vicious circles of attachment and betrayal.

Seldom do people attain the kind of success Gulab did. A Padmashree award is no small matter. Yet the moral universe she inhabited was barely acknowledged by the award-givers, far less respected. The citation described her as 'Mrs Gulab Bai'. For a woman who never married, yet had four children, perhaps this is—in the eyes of its composers—a signal honour. Yet from the perspective of Gulab and her community, this nomenclature indicates sheer disrespect—a refusal to accept their daily reality and way of life as valid.

Gulab lived a double life. I wanted to explore the seamless shifts between the two lives: the public and the private. Gulab sought refuge in art—she entered a form hitherto proscribed to women, thus expanding the spaces women could move into. Yet even as public spaces expand, women seem to be increasingly subjected to male gaze. Do they have to submit ever more closely to hegemonic moral codes and patriarchal expectations? Does a Gulab Bai don masks, expressing herself through many borrowed identities? Is there a core, an essence—or just a series of fractured, ambivalent selves?

2

Through Others' Eyes

Women in north India are usually projected as weak and oppressed, victims ad infinitum—docile, housebound, trapped within patriarchy, identities squashed from infancy to old age. Gulab Bai presented an alternative image. Her figure bespoke other possibilities, plural identities and norms, rather than a monolithic orthodoxy.

Gulab had children though she never married, yet nobody mentioned this to me in a loose or disrespectful manner. People look upon her with admiration and respect, tending to focus on her varied talents and regal persona rather than the more mundane—or scandalous—aspects. As one fan put it, 'A lotus blooms in murky waters.' He added, 'Everybody is born the same way,' and then tossed in for good measure, 'She was never anybody's "keep". Why, if she wanted to, Gulab Bai could have "kept" any number of men!'[6]

*

It wasn't easy to recover Gulab's life history. Unlike actress Binodini Dasi or singer Malka Pukhraj, Gulab left behind no written record of her experiences. But there were many people willing to speak about her. Reconstructing her story involved going places, meeting people, piecing together testimonies: an exercise in oral history.

I went to Kanpur, Balpurva, Tera Mallu, Unnao, Beeghapur, Kannauj and Makanpur in 2002 and 2003—packed trips yielding a rich harvest. Gradually we gathered a number of oral-history narratives from people who had known Gulab.

The people we met had intimate connections with Gulab Bai and/or the Nautanki world. Their stories came pouring out, enabling me to understand the person she was, and the contexts in which she lived and worked.

People's emotions and perspectives were reflected in the way they remembered details and incidents. Descriptions of Gulab Bai often revealed their own feelings and ideas. Everybody who spoke to me expressed strong opinions about Gulab Bai. Some doted upon her, while others didn't even like her much. Many thought she was great, while others didn't quite agree. Yet everybody recognized her as significant. She had made an impact; she could not be ignored.

*

Asha and Madhu related the course of their mother's life, emphasizing various dimensions. Madhu, the more eloquent of the two, often simply said her mother was 'different'. Rising from grinding poverty, she became an artiste to reckon with, provided common people with much-needed entertainment, and cared for those close to her. The government recognised her great talent, yet she struggled through her life, and suffered right up to her dying day.

Gulab's sisters Paati Kali (the third of five sisters) and Sukhbadan (the fourth) spoke of their days in Nautanki. Paati Kali was moderately successful, playing side-heroine roles in many dramas. She retired early to keep house for her children, as well as for Gulab and Gulab's children:

they lived together in a house in Rail Bazar, Kanpur. Paati Kali recalled her eldest sister with fond affection.

Sukhbadan did not care to talk much about Gulab–preferring to wax eloquent about her own days as heroine. She remembers Gulab less as her teacher in the art of Nautanki, and more as a fast-fading competitor: 'I sang so well that when Didi forgot a tune, she would ask me how to sing it!'

Paati Kali's daughter Munni Bai nee Nanda Devi often recalled Gulab's exceptional generosity as a teacher. But her mausi was strict too—'If I mispronounced a word she would grow furious and make me sing the entire part again!' Munni Bai would fall into a reverie and say, sighing with wonder, 'There is nobody like my mausi! Never again will there be anybody like her!'

In Balpurva village, where Gulab was born, her niece Shaila related ancient family lore—including the story of Moti Jaan, Gulab's father's sister. This history proved to be a wonderful frame for understanding Gulab's ancestral and extended family connections. Shaila continues to live at the same spot, in a haveli built by her eldest sister Krishna Bai, who was also a celebrated Nautanki heroine.

The two havelis are grand buildings, standing apart from the rest of Balpurva village. Other houses huddle together as if reluctant to display any trace of individual identity. The remarkable stone havelis rising into the crisp village air bear a faint resemblance to Mughal architecture and medieval ruins that still dot the region, redolent of past glory.

After narrating her stories, Shaila asked her daughter to fetch the key to Gulab Bai's haveli. She opened the gigantic lock and showed us around the imposing stone mansion that Gulab had built for her parental family.

The names 'Gulab Jaan' and 'Chahetan Jaan' are prominently carved at strategic points on the stone terrace. Chahetan was Gulab's second sister. The two sisters' earnings as Nautanki artistes supplied the funds for building these mansions. This fact was acknowledged through the names boldly carved in stone, like authorial signatures.

The terrace boasted intricate carvings with goddess Lakshmi as frontal centrepiece, two elephants by her side, flanked by British officers. On the ground floor were several rooms, while the first floor had one large, airy hall.

The sound of ghungroos seemed to echo in this hall. Did Gulab sometimes dance here—a mehfil for local landlords and noblemen, petty British officers and policemen? Did her sisters dance here, holding mehfils to supplement Gulab's earnings in her early days as an actress? Perhaps this is pure imagination on my part—but then: why the British gentlemen in their topis, atop the haveli? And why the huge hall?

Certainly, this haveli once bustled with bright life. Munni Bai mused, 'At Diwali people came from miles around to see the diyas lighting up this haveli. Now it lies in ruins! There is nobody to maintain it!'

As we walked away from Gulab's haveli, a wiry grey-haired man peered at us from his shack. It turned out Ram Singh had spent much of his life at this spot, from which he could look out upon his fields and beyond at Gulab's old home. He said, watery eyes sparkling, 'I played with Gulabiya when we were children. She was a year or two older than me.' He was from a prosperous upper-caste family whereas she grew up in a tiny hut on his family's land. His father filed a case against Gulab's father and cousin, but eventually lost the case.

Ram Singh betrays no rancour or ill-will. Over the years he has watched the world change completely. Gulab's haveli came up in front of his eyes. He witnessed her Nautanki shows: 'She brought her company to Balpurva to perform', he explained. 'The first show of every season was performed at Phoolmati Maiya's temple; next day there would be another performance on the other side of the haveli. The Nautankis were very good! They provided knowledge. They taught us our history—about Raja Harishchandra and Amar Singh Rathore . . .'

The pujari at Phoolmati Maiya's temple—a stone's throw from the haveli—said, 'Gulab Bai got this temple made. Earlier it was just a sacred stone. She got the central shrine constructed, and the rooms for priests. She raised the boundary walls before she died.'

In village Tera Mallu we met Dashrath Devi, widow of Gulab's brother Haulu. Haulu died many years ago. Although Dashrath Devi was always homebound, barely ever stepping out of the village, she was very close to Gulab. 'My *nanad* was very good,' she said nostalgically. 'She never let me remain in want.'

*

Back in Kanpur we met Shanti, a dour, ageing woman, who was fifteen when Gulab first saw her sing and dance at a *numaish*[7] in Etawah, and asked her to join the Great Gulab Theatre Company at a monthly salary of Rs 200. Shanti moved in with Gulab's family, where she and Gulab's brother Subedar soon fell in love. Gulab arranged their wedding, and Shanti continued to act for several years. She reminisced, 'Gulab Bai never spoke of her own troubles. She always looked after us. I took care to see that she ate properly, and washed her clothes if needed.'

Harmonium player Ram Prasad was working in Ram Lilas when Gulab offered him a job. A Brahman from Singahi, he had watched her Nautankis and admired her work from a distance. After three years Gulab promoted him to the post of music director. He married Gulab's niece Mangala. He said, 'Bai was very good. She treated me like a son.' He travelled with Gulab's company to Trinidad and Tobago some months before her death. To the end, he was her trusted 'bajamaster'.

Harishchandra played dholak and nagara in Gulab Bai's company. Ustad Rashid Khan, who worked with Gulab Bai until his last days, taught him to play the nagara. Harishchandra noted, 'Gulab was very dignified —and that is not true for all Nautanki people!'

Hafiz grew up in Aligarh district and came to Kanpur in 1977 to work with Gulab Bai. He said, 'There was nobody like Gulab Bai. She was very particular. I was careful to make no mistake when performing in front of her.' Hafiz became a well-known hero while working in her company. He worked in several companies—Krishna Bai's, Shanti Varma's, Radharani's and Chanchala-Mala's. He played lead 'Raja' roles in at least forty to fifty dramas including *Sultana Daku, Harishchandra, Bhakt Prahlada, Srimati Manjari, Shirin Farhad, Indarharan* and *Satyavan Savitri*.

Binda Prasad Nigam 'Sherdil' played hero roles too, in a number of companies. In Gulab's company, he played opposite Sukhbadan, whom he remembers fondly. Later in life Binda Prasad co-founded an organization to protect the rights of Nautanki artistes. 'When I worked with Gulab Bai's company I had no problem,' he recalled. 'But later on one or two artistes came to us and said she was underpaying them. We tried to sort it out . . . . this kind of thing happened in every company. We provided a forum for the workers. Otherwise company owners always had the last word.'

Shiv Adhar Dube was Gulab's company manager for several decades. He hailed from village Thathiya, next to Balpurva. He recalled seeing Gulab dancing as a young girl on village paths, collecting money from door to door. Decades later, after Dube joined Gulab Bai's company as manager, she trusted him with much of the administration and finances. Though her faithful lieutenant, he never had a steady income: 'She just gave me 500 or 1,000 [rupees] whenever the company earned something.'

Munni Bai grumbled too: 'If there wasn't enough money, we weren't paid properly. After all, we were in the family! But Gulab Mausi was good to everybody. If somebody came hungry, she would hand over her plate to him. She could not bear to see anybody hungry. She would make a person sit next to her and ask, "How is your family, brother? How are your children? Is everything well with you?"'

Chandrika Prasad 'Nidar' grew up in Bhagvantpur, near Takiya. A cattle fair held annually at Takiya attracted many Nautanki companies. Chandrika Prasad saw Krishna Bai and Gulab Bai acting together one year. Krishna Bai played the part of Majnu, and Gulab was Laila. They were hardly twenty years old. Krishna was wearing a loose man's kurta, Gulab a woman's kurta. Chandrika Prasad reminisced, 'Nautankis were so popular that the best companies charged more than talkies. People queued up for Nautanki tickets costing up to two rupees.'

Chandrika Prasad was charmed by Gulab Bai's singing, which he heard on several occasions. He compared her to goddess Saraswati—calling her 'Kalyug ki Saraswati', emphasizing her virtues even in the present dark age. He once visited Gulab, whom he was in awe of, in her Rail Bazar home. He was struck by her gracious manner: 'She asked me to sit, inquired about me and my family. She offered me paan. That's the kind of person she was. I might be a small man, but she made me feel important, made me feel she cares. No wonder everybody respected her. Why do you ask me about her personal life? People say she had her children with a seth, then with a Nautanki actor. Bai had dignity. She was a great artiste. Apart from that, she had her own life.'

Chandrika said that even in the 1990s at the Takiya mela people would shout for Gulab's songs. She had grown heavy and could hardly walk, but people would say they wanted her, and only her. She would come on stage supported by two people, sit on a chair and sing, and the audience would scream and clap. The audience really loved Gulab Bai, he said, right till the very end.

Hasina Banu Lucknowvali explained she learnt Nautanki from Gulab Bai in the 1960s. She was fourteen years old when she joined. She worked in Krishna Bai's company too. She says, 'In those days they trained artistes so well, like teaching their own children. That's how they trained us and made us first-class heroines.' She exclaimed that several songs Gulab Bai sang were hits—superhits.

Nautanki actress Nargis nee Saira Banu said, 'Gulab was a wonderful singer. If she sang you felt like sitting with your eyes closed, just listening. But she did not have much knowledge of *haav-bhaav*, of finer nuances of acting. She was not that great an actress, after all she was not khandani.' Nargis herself is khandani—born into a lineage of tawaifs, whose occupation was singing, dancing and the arts of entertainment. She feels that Gulab and others from the Bedia caste were lowly street-singers in comparison to tawaifs who were refined singers.

Siddheshwar Awasthi, a well-known theatre director, knew Gulab Bai over the years. Describing 'deredar tawaifs' as cultured and accomplished women, he said, 'Some Bedins [women of the Bedia caste] like Gulab Bai, were similar. Many Bedins were prostitutes, but these women– Gulab Bai, Krishna Bai, Jaddan Bai Calcuttavali (film actress Nargis' mother)—were not. They had character. They were not "available". They did their riyaz for hours everyday, sang and taught music. But the public sometimes thought they were "available". Performing in public was considered obscene—even if a woman was fully clothed.'

Rajkumar, Gulab's nephew, discussed his knowledge— gleaned from family elders—of the origins of the Bedia caste, and of Nautanki. He situated the Bedia caste within wide socio-historical contexts, tracing the social customs and lifestyle to their being a fugitive people, often hunted down by powerful regimes. He noted that they are weak today— their backs broken by centuries of persecution and penury.

Chinha Guru, of Beeghapur village, often saw Gulab Bai perform heroine roles in Tirmohan Ustad's company. He said, 'We know Gulabiya's origins. Tirmohan found her when she was a mere slip of a girl, wearing a little lehenga and blouse, singing songs for money. He took her in and trained her. Much later she started thinking too much of herself and started her own company. That hurt Tirmohan Ustad very much. He got a new instrument— the clarinet, and persuaded Gulab Master of Agra to play it at the next mela. Because of this new instrument people flocked to Tirmohan's tents, abandoning Gulab's shows.'

Actor Saajan expressed anguish at the state of Nautanki today. Frustrated that he cannot perform and look after his mother, Hiramani, as he would like to, he said plaintively, a note of anguish in his voice, 'Gulab Bai has gone! Where will we find such a gem again?'

*

While co-artistes and spectators have vivid memories of Gulab Bai, neither photographs nor her music is easily available today.

Searching for her music was a journey in itself. Though her songs were professionally recorded, the records are barely accessible.

I finally located Gulab Bai's songs through a unique music-lover's mecca in Delhi—the Shah Music Centre. Tucked away inconspicuously in the midst of a metal tools market at the foot of Jama Masjid in Old Delhi, the shop is able to produce any record or cassette cut by well-known singers, in films or outside, especially from the earlier years of music recording in India.

Musicologist Jyoti Pandey introduced me to the Shah Music Centre. Picking our way past goats, tool-shops and tea-stalls, through a network of tunneled low-roof shops, we stopped at a shop very different from the rest. It was stacked high with music cassettes, records and a couple of players; even its low ceiling was plastered with old records.

Gulab's records, said the affable and knowledgeable Ahmad Shah, were buried in enormous mountains of music. The Shah family owned six godowns full of records piled high. It would be an extremely arduous task to locate somebody like Gulab Bai whom few people today ask for.

With a flourish he produced the jacket of Gulab's record. He was adamant about the music itself being really difficult to reclaim. It would be easier to make a recording from a recording Shah had once made for Pandey. I agreed to this, and as it turned out, I soon possessed a treasure trove—sixteen songs sung by Gulab Bai.

I listened to them often, absorbing the tones and nuances, charmed by her sweetness, and by her ribaldry. These are dadras and rasiyas—folksy and robust. She sang full-throated—used to singing in the open air to thousands of people with no microphone. Singing to a machine in a little studio must have felt decidedly odd.

Listening to her brought me closer to Gulab Bai. As I listened to her strong voice belting out songs with many different moods—from the sublime to the bawdy—I wondered about her multiple facets. The songs are lively—sparkling with energy; sometimes sad, imbued with pathos.

*

In the Sangeet Natak Akademi, New Delhi, I found a bunch of relevant audio and audio-visual recordings. The Akademi was, unexpectedly, a haven. Shrabani Mukherji, who headed the music section, appreciated my project and related vignettes about Teejan Bai and other women folk artistes. I listened to recorded music in a wonderful, snug sound-room. The equipment worked beautifully, headphones fitted well and records in the catalogue were actually available.

Here I heard as well as saw Gulab sing her most popular dadra—*Nadi naare*. It was delightful. I heard it repeatedly, entranced, letting the music and words soak into me as I reflected on this as a work of art charged with meaning. Its resonance with events in her life began to emerge in my consciousness.

I heard other Nautankis in this womb-like room—*Indar Haran, Amar Singh Rathore, Dahiwali*.

Upstairs in a studio I was treated to audio-visuals of Nautanki performances, especially the Nautanki *Dahiwali* performed by the Great Gulab Theatre Company, with Gulab's elder daughter Asha in the lead role.

Back in 1996 I had seen recordings at All India Radio: the play *Puran Bhagat* by Krishna Kumari Mathur and Company, and *Bahadur Ladki urf Aurat ka Pyar* by Gulab Bai's company. I had also seen a brief television interview with Gulab Bai in which she described her life, from joining Nautanki as a ten-year-old to her ascent to success, when she set up her own company and trained others.

*

When I approached the Sangeet Natak Akademi for photographs, it again rose to the occasion. The enthusiastic Prithpal Singh, whose job it was to help provide information to researchers like myself, took barely a few minutes to locate two bulky albums with pictures of Gulab Bai (and some other artistes). We went through the albums and I noted down the photos I wanted. Within a couple of weeks, these were ready. The photos are all from Gulab's later years—1980s and 1990s.

Unfortunately, I was unable to access any photos of Gulab's younger days from official or unofficial sources. Newspaper clippings I did locate—but from her later years, after she had been awarded the Padmashree.

*

The literature available on Gulab Bai is sparse. There are only three articles devoted to her. One by Ravindra Nath Bahore, '*Ye parampara hamesha chalti rahe!*: Padmashree Gulab Bai' is based on a long interview conducted for the UP Sangeet Natak Akademi.[8] The article focuses on

Gulab Bai: a portrait

Nautanki music as practised in the Kanpur style, and briefly touches on the history of Nautanki as well as Gulab's desire to pass on the tradition to the next generation. Said Gulab, 'I would like a centre to be opened in Kanpur in which young people will be taught so that this tradition remains alive not just for a few days, but forever! Some artistes should be given a stipend to enable them to learn, because the people who will come to learn will be very poor.' She elaborated further, emphasising that taveel, chaubola, lavani and all the various raga-raginis would of course be taught.

Kailash Gautam's article, entitled '*Nautanki ki parampara*: Padmashree Gulab Bai', attempts a brief sketch of her life. His admiration for her is evident. More hagiography than biography, the article is packed with adulatory passages such as:

> ... She looked like a desi rose. Her voice was matchless. Sometimes when her little brothers and sisters were very restless due to hunger and thirst, Gulabiya would soulfully sing sweet bhajans for them. They would forget their hunger and thirst and gaze unblinkingly at Gulabiya ....

and

> Gulab would practise her roles for ten hours at a stretch. Before a show there would be two or three full rehearsals, with no prompting. Gulab loves to recall the hectic pace and hard work of those days. There was so much desire to learn, such enthusiasm and courage. Rehearsals would continue all day and all night without eating anything in-between. Riding in a bullock-cart, she would be going towards a railway station, worried that she might miss the train. Exhausted, she would fall asleep in the bullock-cart! In those days there was real joy in living. She had youth on her side, people around her, and a great need to earn ...

The third article, '*Ek thhee Gulab*', is based on its author Krishna Raghav's interactions with Gulab Bai during the weeks prior to her death. It is a beautiful, evocative piece of writing, describing his own lifelong fascination for Nautanki, and the step-by-step unfolding of Gulab's personality as he came to know her. He paints a lively portrait of Gulab, with hearty enjoyment as well as delicate sensitivity.

Recent sociological research has helped fill in gaps about Gulab's caste customs and social background. Particularly useful has been Anuja Aggrawal's Ph.D. thesis, an ethnographic study on Bedias in contemporary Haryana. Syeda Hameed has an insightful sketch of Bedia women's lives in one chapter of her book *They Hang: Twelve Women in My Portrait Gallery*.

As for useful writing on Nautanki, Kathryn Hansen's *Grounds For Play: The Nautanki Theatre of North India* deserves special mention. Meticulously researched, Hansen's scholarly work describes Nautanki as a cultural organism living and dying within a community of related forms. She argues that Nautanki was anything but marginal to social and cultural processes in north India. She weaves her discussion of Nautanki into a well-defined historical fabric, developing a chronological account of texts, themes, schools, music and metre. She examines a range of Nautanki narratives, exploring the play of multiple meanings within dramatic texts, illustrating how Nautanki confronted as well as colluded with established values and reworked the conflicts that riddle human existence.

The edited collection *Loknatya Nautanki: Kuchh Prashna* is an excellent anthology on the Nautanki form. Articles by Krishna Narayan Kakkar, Urmil Kumar Thapliyal, Mudhrarakshas, Kaushal Pandey, Yuktibhadra Dikshit, Krishna Mohan Saksena, Anand Kumar Mishra, Suresh Kala, Raghuvir Kushvaha, Vijay Bahadur Shrivastava, Suresh Salil and others provide ample food for thought—information as well as reflections on the past, present, and future of Nautanki.

Scores of Nautanki booklets, each with one drama script, have been a source of unlimited entertainment. The intricate plots and lively language continue to draw me ever further into the fold of Nautanki.

Suresh Awasthi's book on performance traditions in India, Balwant Gargi on folk and classical forms, Hanne de Bruin's article on hybrid-popular theatre, and my own fledgling documentation of the Rajasthani Khayal afforded insights into Nautanki as one among several related forms. Garcin de Tassy's work on Muslim festivals in India provided historical grounding for the Sufi ethos prevailing in north India, especially Makanpur—where Gulab saw a Nautanki for the first time.

Lives of other performing artistes have provided a comparative perspective while writing of Gulab. The autobiographies of Binodini Dasi and Malka Pukhraj reflect sensitively the continuities and disjunctions between personal and professional life faced by female performing artistes. Dasi was an actress in early twentieth-century Bengal, while Pukhraj danced and sang in Jammu and Kashmir, and later Pakistan. Biographies of the stage actor Bal Gandharva, classical singers Tansen and Siddheshwari Devi, cine stars Madhubala and Guru Dutt, and interviews of a number of singers and dancers by C.S. Lakshmi have all provided ways of looking at gender issues in the performing arts. Many silences and sexualities are interrogated, and subtle forms of subversion deftly explored.

Zohra Sehgal, Sukanya Rahman and Felicity Kendall's autobiographies are a rich mine for sundry historical facts and inklings about women in the performing arts. Shovana Narayan's book on Kathak focuses on the dance form that has vitally contributed to the artistry of tawaifs, as well as of Nautanki artistes. Vidya Rao's examination of the thumri, a form identified with women singers including

Gulab Bai, takes us into the realm of linking musical meaning with the intimate life experiences of the singers.

Against All Odds, a novel by Kishore Shantabai Kale, explores the lives of women in Maharashtra's Tamasha, indicating some strong parallels with the lot of Bedia women in Nautanki. Other novels with fascinating comparative insights include *The Woman of Basrur* by K. Shivarama Karanth, and *The Nautch Girl* by Hasan Shah. Both dwell on the lives of courtesans. *The Nautch Girl* (*Nasthar* in Urdu: reputed to be the first Indian novel) is about Khanum Jaan, who entertained officers of the East India company in late eighteeenth-century Kanpur. *The Woman of Basrur* brings alive the world of Manjula, celebrated courtesan living in Basrur, off the Kanara coast in south India. Like Gulab Bai, all these women lived by singing and dancing on the margins of society—and yet integral to it.

The films *Umrao Jaan* (based on the novel by the same name) and *Teesri Kasam* are classics—beautifully rendered tributes to such women. The heroine of *Teesri Kasam* is a Nautanki dancer—her personality and life resonating powerfully with Gulab Bai's.

A dance-drama mono-acted by Rita Ganguly called *Akhtari Bai* evokes the figure of Begum Akhtar. At one point the heroine laments, 'If a man sings well here, he is called an Ustad. If a woman sings well, she is called a Bai.' The term 'Ustad' signifies masterly accomplishment whereas 'Bai' denotes an available woman. The 'Bai' in 'Gulab Bai' has its own peculiar nuances—marking her out as a singer and entertainer, at the same time signifying that as a 'public woman', there is something inevitably disreputable about her.

*

This book is a biography of Gulab Bai, but also, at the same time, a rudimentary social history of the Nautanki theatre. The final chapters especially explore the state of Nautanki today, including the critical interface between gender and genre.

Putting together the information gathered from varied sources was like trying to make a complete picture out of sundry jigsaw-puzzle pieces. Inevitably some pieces were missing. I visualized, projected and imagined. A blurred image would emerge—then I would return to my sources to check out the facts. Many gaps remained. Despite the missing pieces, I formed a picture I could share with others—smudged and disfigured at places, yet on the whole lively and interesting.

A vivid image of Gulab Bai has emerged—a colourful personage moving and singing within the context of Nautanki, wearing its evocative costumes—those of a queen in a modern-day fairy tale. The picture is part myth and part reality. Yet it is cohesive; it holds.

Fact and fiction, biography and story—the boundaries are blurred. In any case, is there ever anything purely factual? Or, for that matter, is there ever at all anything that is purely fictional?

PART II
GULAB'S STORY

Nomadic Past

Shaila (Gulab Bai's niece): *Sometimes my father, Kallu Seth, related the story of his mother, Moti Jaan. For many years she lived in a royal court that side of the Ganga. She sang and danced. Those were the days of tabla and sarangi, when music and dance was valued in the courts.*

Moti Jaan had a son. The Rani—the king's wedded wife—was jealous of Moti Jaan and got the child killed. After this my grandmother had three more children. But her life was in danger because the Rani was jealous. One day the bhagat [the magic-and-medicine man] did his bhagatai, that is, he made a prophecy. He told Moti Jaan the Rani was planning to kill the three children. He said, 'To save your children you should escape immediately. These children will not survive the night if they remain here.' My grandmother took the children and left that very night. She knew of a tunnel leading outside the palace. In the dead of night, clutching her children, she descended into the tunnel. She kept running until she reached the other end. She was out in the open, but still kept running. Otherwise the king's men would have caught and brought her back.

She kept running for several days carrying her children with her—a girl and two boys. She touched people's feet to beg a little food for the little ones. She asked for shelter, slept in the dark and kept running the next day. She crossed the Ganga. Only then was she at ease. Once she had crossed the Ganga she knew she was out of danger. She stopped to rest at this village, Balpurva. It was a simple village this side of the river.

She started living at this very spot. She built a tiny hut with mud and thatch. She sent word to her family. Her brother Lal Bahadur came to see her. After he lived with her for a few days he too settled down here.

(Balpurva, May 2003)

Gulab is Moti Jaan's niece – Lal Bahadur's first child, born in 1920.

Everybody is born into somebody else's story – and becomes a character in it even as the script of her own life gets written. Gulab was born into the story of Moti Jaan's life, and went on to create her own script – with herself as heroine.

Moti Jaan's tale is well hidden by most of her family— perhaps they are too busy to keep track of historical detail. Gulab's daughters may or may not even have heard of it. It was left to Gulab's niece Shaila, who leads a retired life in Balpurva, to bring this skeletal fairy tale out of the cupboard. Shaila and her children are the only people still living at the spot where Moti Jaan built a home a hundred years ago.

To understand the ethos Gulab was born into, we will retrace our steps, returning to Moti Jaan and her brother, Lal Bahadur. In the early years of the twentieth century, they were two lost souls seeking a home, a place to drop anchor.

Moti Jaan and Lal Bahadur grew up on the roads rather than any settled home. Like others of the Bedia caste, Moti began singing and dancing as a young girl to earn for the family. Lal Bahadur, her youngest sibling, was born some fifteen years after her. Their mother spent her days cooking and caring. Moti learnt performing arts from her *buas*—father's sisters. Her father hunted for game in the jungles and tried to keep track of news and events in the world outside. The family moved from one village to the next, girls and women performing in exchange for grain and clothing.

Moti's comely figure drew the attention of a wealthy landowner of Hardoi district. He already had a wife but Moti Jaan—an energetic twenty-year-old—became the current favorite. She moved into his palatial estate, her family receiving substantial gifts in exchange for parting with her. This happened during the last years of the nineteenth century. Around the turn of the century Moti Jaan gave birth to a son.

*

Rajkumar (a distant relative of Gulab Bai's): *Our fathers and grandfathers told us this story about our origins. I don't know how true it is. Our ancestors are from Chittorgarh. In Akbar's time we were in Rana Pratap's army. When Akbar won we left Chittorgarh with Rana Pratap. We moved from village to village. We vowed not to settle anywhere so long as alien rulers ruled our kingdom.*

Our ancestors became wanderers. They walked across Rajasthan and went into [what is now] Madhya Pradesh and Uttar Pradesh. They took up some livelihood or the other. They became Banjaras, Kols, Bhils, Kanjars, Bedias, Nats . . .—twelve castes in all. Amongst us—

*Bedias—women sang and danced. The men were latthaits
[musclemen–literally: wielders of the lathi or bamboo stick].
Bedias were employed in royal courts, or just here and there.*

*Those who can wield the lathi are the ones who can
appreciate music. This is human psychology. Is it not?*

*Once we were a brave and valiant people. Now we are
weak. If we cannot even earn two paise, are we not weak?*

(Kanpur, May 2003)

Bedias, according to Rajkumar, descended from soldiers belonging to Maharaja Rana Pratap's army in the sixteenth century. Rana Pratap's defeat at the hands of Akbar was a mortal blow to his soldiers. Even as the king wandered incognito, living in penury, eating only grass for a whole year, his soldiers wandered with him over hills and valleys, jungles and rivers. They vowed to wander, homeless, so long as the land was under alien rule.

Similar stories abound among related tribes and castes. For instance, the story goes that Rani Padmini left Chittorgarh with a devoted band of soldiers and maids when Sultan Allaudin Khilji tried to capture her, and her husband Ratansen died in battle.[1]

Local history has it that though defeated in battle, these people kept the flame of freedom alive over the centuries. Only a few settled down in villages along the way, submitting to the reigning powers. The rest remained nomadic. They moved eastwards towards Bundelkhand, dodging imperial soldiers and police along the way. In the nineteenth century many walked northwards towards the Doab. Some ventured as far as Avadh and Purvanchal.

They took up various occupations to make a living. Gadiya Lohars made iron implements for household and agricultural use. Nats were nimble gymnasts, performing stupendous rope tricks and dizzying pole vaults. Kalbeliyas kept village audiences spellbound with dances in which they twirled around countless times, feet and skirts flying at the speed of light. Banjaras traded in foodstuff. Moghiyas were healers and herbalists. The Bedias sang and danced vigorously—their movements requiring grace, stamina and acrobatic skills.

Bedias, Nats and Kalbeliyas brought with them a tradition of music and dance, so pervasive in Rajasthan. Earlier they would sing to celebrate births, weddings and festivals within their own families and villages. As they moved through other villages, young women began performing at functions and festivals to earn some food, shelter and clothes for the family.

For a night programme kerosene oil would be lit in glass bottles to provide illumination. If possible a rug was spread out on the ground for the audience. Everybody in the village gathered to watch the dance. The Bedia dance style was called 'chhapka' or 'rai' at different sites. It demanded a great deal of agility, including twirls and leaps high into the air.

Bedia men were fighters. On the face of it, male fighters and women entertainers make an odd combination. Yet both disciplines require rigorous body culture and sustained practice. The Bedias honed their skills systematically, despite the itinerant lifestyle.

Bands of Bedia and other nomadic communities continued to rebel against imperial forces, and were captured and punished from time to time. The Mughal and later British armies hounded and tortured them. Repression proved incapable of crushing them. Then in 1871 the government came up with a new strategy. It prepared a list of 'criminal tribes and castes', including all the itinerant ones. Entire tribes and castes were declared criminal. Their members were required to register at police stations wherever they were. Failing this, they could be arrested. Thousands of men were probably captured and killed by the state using this stratagem.

Male Bedias were the most vulnerable. Men concealed their identities and hid in thick jungles. Over the years women became the central earners. Men occupied a relatively peripheral role in the domestic economy. Initially Bedias travelled as caravans or extended groups. Later when imperialist forces hounded them mercilessly, they split into small family groups to escape notice. They moved through thick jungles, often at night, walking routes used by fakirs and mendicants, making detours to cover remote villages. They would camp outside the village margins, and villagers would gather in the evening to see the women perform. In exchange, they were offered food and shelter.

By the late nineteenth and early twentieth centuries Bedias increasingly settled down. The colonial state favoured settlement of the 'criminal tribes and castes', considering their wandering lifestyle to be conducive to engagement in criminal activities over widespread areas. Some men sought employment as guards or soldiers in princely estates, changed their caste name and settled down. Others became tenants-at-will or sharecroppers. Settlers had to secure the support of the local elite for land and protection.

We have on record about Bedias in 1915 in the Central Provinces: 'In Saugar the women of the caste are the village dancing girls and are employed to give performances in the cold weather, especially at the Holi festival, where they dance the whole night through, fortified by continuous potations of liquor. Their dance is called "rai" and is accompanied by most obscene songs and gestures.'[2] This dance was also called 'ravla' in the Bundelkhand region, while in the Braj area the dancers were called 'bhavaiyas'.

Some women moved from dancing and singing to sex work—forming liaisons with wealthy patrons. Bhola Baba, a Bedia in Bharatpur, explained recently, 'Earlier there was no prostitution. If any girl lived like this, she never went to ordinary men. Our father's sister lived with Raja Jaswant Singh . . .'[3] Part of the community became dependent on women's concubinage. The arrangement was distinct from prostitution or sex work in that a woman would be 'kept' by just one wealthy patron. Later this system eroded and gave way to open sex work: the women became available to more than one client. These shifts in women's work were also linked to the community's move to a sedentary lifestyle.

The entire community experienced a delicate balance between danger and survival. Women took over the role of frontline soldiers in this battle for existence. They went into melas and mehfils, danced and sang and bartered sexual favours. Their work provided a means of livelihood to the entire community.

Sexual ethics evolved within this situation. Women who sang and danced remained unmarried. They set up liaisons, but remained strongly bonded to their natal families. Bedia men married women from related castes like Nats and Kanjars. They also married Bedia women: those who did not sing and dance for a living. Some Bedia girls were brought up the 'normal' way—trained in domestic skills and expected to marry.

Moti Jaan, of course, was one of the performers and providers. From earliest childhood she learnt to use her wits and fend for herself. Many Bedia women worked as street entertainers without pause, for years on end, with brief liaisons here and there. Moti Jaan made a better bargain—or so it seemed in the early years. As time went on, intrigues within the estate shattered her peace of mind.

*

Hardoi was one of twelve districts collectively known as 'Avadh' (officially spelt 'Oudh' during British rule). From 1775, the British conquered and annexed one region after another, until by 1856 the entire UP (United Provinces of Agra and Oudh: nearly congruent with present-day Uttar Pradesh and Uttaranchal) was included in their empire.

Tensions between landlords and tenants escalated over the decades, particularly in Avadh and east UP. Avadh had the most exploitative tenurial arrangements in the province. After 1857 the British allowed zamindars and talukdars every leniency in order to enrich themselves, in return for their loyalty. Though not kings, the zamindars and talukdars were referred to as 'Rajas'. They were feudal landlords, moneylenders, local lawmakers, tax collectors and judicial authorities all rolled into one. Individual landowners were the units of settlement. They collected rent from their tenants and paid revenue to the state. Most peasants lived in poverty. Evictions and rack-renting were common, as were all manner of exorbitant cesses. Landless labourers, tenants and poor peasants were uniformly from the lower castes.

Bedia families like Moti Jaan's fell outside the agricultural hierarchy altogether. When Bedia families settled, it was at the edge of the village proper. They were outcastes.

They still had no means of survival apart from song, dance, petty pilfering and some form of sex work.

Few Bedia men would deign to work on the land. Many boasted that they were descended from Rajputs and had blue blood flowing in their veins. In a sense this was true, since parentage was generally mixed. The men refused to join a hierarchy in which they would be placed on the lowest rungs. In any case there was strong social stigma against the community, and Bedia men were not welcome as agricultural workers. Thus they remained located, at best, at the margins of village life.

*

Young Moti Jaan's family was scattered over the fertile countryside. When she had moved into the estate in Hardoi she entered a life of relative isolation. The Raja barely tolerated any mention of her parents or other relatives. He did not want to be bothered by them. Yet her father and brothers visited her frequently. Moti Jaan loved to have them over. She would smuggle out good food and expensive gifts to place in their hands. If they needed money, she would often procure it through some clever stratagem.

Her daily routines changed dramatically from the earlier nomadic life. She absorbed the new ethos and tried to fit herself in. She observed the details of daily life, and began to help in the kitchen—cooking and serving food to the master. She dressed impeccably and chose her jewellery with care. Sinking into her role as 'Rani', she considered herself lucky.

She was no longer expected to sing or dance. She lived in luxury, but had to submit to the whims and fancies of the king. Sometimes he treated her like a queen but at other times shamed and commanded her as if she were a lowly maidservant. Her sense of dignity was often shaken. She had earlier suffered shabby treatment from many people—commoners as well as government functionaries. Bedias were habituated to such treatment. They resisted it when possible, but were hardened to the fact that upper castes looked down upon them and often treated them like vermin.

Within her family and community, nobody had ordered Moti around or treated her as shabbily as her 'husband' sometimes did. After all, he was a feudal lord and no doubt considered himself far her superior. Basically there was no comparison in their status, and they both knew it. At such times she would long for her family and her own people.

Moti Jaan had seen wretched poverty. Her family owned less than poor settled villagers who owned at least a thatch hut for shelter. Living in the estate she saw the other side of the picture. She understood that the rich live off the fat of the land, taking luxury as their birthright. She had become part of the setup, although a sensitive and rebellious streak within her questioned the whole position.

Jealousies, brutality and cold-blooded murders were all present in this house of wealth. According to Shaila's oral-history version, Moti Jaan became a focal point for the elder Rani's jealous fury. Perhaps the elder Rani tried to poison the Raja's mind against his 'keep'. Maybe she paid some loyal maids and courtiers to harm Moti and her children.

Moti Jaan's first-born was probably a sickly baby. She missed her mother then, and the ministrations of other women of the family. The baby never gathered strength. Day by day he lost weight until he passed away. With a heavy heart, Moti Jaan let go of the precious bundle. She heard rumours that the Rani had invoked black magic against the infant. Perhaps—who knows?—she had sent a drop of deadly poison through a trusted servant to mix in the baby's milk.

Moti Jaan was young and naïve when she had the first baby. With her second child, she took greater precautions. She was delighted to have a daughter, whom she called Chandrabaga. The child was born healthy, and thrived under her watchful gaze. The next year she gave birth to a son, Kallu. The children grew up healthy, safe and sound.

As the years passed, the Raja no longer favored Moti Jaan with his attentions. Distracted and tired with her mothering duties, she was no longer attentive to his every desire. Physically and emotionally, she had changed. His passion waned—he was no longer the ardent lover he had once been. He visited her quarters only occasionally.

It is likely that at this time the Raja began inviting dancing girls to the estate. He was fond of organizing mehfils. He scoured the countryside for young, glamorous dancers. Moti Jaan was interested in seeing these beautifully made-up young women, wearing glittering costumes. She was even more fascinated by their styles of song and dance. They sang ghazals and thumris and danced languorous, slow numbers, the tempo picking up as the song proceeded. They wore diaphanous lehenga-cholis or angarkha-churidars.

Moti herself had danced—like other Bedia women—to a uniformly faster tempo, singing vigorous dadras and kaharwas as she danced. Different musical instruments were used for accompaniment: these women danced to the tabla and sarangi while she had danced to the rustic dholak. Yet often the sentiments expressed were similar—longing, pain, desire, erotic teasing and fulfilment.

The women coming into the estate to sing were mujra dancers or 'nautch-girls'. They originally came into UP from Bengal, Punjab or as far as Kashmir, during Mughal times, and adapted their local styles to the forms appreciated and encouraged by Mughal emperors and noblemen. They contributed to developing the arts, especially ghazal, thumri and Kathak dance. Many performed for the British officers of the East India Company, and later soldiers of the British army.

By the late nineteenth century the Mughal empire lay in ruins. British officers were trying to refurbish their image. Laws had been passed against 'obscenity' in the arts, even as puritanical ethics became increasingly influential. British women came into India in larger numbers than a century ago, and the presence of their own country women—often wives or daughters—restrained British officers from indulging in mujras. Their presence also partially compensated for the lessened opportunity to interact with dancing girls. Thus the demand for nautch-girls declined. These women were at large. Zamindari estates stepped in to fill the gap. They provided the requisite patronage.

Moti Jaan probably befriended some of them. She made sure she had an opportunity for informal interaction with them when they came to her estate to perform. Of course she could not be part of the mehfil herself. But she could sit by when they practised to the accompaniment of tabla and sarangi. She felt—and was!—*dehati* (a village bumpkin) in comparison to these urbane, sophisticated women. Their musical practice was more disciplined and sophisticated.

Moti encouraged her daughter Chandrabaga to meet these women and attend their performances. The little girl was quick at memorising lyrics and melodies. She would practise dance steps wearing small ghungroos and a ghagra. Despite living on the estate, Moti Jaan wanted to pass on the heritage of dance to her daughter. She felt it was important that her daughter learn skills by means of which she could earn her livelihood as and when she needed to. Moreover, in her youth Moti had enjoyed singing and dancing, and was pleased to see how graceful her little daughter was.

*

Moti Jaan knew her influence over the king was waning. The senior Rani still saw her as a thorn in the flesh. As legend goes, the elder Rani hatched a plan to kill Chandrabaga and her brother Kallu.

The royal bhagat read Moti Jaan's future and revealed the sinister plot. Matters, according to his predictions, had come to a head. The children's lives were in grave danger. He advised her to leave the palace immediately in order to save them.

Rather than wait for the worst to happen, Moti Jaan decided to take matters in her own hands. The thought of escape had been lurking in her mind for a few months. That very night she and her children left the palace forever. The Raja's estate had a secret tunnel. Moti Jaan knew of it.

At night she descended into the tunnel and ran through its dark and ominous length, holding the children close. It was eerie. But at the same time it was the passage to a new life. At the other end of the tunnel she climbed out into wilderness. She knew the king would have her tracked. He would not allow her to just leave. If captured, she might be severely punished. She had seen labourers tied and beaten until welts rose on their backs and they collapsed, unconscious.

She walked southwards as fast as her legs could carry her–through fields and villages and forests until she reached the river Ganga. The children walked with her, bodies matted with dust. They begged for scraps of food and people gave a few rotis or chana and jaggery so the children could eat. She touched people's feet and appealed for shelter.

She was a nomad once again. With every step childhood memories welled up within her. She was back to traversing jungle and road, lanes and by-lanes. Her children kept pace with her. They crossed the Ganga by ferry. Once she had crossed the river she breathed easy. Now she was beyond the king's reach. His territories and power did not extend beyond Hardoi. Now not only Hardoi but the entire region of Avadh was behind her.

This side of the Ganga was known as the Doab region. It was a fertile land lying between the '*do ab*' or two rivers—Ganga and Yamuna. Here too land ownership patterns were inequitous and poor peasants and landless labourers lived in penury. Yet land tenure arrangements were a shade better. Under the 'mahalwari' system in place here, estates, rather than individual landowners, were units of revenue settlement.

Moti Jaan stopped at Balpurva village, a few kilometres from the river. She was worn out and decided to camp in the village. Seeing her disheveled appearance and starved children nobody grudged her the square metre of land on which she spread out some *pual* and fell off to sleep. This was at the edge of the village, on land belonging to a Thakur family.

As soon as she regained her strength she set to work—singing at a birth here, a wedding there. Habituated to a settled life, the charms of continuous wandering no longer appealed to Moti Jaan. Making two ends meet was enough of a challenge. She picked up the threads of the only occupation she knew—and found the energy to sing and dance come surging back. When she went out to sing, she would wear the colourful lehenga choli and shiny jewellery she had carefully carried from the estate in a cloth bundle.

Because she had been out of practice for so long, her singing was a little shaky. But she had not forgotten her old art. She had picked up some new styles and movements from the nautch-girls, and presented an eclectic mix. Elderly village men asked her to sing for them. So did upper-caste families from Thathiya, an adjoining village.

Makanpur town, close at hand, had an annual mela where singers and dancers gathered, performing to large audiences. During the next few years, the mela offered an important opportunity for Moti Jaan to earn.

Moti Jaan sent word to her family, and two brothers soon arrived. She had three brothers, all younger than her. Lal Bahadur, a lanky youngster, settled down with her. Her relatives were quick to reclaim her as their own, and she found the network comforting.

Moti Jaan had camped on land belonging to a well-off Thakur family. With tears in her eyes, she begged for a small piece of land on which to squat. The old patriarch granted her that.

She set to building a hut of bamboo, mud and thatch. The children did what they could. Chandrabaga was eight or nine years old at the time, and Kallu a year younger. Lal Bahadur was some thirteen or fourteen years old.

Thus began a new phase in Moti's life. She was independent of palace intrigues, but had to fend for herself and struggle for every morsel of food. In the palace she had food aplenty, and luxurious clothes. Yet she was glad to have escaped. She enjoyed the open fields, trees and birds, and freedom to organize her days. It was her job to earn a living for the family, and she set about this spiritedly. Within the next few years, their life settled into a steady pace.

4

Gulab is Born

I think ever since the earth was made and human beings were moulded, it has been happening that if two people like one another, they want to have each other. Some are married according to their parent's choice. Others go in for love marriage. This is what I have been seeing all along.
—Munni Bai

Ye kudrat ki baat hai ki dehat mein ek gulab ka phool paida ho gaya . . . . [It is a phenomenon of nature that a rose blossomed in the village air]
—Shiv Adhar Dube

Gulab Bai's mother was Kurmi. Father was Bedia. The union of the two made a khichdi.[4]
—Dube

Gulabiya was born in Balpurva around the year 1920. Gulabiya's father was Lal Bahadur—Moti Jaan's brother. Over a decade had passed since the day Moti Jaan first arrived in Balpurva.

Lal Bahadur had grown into a wanderer. Although he lived in Balpurva, he spent most days roaming around the surrounding countryside. He hunted in the forests, bringing home small game like rabbits or birds. He visited villages and met his numerous acquaintances and cronies.

He was a strapping young man, and a part of the male-Bedia ethos in his refusal to work for a livelihood. Often he indulged in petty theft—sugarcane from somebody's field or green vegetables from another's. Kallu—just a few years younger—often accompanied Lal Bahadur.

One day Lal Bahadur noticed tall, shy Jehangira while wandering through a village commons. He began frequenting that village. He would hang around the path she took to fetch water or carry clothes for washing. One day he found her without the usual gaggle of girls and waylaid her. Moved by the desire to marry, he built a hut next to the one he had been sharing with Moti Jaan and her children. A few days later he captured and brought Jehangira home.

Bedia men often indulged in 'love marriage' – usually in this case a euphemism for marriage-by-abduction. Bedia women seldom married, so the Bedia men brought in women from other castes. The Bedia men usually married into related communities like Sansis, Nats and Kanjars. Sometimes they abducted women from higher castes.[5]

Jehangira is reputed to be from a higher caste, Kurmi. Probably her mother was a Bedni or Nat, and father Kurmi.

Moti Jaan was well pleased with her brother's choice. But Jehangira's brothers felt the abduction was an affront, and sent some cronies to capture and bring her back. They would probably have done so—nipping the marriage in the bud—had Chandrabaga not intervened.

Though just nineteen years old, Chandrabaga had already made a mark as a singer-danseuse. She had a confirmed circle of admirers. One of these was Darghai Lal, an influential and wealthy man from Thathiya, a village adjacent to Balpurva. She asked him for help to tide over the crisis. Darghai Lal provided shelter to Jehangira and Lal Bahadur and sent for Jehangira's elder brother. Jehangira's family was poor. Darghai Lal was wealthy and powerful. When Dargahi Lal advised Jehangira's brother to accept the match, the poor man relented. He agreed to condone the marriage.

Jehangira's brother approached Moti Jaan with the good news. They arranged a simple ceremony in which bride and bridegroom exchanged garlands, the families shared a meal and exchanged clothes.

After this, life carried on, the new arrangement well in place. Lal Bahadur and Jehangira built a new hut, next to the one in which Moti and her children lived. Within the year Jehangira gave birth to a baby girl. Moti Jaan took one look at the petulant screwed-up little face, and named her Gulab.

The birth was joyfully celebrated. Moti Jaan sang joyous sohars and Chandrabaga danced, accompanied by the vigorous beat of the dholak. Unlike most castes, Bedias were thrilled when a daughter was born within their family. The birth of a boy was simply accepted as 'destiny', while the birth of a daughter was a tremendously happy occasion, celebrated with song and dance.

By the time Gulab was born, Chandrabaga was the main earner in the family. She performed at village festivals and functions, mehfils and the occasional mela, and shared whatever she earned with the whole family. It might have been a sack of foodgrain, some clothing or a few annas.

The family's existence was fragile. They lived from hand to mouth, yet dreamt of better days. The only road to riches they could foresee was through the girls born into the family.

*

Chandrabaga had learnt some music at Hardoi. After settling at Balpurva, Moti Jaan was determined to continue with Chandrabaga's *taleem*. This was a tall order, given the family circumstances.

Moti Jaan had brought some of her jewellery with her from Hardoi, carefully wrapped in an inconspicuous cloth bundle. She mortgaged or sold a bracelet or anklet, ring or necklace when the going got particularly rough. A sizeable chunk went into paying for Chandrabaga's musical training. The rest went into emergency needs—food or medicine.

Chandrabaga learnt music from an ustad from Ferozabad who also taught two sisters belonging to a wealthy family in Thathiya. Twice a week Chandrabaga trooped down to the village and joined the two young girls in their home. Moti Jaan arranged this—only she knew how! Chandrabaga learned scores of folk songs from her mother—rasiya, alha, dadra, hori, chaiti and sohars. The Ustad taught her ghazals and thumris, to the accompaniment of tabla and sarangi.

In the early years at Balpurva, Chandrabaga accompanied her mother when Moti Jaan was invited to sing at festive events. As she blossomed into a youthful beauty, people began to invite Chandrabaga independently. By the time Gulab was born, Chandrabaga had been performing on her own for at least four or five years. By then she was a seasoned artiste. She kept up her taleem and her riyaz[6].

Kallu often escorted his sister Chandrabaga when she went out to perform. But he never tried to pick up musical skills—playing dholak or tabla, manjira or sarangi. Nor did Lal Bahadur make any attempt to do so. They considered such work, or indeed labour in the fields, below their dignity. Moti Jaan left them to their own devices.

Gradually Lal Bahadur and Kallu became inseparable. In the neighborhood they were known as the *mama-bhanja* (maternal uncle and nephew) pair. They spent most of their time wandering hither and thither, talking to various people and dreaming of wealth and luxuries.

Kallu, having spent the early years of his life in the estate at Hardoi, was obsessed by the image of his rich father and the property he could have inherited. He felt superior to other villagers because of the blue blood running in his veins.

*

From the day Gulab was born she became the centre of attention. Her daughter Madhu related a story much recounted in their family: 'The day Gulab was born her father Lal Bahadur heard an akashvani (divine pronouncement). The voice said, "Lal Bahadur, Lakshmi has been born into your house. Now you must leave your dishonest ways. You must reform yourself." Ever since that day Lal Bahadur gave up dacoity, theft and the telling of lies.'

It may be unlikely that Lal Bahadur heard any such akashvani, and even more doubtful that he actually did reform his ways. But there is certainly more than a grain of truth in the notion that Lal Bahadur hoped his daughter was Lakshmi incarnate: the goddess of wealth and prosperity!

Lal Bahadur encouraged little Gulabiya to sing and dance. It seems she began to sing before she could talk, and dance before she could walk. As she danced away the moments of each day, day after day in the open village air, Gulabiya had little inkling of the dreams being woven around her—dreams she was destined to fulfil.

5

Music in the Air

Sukhbadan Bai (Gulab's sister): *One day Chandrabaga was sitting outside the house on a string cot when a police officer passed by, riding his horse. She was lounging in the shade of the mango trees, long hair open, relaxing between sessions of practice and hard work. The policeman—employed by the British raj—was in the habit of barking threats at local poor people. He stopped when he saw the beautiful young woman. In order to trouble her he rudely asked, 'Hey you, what do you think you are doing?'*

Chandrabaga flared up. She was not one to take an insult, especially when she was doing nothing wrong, nothing that could even remotely be described as criminal. All she was doing was resting in her own home. But the uniformed man continued upbraiding her, 'Whose land are you sitting on?' As far as Chandrabaga was concerned this land belonged to her family. She confronted the uncouth man, least daunted by his regalia. She spoke sharply, her eyes flashing, 'I am sitting in my own house. Don't you have eyes that you cannot see? Who are you to talk to me so rudely when I am sitting in my own house? What are you doing here? Shall I call my father and brothers and have you beaten to pulp?' The police officer sped away on his horse. He avoided coming by that path ever again!

(Kanpur, 2003)

Chandrabaga was every bit her mother's daughter—beautiful and free-spirited. She too began working at a young age to support the family.

The family was growing. Lal Bahadur brought in Jehangira, and they had their baby, Gulabiya. Chandrabaga's brother Kallu married around the same time. He was just eighteen years old and his bride was even younger. They began a family immediately.

In keeping with his status as a married man, Kallu began calling himself 'Kallu Seth', a pompous appellation that gave him great satisfaction. Others too began referring to him as Kallu Seth.

Kallu's daughter Krishna was just a few months younger than Gulab. The next year Gulab had a sister: Chahetan. Another year later Krishna's sister Kashi was born. Then Gulab had a brother, and Krishna another sister. Kallu Seth's wife died, but within a few years he married again.

Chandrabaga worked hard to earn for the entire brood. Moti Jaan, well into her forties, no longer danced. Occasionally she sang at domestic events in the village, in exchange for a bundle of clothes or a sack of coarse cereals.

*

Gulabiya, Krishna and Chahetan were playmates. They also helped their mothers cook, run the household and look after younger siblings. Chandrabaga was their role model. They were entranced by her dance steps and would twirl around imitating her, lehengas swirling gracefully.

Chandrabaga worked most days. Gulab would want to go out with her. By the time Gulab was five or six years old, Chandrabaga began to take her along occasionally. Sometimes Krishna, Gulab and Chahetan together went out with Chandrabaga. Thus the sisters became familiar with the tinkle of ghungroos, the beat of the tabla and the appreciative gaze of wealthy men.

*

Before she knew it, little Gulabiya had ghungroos on her feet. She tagged along with Chandrabaga, joining in where she could. At melas or village streets she would beat her little feet in a thumki, twirl round and round with her lehenga flying in the air.

Chandrabaga had a varied repertoire and performed as suitable for different occasions. She danced the Bedia-style chhapka and rai, as well as mujra items close to Kathak. She sang a wide range from folk to semi-classical songs.

When Krishna Bai and Gulab Bai were seven or eight years old, Lal Bahadur and Kallu Seth began taking them out with a dholak player from the village. The little party would stop at people's doors or under a pipal tree and begin their musical feast. People would look out of their doors or stop on their errands to see the energetic dancing and hear the sweet singing. The party earned a few coins every time they went out on a round.

In later years Gulab's relatives often romanticized her affinity for song and dance, projecting it as a God-given talent. For instance, her niece Munni Bai waxed eloquent on the child Gulab: 'She sang as she washed clothes, she sang as she cleaned utensils. She sang as she went to fetch water from the village well. She just had this natural talent in her!'

In fact, the family was poor and their fathers put them to the task of generating an income as soon as possible. Their innate musical talent was carefully nurtured and actively encouraged. Gulab, Krishna and Chahetan did not think of the labour they put into earning a living as unwarranted, harsh or exploitative. They took it in their stride. They enjoyed dancing and appreciation made it all the sweeter. It probably bestowed a sense of identity, and developed a quiet self-confidence. This stayed with Gulab throughout her life.

In later years a drama critic, Kailash Gautam, sketched a poignant image of Gulabiya's singing prowess and the early use to which it was put: '...What can one say about a voice as sweet as hers? Sometimes when her little brothers and sisters were very restless due to hunger and thirst, Gulabiya would soulfully sing sweet bhajans for them. But Gulabiya knew her voice would not attract them forever. What would happen once they got bored...?'

Lal Bahadur and Jehangira had ten children in all: five girls and five boys. There was seldom enough to go around the circle of children—an ever-expanding circle.

There wasn't enough clothing to protect the children from the cold in winter. Gulab told her younger siblings and children an apocryphal story that they often repeated when describing the early poverty of their family. As Gulab's daughter Madhu describes it, 'When Amma was young her parents were so poor that at night my grandmother would spread pual and the ten children would line up and sleep on this. She had two lehengas so she wore one and spread the other one over the children.'

Kallu had three children by his first wife, and two—Shakuntala and Shaila—with the second. The second wife died, and Kallu married a third time. With his third wife, Kallu had one daughter, Munni.

Most days there was just enough for one square meal. But the air was sharp and fresh. Stretching in all directions were zamindar's fields with millets and mandua, barley and maize, mustard and lentils. The Bedia women grew vegetables on a patch of land next to their huts. The men sometimes hunted—a wild rabbit or deer, pigeon or partridge—and brought the meat home to cook.

The family muddled through, struggling against the odds. Jehangira kept house, fed her husband and brought up their children. Kallu's wife would carry out the same housewifely chores. Wise, experienced Moti Jaan was the one to take important decisions, provide advice and support. Chandrabaga was the bread winner. Increasingly she sang at intimate soirees in the homes of select patrons: local landlords and moneyed upper-caste men. She sang ghazals and thumris and was paid well.

Chandrabaga's popularity grew day by day and the family's fortunes were on the rise. The fortunes of a Bedia family would rise or dip depending on the income generated by its professional girls and women. The women could earn well only when they were fifteen to thirty-five years old.

With Chandrabaga's takings expanding, the family improved and extended the humble huts they dwelt in. They cleared wasteland near the huts and began to consider it theirs. They laid claim over the land they lived on.

Mango trees spread their wide shade just outside their home. The family enjoyed the fruit of these trees and sat under the shady canopies for protection from the summer heat. The land was legally owned by an upper-caste family, which later filed a case to get them evicted. The case went on for decades. Finally—well after Independence—Gulab's family won the case.

*

When Gulab was about ten years old, Chandrabaga left Balpurva to live with her patron Darghai Lal. This was a blow to the family's finances. Darghai Lal paid a handsome dowry, but Chandrabaga no longer provided the daily income.

Lal Bahadur and Kallu were masters at squandering any cash that came their way. The dowry was soon spent. From time to time Chandrabaga sent some foodstuff and clothing to help Moti Jaan and Jehangira, and Kallu's wife, to run the large household and look after their brood of children.

Darghai Lal did not want Chandrabaga to perform. Being a second wife, Chandrabaga had her hands full managing her interests within Darghai Lal's household. Mingling too much with her natal family wouldn't have helped matters. She stopped performing, stayed at home and had children of her own.

Chandrabaga sometimes visited Balpurva but never moved back to live in the village. Gradually she lost touch with the family. Years later, nobody in the family seemed to know anything definite about the rest of her life. Sukhbadan just said Chandrabaga had gone off with Darghai Lal and then never came back. Shaila had an impression that Chandrabaga died quite young. She vaguely recalled hearing that Chandrabaga gave birth to two or three children, but knew nothing about them or their whereabouts.

6

Village Deity

My Gulab Mausi always said that whatever she achieved is due to the blessings of Phoolmati Maiya. She was never arrogant or proud. She said whatever she has is because Phoolmati Maiya gave it to her. Otherwise how could she have done so much all on her own?

—Munni Bai

A 'Devi' gave to a 'Bai'.

—Krishna Raghav

Gulab grew up within a network of strong women. Moti Jaan and Chandrabaga provided the child with an atmosphere where she absorbed music with every breath she inhaled. As performing artistes they wielded significant influence over the young girl. They recounted varied stories the children listened to, spellbound. They had been to many places, participated in varied events and met all sorts of people.

When Gulab was ten years old Chandrabaga virtually disappeared from her life. Just three or four years later, Moti Jaan passed away.

*

Gulab was deeply influenced by Jehangira, her mother. Jehangira knew nothing of the arts of song and dance. But she supported her daughters in whatever they wanted to do. She was there for Gulab through thick and thin. Sensitive, and committed to the welfare of her children, she suffered privations and endured hardship for most of her life.

'My grandmother Jehangira was a simple woman, always in ghunghat,' recalls Gulab's daughter Madhu. 'She was in purdah even with the men of the house. She never sang and danced. She never even went for any of my mother's programmes or performances.'

Gulab Bai's elder daughter Asha, who bears a strong resemblance to her mother

Gulab was a professional artiste during the best part of her life, but her mother Jehangira remained confined to the four walls of the village home. Despite the profound differences in their experiences and exposure, mother and daughter remained closely bonded throughout their lives.

*

Another powerful influence on Gulab was Phoolmati Maiya, the village deity. Everybody in the village worshipped Phoolmati Maiya. She had always been the gram devi or village deity. Phoolmati Maiya's tiny shrine stood a few hundred yards from Gulab's home. Every morning the young girl gathered flowers and ran down to the temple to offer these to the Maiya. She had been doing this ever since she

Phoolmati Maiya's temple, Balpurva, a stone's throw from Gulab's village home. When Gulab was a child, it was just a tiny shrine.

could remember. 'Phool' means flower: this devi was especially associated fragrance, colour and a sense of beauty.

Even years later, when Gulab was rich and famous, she always expressed gratitude to Phoolmati Maiya. She firmly believed the Maiya was responsible for all her achievements.

Every few years Gulab made an addition to the original shrine. A graceful structure with a white marble dome came up to house the main shrine. A yagyashala was made for performing purifying rituals. Rooms were constructed for the temple priest and his helpers to live in. She got a well dug and sponsored the construction of a gate and low wall all around the temple compound. Flowers were planted in the compound.

Whenever Gulab Bai started on an important venture she went to Balpurva to take the blessings of Phoolmati Maiya. When she ran her own company—the Great Gulab Theatre Company—she brought the entire staff to Balpurva for the first show of each season. She would get a yagya performed, hold a feast for the villagers and enact the new play at the feet of the Maiya. She offered it to the devi and sought her blessings for the entire season.

Whenever her company held a show, anywhere, Gulab Bai lit incense, made an offering and intoned a prayer. She remained pious throughout her life. Deeply attached to simple daily rituals of worship, these provided her with solace and a sense of continuity.

Krishna Raghav, who made a film on Gulab Bai shortly before her death, visited the temple in 1996. He mused, 'A Devi made Gulab into a Bai!' Phoolmati Maiya was no Brahmanical goddess imposing strict puritanical ethics. Her persona was playful and sensuous, with aesthetic depth and a touch of the erotic. She was a devi of the Dalit castes, rather than keeper of high-caste ethics.

Gulab was a devotee of Lord Krishna too. She loved to sing Krishna bhajans. She sang for various gods and goddesses including Saraswati and Ganesh. Her Nautankis always began with a vandana (invocation) to these and several other deities. Some Nautankis had the Muslim salaami as well.

Evidently Phoolmati Maiya was not a jealous goddess. She left her devotees free to wander where they would. The goddess—a beneficient force immanent in all nature—could be worshipped alongside other deities. There was no contradiction.

Gulab remained Phoolmati Maiya's devotee for life. At the same time, in the course of a long and colourful life, she mixed and mingled and had intimate friendships with people from various cultural backgrounds. She had a lively interest in their different beliefs, practices and ways of life.

Going to the Fair

Madar is the most celebrated Muslim saint of India. The Hindus are one with the Muslims in celebrating his cult . . . He died on the 7th of Jamadiul awwal, 837 (20 December 1433) and because of his reputation as a pious man and his power of working miracles, the anniversary of his death has been celebrated ever since then with a large number of people gathering at Makanpur. Madar's tomb—built by Sultan Ibrahim Sharqi—is raised in the middle of a large square building at each side of which there is a window. It is covered with golden cloth. Over it there is a canopy of the same fabric, which is heavily perfumed with the essence of rose, 'itr'.

—Valentia, in Garcin de Tassy, 1831

Musicians beat a kind of big drum, 'dhol', while fakirs dance, walk through fires lit up for this purpose, singing songs in praise of the saint. A huge crowd fills the town; pikes are raised on all sides, and in the night a great number of lamps and lanterns dispel the darkness. They all carry pikes to Madar's tomb and each one seeks grace or fulfillment of a wish.

—Jawan, 1812, in de Tassy

Shah Madar is venerated very much, particularly by low-born people. Some of them play the instrument called 'rabab'. The pilgrims stay near the saint's tomb for several days, busy offering the saint presents and asking for boons; at the end of the seventeenth day of this month they return home.... The practice of visiting Makanpur is quite old but it is not known who established it.

—Afsos, 1808, in in de Tassy

... The principal practice of the Madarias (those belonging to the sect of Madar) is the use of 'bhang' (intoxicating liquor extracted from hemp leaves or the exudation of its flowers), in the hope of conjuring visions.

—Garcin de Tassy, 1831[7]

Gulab Bai: *'There was a mela at Makanpur, in Kannauj district. I told my father I want to go there. He said, "Alright", and we went in a bullock-cart. Mother, father and I went.'*

—Krishna Raghav, 1996

Gulab's visit to the fair was a turning-point in her life. She was twelve years old at that time. In later years she would often describe her visit to the Makanpur mela, in 1932.

This annual mela has a history spanning the centuries. Various scholars including De Tassy, Valentia, Jawan and Afsos visited the mela over a hundred years before Gulab, and it made an impact on them, as is evident from their writings. People are believed to have gathered at the tomb of Madar Shah, a Sufi saint, on his very first urs (death anniversary), that is 1434. So at the time Gulab visited the mela at Makanpur, the tradition had already been in place for nearly 500 years.

Turbulent crowds continue to celebrate the urs of Madar Shah. Even today thousands of Muslims as well as Hindus gather from far and wide, staying at Makanpur for several days of worship and revelry. The mela is held every year around the start of winter.

Gulab's family members were regulars at the mela. Makanpur was just a stone's throw from Balpurva. The family would have gone not as ordinary revellers, but in order to make a quick buck. The girls and women would have earned by performing, while Lal Bahadur and Kallu kept their eye trained on opportunities to swindle and pick pockets.

Munni Bai spoke of 'Madar Baba' with affectionate familiarity when we passed by Makanpur in 2002. She herself performed Nautankis at the mela during the 1960s and 1970s. She explained emphatically that very strict timings have to be maintained at the Dargah, or else Madar Baba can fly into a rage. His reputation as a hot-headed saint is such that even birds don't fly overhead in the afternoon at the designated rest time.

Gulabiya's imaginative world expanded listening to local histories and legends such as that of Madar Shah. He was supposed to have come from Aleppo and was a descendant of Hussain. Apparently he made a pilgrimage to Mecca and Medina at the age of 100. Prophet Mohammed asked him to go to Makanpur to quell the demon Makan Deo who had turned the place into a wilderness. Madar imprisoned the evil spirit and rendered the place habitable. He stayed there until his death, which is reputed to have happened at the ripe old age of 400.

Madarias believed that even Mohammed would have access to paradise only if he uttered the words 'Dam Madar' or the breath of Madar. 'Dam Madar' was also a war cry used by Muslim soldiers. Another sect of Madarias wore only black and carried black flags. Many Madarias were jugglers, and reared tigers, bears and monkeys to show them to the curious. They would make the animals dance and execute skillful feats. Some donned black garments and plaited their hair, while others rubbed cow-dung ash on their bodies and went about naked with iron chains around the waist and neck.

At the gatherings in Makanpur, De Tassy found 'faqirs, devotees of all classes, musicians and jugglers, prostitutes and dancing girls, magicians and libertines, rascals and thieves'. Although the mela changed over the centuries, it remained fairly wild in the 1920s and 1930s when Gulab frequented it as a young child.

Merchants would erect stalls selling delicious sweetmeats and breads, meat roasted in several styles and rice cooked in different ways. Stalls were heaped with fresh and dried fruit, and betel leaves in hundred-leaf packs. Musicians played countless different instruments. Madarias were sure to have a dafli (tambourine) in one hand, jingling it vigorously to accompany their singing. Dancing girls and rope-dancers would perform remarkable feats. No doubt many of these were Bedia and Nat women. Intoxicants like bhang were freely available.

Everybody who came for the mela paid homage to the Sufi saint. They offered flowers, ghee, mustard oil, molasses and other sweets at his shrine. Singers and musicians expressed devotion through their arts. Devotees lit Madar's tomb with lanterns and candles, and spread lotus and cypress flowers all around. The tomb was covered with gold cloth and soaked with rose itr. A canopy over the tomb was similarly dressed, exuding the heavy, soothing fragrance of local roses.

A considerable number of Dalits had converted to Islam during previous centuries, partly under pressure during the Mughal empire and partly attracted by syncretic Sufi culture. Sufi festivities borrowed a great deal from the practices of song, dance and worship that the Dalit Hindu converts brought with them.

The presence of dancing girls was a feature of all significant melas in this region. Even Moharram processions in north India were preceded by a troop of musicians and a band of dancing girls reciting marsias. The French used the word 'bayaderes' for these dancing girls, adapted from the Portuguese 'bailadeira'. Since the caste name 'Bedia' has no ancient references, it is plausible that it was an adaptation of the French and Portuguese terms for dancing girls. After all, this dancing is what marked them out as a distinctive occupational group[8]. Female dancers were also called 'ramjani', 'nautchi' or 'kanchani'.

Erotic episodes were not uncommon in the free-flowing atmosphere of these melas. Badauni describes his experience when he went on pilgrimage to the Makanpur mela: 'I was captured in the net of desire and lust, and the secret contained in the ancient writing of fate was revealed, and suddenly in that shrine I committed a terrible piece of impropriety.... God granted to some of the relatives of the beloved to overcome me, from whom I received nine sword-wounds in succession on my head and hand and back.'

Such dramatic real-life episodes seem to have intermingled with song and dance, mimes and plays, wine and various herbal intoxicants.

*

In the early years of the twentieth century, Nautankis became a new form of entertainment in the north Indian plains. The form took shape in Hathras (some 100 miles west of Kannauj, which is next to Makanpur and Balpurva) during the latter half of the nineteenth century. By the turn of the century Hathrasi Master Natharam Gaur's Nautankis sometimes travelled to Kannauj.

A young lad by the name of Tirmohan Lal had run off from his middle-class home in Kannauj and joined Natharam's akhara, in which the Nautanki form developed. Akharas were sites for training young men in physical discipline and body culture—including wrestling, body building, dance and theatrical skills. Tirmohan Lal trained under Natharam and became a brilliant actor as well as nagara player. He proved particularly adept at playing female roles. After some years in Hathras, Tirmohan Lal returned to Kannauj. He gathered boys from the city and surrounding villages to set up a new company, in the year 1903. Most boys were from Dalit castes that had a tradition of boys and men playing musical instruments, chanting, singing or acting in existing folk forms.

Tirmohan's company performed several dramas in the region during the next many years. By the early 1930s the company was extremely well known. Rehearsals were held in the compound of his family house in Kannauj. Tirmohan also rented a house in Kanpur because the atmosphere there was conducive for the development of his group. A distinctive Kanpur style of Nautanki was evolving, along with a discerning audience to appreciate it.

Tirmohan Lal was over fifty years old at that time. His wife had died, two sons were studying and daughter was married to a farmer in Beeghapur village of Unnao district. In 1928 Tirmohan's company enacted Nautankis at Beeghapur during the last three days of the Dussehra festival—ashtmi, navami and dashami. This proved so successful that it became established as an annual event. The tradition continues to date.

*

Performing Nautankis annually at the Makanpur mela was another tradition in the making. Puppeteers and bards, raconteurs, singers, dancers and actors had always entertained the crowds at Makanpur. Nautankis fitted in smoothly into this creative and earthy cultural ethos.

Young Gulab had already seen amateur Nautanki improvization in her village. Some young boys bought two or three drama scripts that sold in large numbers along with Nautanki performances. They distributed roles and memorised the parts. Utilizing the skills of stray musicians, they had a merry time singing, practising roles and making a huge din.

Gulab had seen these boys rehearse in Balpurva, and was fascinated. She heard that the great Tirmohan Ustad's company would perform at Makanpur and looked forward to seeing his Nautanki. She knew her father had already seen a few of Tirmohan's Nautankis and was an avid fan. Lal Bahadur had even dropped by at Kannauj to see rehearsals and chat with some of the young actors.

Gulabiya and her sister Chahetan went dressed in their finery—lehenga, blouse and dupatta—to attend the mela. Gulab was a charming twelve-year old growing tall and buxom like her mother. By day they sang and danced, earning a few coins. As evening fell, the summer sun vanished and a cold night breeze blew over the jostling crowds. Gulabiya and Chahetan ate hot pilau and meat, then huddled up with their mother in a warm woolen dushala.

Preparations were on for the Nautanki to begin. Lal Bahadur had managed to buy tickets. Gulab Bai later recalled that each ticket cost the astronomical amount of five annas. Years later, Munni Bai's acerbic comment was: 'Sometimes people's brains stop working. Gulab's father earned maybe one rupee a day, and he spent it all on buying Nautanki tickets!' Perhaps in fact he never bought tickets, rather got in by appealing for a 'pass' from actors he was acquainted with, or else smuggled his family in as part of the pressing, milling crowd.

Gulabiya's eyes were riveted to the stage. She had never seen such vivid scenes unfold in front of her. Musicians played their instruments at one side of the makeshift stage. Nagara, tabla, dholak and harmonium were in readiness to provide beat and rhythm through many hours of acting. As the curtain parted, a bevy of actors sang the mangalacharan. After this offering to the gods and goddesses, they performed a salaami, then the Ranga came dancing in to introduce the story. The play that night was the familiar *Raja Harishchandra*.

Raja Harishchandra is the story of an ancient king who is known to be steadfast in honouring his words. One day, sage Vishwamitra, in order to test him, appears in his court and tricks him into making a promise by which he relinquishes all his possessions, including his jewellery, throne, and palace. Unable to pay *dakshina*—a fee offered to Brahmins—he is reduced to serving as a slave at a cremation ground. His wife Taramati joins work as a domestic servant in a rich man's house. A poisonous snake bites their young son Rohit. Taramati carries her dead child to the cremation ground, but cannot pay the fee. Harishchandra refuses to cremate Rohit unless the proper fee is paid. Taramati begs Harishchandra to chop off her head to save her from further pain and humiliation. He blindfolds his eyes and draws a sword. At this moment Vishwamitra appears, admits the glory of the truthful Harishchandra, revives his son and restores him to the throne.

Nautankis based on this story had already been performed hundreds of times. In Hathras Indarman and Pandit Natharam Gaur's groups had performed it since the late nineteenth century. It was one of the most popular dramas in Tirmohan's repertoire. The same story was also performed by other folk theatre forms, such as the Tamasha in Maharashtra. The Tamasha and Nautanki versions probably inspired the first film made in India, in 1913, which had the same name—*Raja Harishchandra*.

Young Gulab sat up all night watching the Nautanki. She was deeply stirred by the story, and even more by the music. Tirmohan Lal had hired excellent musicians to train the boy-actors. Their steady voices carried in the cold winter air, without the aid of any microphone.

Several lengthy breaks were held between drama scenes. Everybody rocked with laughter at the antics and bawdy humour of the 'joker'. They swayed to the familiar melodies of popular folk songs. The show carried on until the early hours of morning.

Gulab had seen many fabulous sights at the mela that day: monkeys in knickers and frocks, enacting domestic scenes; Nats performing incredible acrobatic tricks, their bodies elastic like rubber; fakirs and sadhus with matted hair and majestic robes smoking chillams amid clouds of swirling smoke...but this Nautanki was the crowning glory. Nothing else was anywhere as magnificent!

In a Male Bastion

Gulab Bai: *Boys enacted all the roles–male and female. I liked it a lot so I said, 'Pitaji, 'I want to join this. Tell them to take me.' He wouldn't agree. I insisted. He took me to Tirmohan Lal and said with folded hands, 'Bhaisahab, my daughter wants to work with you in the Nautanki . . .'*

[Here GB began relating the conversation as if she were mono-acting].

T	:	*Arre Bhai, only boys work here.*
GB's Father	:	*So what? My daughter wants to do this.*
T	:	*Oho! Well, there is no earning here.*
GBF	:	*Whatever you want to give–for 'saabun-tel' (basic needs), it's fine.*
T	:	*Okay, we will give her fifty rupees. But she will have to come to Kanpur.*
GB:	:	*I asked my father, 'Take me for a few days to their place in Kanpur.' He agreed. We were scared of the name 'Kanpur'. Still, we went.*

—Krishna Raghav

There are several versions of the story of how Gulab joined Nautanki. Gulab herself recounted different details on different occasions. Sometimes she put her age as eleven, at other times as twelve or thirteen. At times she emphasized her own desire to join Nautanki, at other times her father's. Sometimes she said Tirmohan refused to take her until others in his company lobbied for her. At other times she said Tirmohan took her at once after hearing her sing just one dadra.

Memory plays tricks; we often reconstruct past events based on present desires. In later years when Gulab Bai related the story of how she joined Nautanki, she usually projected herself as the central decision-maker. However, this is probably closer to how she would have liked it to be than the way it actually was. Her father would have played a far more active role than she wanted to acknowledge. It pleased her to think she'd made the choice, but Lal Bahadur is not likely to have simply acquiesced to a twelve-year old girl's wishes on a decision so radical and far-reaching.

It is true that Gulab was strongly attracted to the Nautanki form. For a girl who lived half the time in the world of music and dance, the musical dramas opened up new imaginative space. Gulab's father had hobnobbed with a few Nautanki artistes and realised its potential. It was a successful medium, growing in popularity and likely to be a confirmed money-spinner in years to come.

Lal Bahadur knew his daughter was set in a mould: she would lead the life of a performer. How did it matter, he wondered, whether she sang and danced in and around the village, or joined a travelling company? In fact the latter option was preferable since it would provide her with a far better income.

Bedia economy rested on the earning capacity of women, and it was the role of fathers to develop and exploit this capacity to the fullest. Lal Bahadur played this role to the hilt.

He had grown up with a mother who earned by singing and dancing on the roads, and later lived off a sister's earnings. The notion of women performing in public was not at all extraordinary for him. He had few qualms about sending his young daughter off with a travelling theatre company. Jehangira did not like the idea, but he did not care to take that into consideration.

News had trickled in of women joining theatre companies in Bengal and the cinema in Bombay. Many early actresses were from courtesan families, prostitutes or singer-dancers. Gulab's joining seemed plausible and well in tune with this trend in other parts of the country.

Early in the morning Lal Bahadur went up to Tirmohan Ustad and appealed for work for his daughter. At first Tirmohan wouldn't hear of it. A girl joining the Nautanki troupe! However, one of his artistes had heard Gulabiya sing and was impressed by her talent. He advised Tirmohan to hear the girl before taking a decision. Tirmohan heard her sing a dadra and was charmed. She went on to sing snatches of lyrics from the drama she had just seen.[9] She had memorized lines after hearing them just once. Tirmohan was impressed by her talent.

Tirmohan was a company manager and an ambitious one at that. His organizer's mind began ticking. He realised this girl might be a tremendous asset to the company. She had striking good looks, a simple nature and explosive talent. Her voice soared with exceptional sweetness. With proper guidance and training, she could excel.

Tirmohan's was one of the foremost companies in the field, but it was facing stiff competition. Shrikrishna Pehelwan and Lalmani Numberdar had far better infrastructure in Kanpur and had set up full-fledged companies that were doing very well. Tirmohan recognised the need for new and critical elements to attract an audience. Taking in a talented female performer would be a shrewd move. It could contribute to a dramatic upswing in his company's fortunes.

Imagination fired, he began to quiz the father. He agreed to take Gulab but said he would only pay for her upkeep. She would eat from the common kitchen. Lal Bahadur was a skilled negotiator, and before he knew it Tirmohan had agreed to pay a few annas or a rupee every month directly to the father. Tirmohan said Gulab would have to go with the company to Kanpur. Lal Bahadur agreed. At that time Kanpur seemed a long way away, and village people were scared of its big-city ethos. Yet this was part of the deal: Gulab would have to move with the company wherever it went.

Satisfied with the deal, Lal Bahadur took Gulab home. She was excited beyond words, barely registering what was happening as she bid farewell to her distraught mother and siblings. He brought her back next night, and she sang a dadra during the Nautanki show. Her performance was satisfactory. Within a few days Tirmohan's company left for Kanpur. Gulab went with them. Since she was a girl in an all-male troupe, Lal Bahadur too went with her.

Joining Tirmohan Lal's troupe was a decisive step in Gulab's life, changing it forever. At the same time it was a historical step for the Nautanki form. A girl performed on the Nautanki stage for the first time. What greater novelty could anybody offer? And what better way to draw the crowds?

*

Until Gulab's entry, young boys played the roles of heroines, side-heroines and other female characters. Reputed to be the first woman to join Nautanki, Gulab entered an all-male space. In those days Nautanki had a decidedly masculine ambience. Many boys ran away from home and village in order to join a Nautanki troupe. Gripped by wanderlust and the urge to perform, they left home and hearth for months, sometimes years.

Tirmohan and his artistes maintained a simple lifestyle. Tirmohan had hired a large house in Cooperganj, Kanpur. He lived there and set up quarters for the artistes. When travelling they lived in tents. Gulab's father or one of her brothers stayed with her wherever she was. The boys melted into the troupe, running errands for the actors and musicians and watching Nautanki shows.

Accustomed to living in a large family, Gulab didn't have much trouble adjusting to communal living. Tirmohan and other senior actors and musicians were affectionate and kind. She had enough to eat and drink. Most importantly, she was absorbed day and night in learning music and Nautanki acting.

She did miss her mother and younger siblings, and often felt homesick. In those days a troupe performed for eight or nine months a year. Gulab was away from Balpurva for extended lengths of time—typically the entire eight or nine months. During the chaumasa or four-month monsoon period, unhindered movement and open performances became impossible. The troupe broke up during this time, and Gulab could return home for the monsoon break.

Initially Gulab sang dadras and rasiyas as fillers between Nautanki acts and scenes. When she sang on stage she wore the dress she was most accustomed to—lehenga, choli and dupatta. She seemed born for the stage. After all, she had performed on streets, in melas and homes ever since she could remember. On stage she was lively and vivacious. She was confident, for she had always won appreciation and applause.

Most of her days were spent in learning. Day and night, she watched rehearsals and performances and absorbed the intricacies and nuances of the Nautanki style. She paid attention to the movements and singing of well-known artistes in Tirmohan's company—Naagar, Moti, Mehboob, Fazal, Bade Fazal, Ismail Kunwarji, Vishambar, Baturi and several others.

Her training proceeded systematically. Other youngsters also learned. Tirmohan Ustad taught them the different metres and styles of Nautanki singing. Years later she recalled, 'We would sit comfortably every day and he would tell me, "This is the tune of a behre taveel, this is the way a lavani is sung, this is a chaubala, this is how to sing a chhand." As we heard, we began to sing. It might take one day or twenty days to learn. This is how he taught others too. Once we had learnt a tune, we would sing it to him. Whatever was incorrect, he would tell us how to correct it.'

Mohammed Khan Saheb also provided musical taleem to Gulab. He belonged to Kajreti, a village near Hathras, and was well versed in the classical ragas and Nautanki music. Her early promise as a singer flowered as she absorbed these rich influences.

Gulab witnessed her company perform plays like *Raja Harishchandra* umpteen times. As she watched, the tunes and words flowed into her veins. Soon she could sing all the lines, whichever character they belonged to. Similarly she learnt the words and tunes of *Laila Majnu*, *Puran Bhagat*, *Bahadur Ladki*, *Shirin Farhad* and a number of other Nautankis.

She was given small roles in plays—part of a crowd or chorus. The first distinct role she enacted was that of Rohit or Rohtas, Harishchandra and Taramati's son. She wore a white pajama-kurta and somebody tied her hair into a knot and wound a thin turban on her head. Make-up was applied—white powder on the face, thick black lamp soot around the eyes, and reddish lipstick. She rather enjoyed all the excitement of dressing up and performing on stage. A large part of the time she had to act as a corpse, lying flat on her back or being lifted as a stiff body. But this hardly dampened her enthusiasm. It was a dramatic scene and clearly she was the centerpiece!

She routinely took part in chorus singing and dancing, and scenes where a crowd was required, or a bunch of courtiers. Gradually she learnt to do her own make-up.

From her early acting debut as Rohit, Gulab soon graduated to 'Rani' roles. She played Rani Taramati in *Raja Harishchandra* and Rani Haadi in *Amar Singh Rathore*. In *Laila Majnu* she would play Laila, in *Shirin Farhad* Shirin and in *Heer Ranjha* Heer. Other popular Nautankis in which she played the heroine were *Alam Ara*, *Pukar* and *Bahadur Ladki*.

*

Soon other women began to join the Nautanki theatre. After Tirmohan hired Gulab, Numberdar hunted for women players to enhance the popularity of his company. Within the year he had hired Krishna Bai, Gulab's close relative and childhood playmate.[10] She had a powerful voice and flowered both as singer and actress.

Gulab's sisters followed her into the world of acting. A year or two after she started, her sister Chahetan came into Tirmohan's troupe. Paati Kali and Sukhbadan joined later. In subsequent years Krishna Bai's five sisters also joined Nautanki.

Women joined the Hathras Nautanki too. Shyama Bai and Anwari Bai, or Anno—sisters hailing from Pinahat near Agra—became famous as the 'Shyama-Anno' duo. Radha Rani of Pilibhit became exceedingly popular. These were talented khandani singers, that is from tawaif families where mujras and thumris were passed down the generations from mother to daughter.

Most Hathras Nautankis remained exclusively male—and are so to date. Compared to the Kanpur side, Hathras companies are purists about traditional music as well as the sex of their artistes. Shrikrishna Pehelvan, a giant in Kanpur's Nautanki world, also disapproved of the growing trend of nurturing Nautanki actresses.

*

Braj folksongs were popular as fillers during Nautanki shows. These often reflected the social ethos, local conventions and relationships. For instance, take the following rasiya:

> Patni: *Paanch rupaiya de de balam, main mela koon jaungi*
> *Paanch aana ki pao jalebi, baithi sadak pe khaoongi.*
> Pati: *Kaha kahe kachhu samajh na aavei, ai mere dil ke pyari*
> *Mela dekhan jaya no kartin, bhale gharon ki nari.*

This translates as:

> Wife: Give me five rupees, dear husband, to go the mela
> I'll sit by the roadside and eat a pao of jalebis for five annas.
> Husband: I can't understand what you say, dear mistress of my heart

For girls from respectable families don't go to any melas.

Women who came into Nautanki were either from Bedia or tawaif deredar Muslim families. Both communities had a well-established tradition of women earning their livelihood by singing and dancing. In both these subcultures, women did not marry, led unconventional sexual lives and provided for their natal families. Both caste groups were considered somewhat beyond the pale of respectability.

Women from 'respectable' families were supposed to keep at a distance from such tainted and independent women. Men from their families might choose to frequent melas and Nautankis—although it was generally frowned upon. The women did go to melas, but usually only in the daytime. They were not privy to many of the Nautanki shows that took place at night. Obscene gestures and words with double meaning ostensibly rendered Nautanki out of bounds for women from respectable families.

Nautanki's cast and audience were largely Dalit. Its whacky characters, intricate plots, earthy humour and erotic lyrics were highly appreciated. It projected conflicting social mores and contentious constructions of self, sexuality and womanhood. Normative Brahmanical codes were explored, sometimes as a model but at other times in conflict with relatively flexible popular cultural practices.

Although most Nautanki actors and musicians were from Dalit classes and castes, over the years several upper-caste men joined. For instance Natharam Sharma Gaur was a Brahman. So was Lalman Numberdar. Shrikrishna Pehelvan was a Khattri, his full name being Shrikrishna Mehrotra. Tirmohan Ustad was a Kurmi.

Company managers made sure their women were well protected. Presence of male relatives was one way to safeguard women's safety. But this wasn't possible for many women, for instance those whose homes were far away like Shyama and Anno. An old-timer recalls a scandal from several decades ago–some students from Aligarh abducted Vidya Bai, a heroine in Lalmani Numberdar's company, because they wanted to see the Nautanki actress from close. Whether or not this was a true incident, we can only conjecture. But just as there is no smoke without a fire, we can assume that some incidents of sexual harassment of Nautanki actresses did indeed take place.

The Bedia family structure facilitated the presence of men as escorts and guardians, since males habitually did no independent work. Their presence was presumed to be protective for their sisters, and no doubt this was so in several situations. Given the overwhelmingly patriarchal ethos prevailing in regions where Nautankis were performed, the simple presence of a male relative would certainly have a sobering and restraining influence.

Several Bedia men were quite comfortable performing ancillary roles, and enjoyed the opportunities provided. By accompanying their sisters, they could move out into the world. If their sisters did well, the men too could access various privileges.

Over the years Gulab's brothers came close to the Nautanki world, although not one developed any skill in singing or acting. Their role remained, at best, that of protective support persons. From time to time they degenerated into the opposite—alcoholic, thieving and womanizing dependents. Some proved themselves to be lifelong parasites.

Company managers developed yet another strategy to safeguard their women. This was to keep the women virtually in purdah. Women were not allowed out during the day, and instead were kept within the confines of their tented rooms. Managers would say, 'If men see you in the daylight, what will they come to the Nautanki for at night?' Keeping the women concealed by day was considered a shrewd business move.

Performing all night, Gulab and other performers would wake up by noon the next day. They ate, chatted and caught up with their chores—stitching, washing, looking after young children and ill people. Male actors were free to wander around outside, hang around in the bazaar and catch up on local gossip. The entire staff would meet in the evening to rehearse and begin preparations for the next show.

Though women were supposed to be in purdah, they did often take the opportunity to slip off for a secret rendezvous. Recalled actress Paan Kunwar, 'We lived in purdah during shows—for months. But Seths would give a thousand rupees to see us and talk to us. All this was done secretly so that the maliks (company owners) wouldn't get to know.'

9

The World of Travelling Theatre

On hearing Tirmohan Lal's nagara playing, people left their fields and came running, Seths and moneylenders would forget their business and commerce. Big zamindars and wealthy people got nautankis performed over several weeks in their villages, kasbas and cities. At some places crowds of up to twenty thousand sat by watching a show until sunrise. The crowds included women and men, boys and girls, elderly people and middle-aged. Tirmohan Lal's nagara could be heard echoing over miles. People ran helter-skelter, uncontrollably towards the sound.

—Kailash Gautam

Nautankis became the rage during the 1930s and 1940s. They were a regular feature in melas—big or small. Hundreds of melas were held every year in the north Indian plains—primarily the United Provinces of Agra and Oudh. Many melas were of limited and local interest while others like the Makanpur, Bahraich and Devi Paatan melas drew thousands of pilgrims and revellers every year. The Bahraich mela commemorated the urs of Salar Ma'sud Ghazi. The Devi Paatan Mela was held during Dussehra.

Nautanki—earlier known as 'Svang'—became easily the most popular form of entertainment in the United Provinces. Entire villages—men, women and children—

watched spellbound, eyes glued to the makeshift stage, from late night into the early hours of next morning. Amongst the Dalit castes there was no taboo on women seeing Nautankis or attending the melas.

Gulab travelled far and wide performing in Tirmohan's company. In the mid-1930s, a woman's presence on stage had a touch of novelty, and excited audiences surged towards the shows. Her beauty and talent kept them captivated. Most performances were held in the open with no tents or tickets. Performers used natural locations and spatial levels to advantage. When a play was performed in a village square or city street, the balconies, housetops and platforms would become the tiers of a palace. A princess might sit at the upper window of a house. The dauntless hero would belt out a love song from below, fix a ladder and climb up to meet her.

In villages plays were usually performed in the middle of an open field. A waist-high rectangular platform would be positioned as the stage. The orchestra sat on a side of the platform in a semicircle. Actors moved freely on all sides. When off-stage they sat near the orchestra—smoking bidis, chewing paan and getting up when their turn came.

In the early days, costumes, make-up and props were simple and could be carried in two or three tin trunks. A chair would be solicited and transformed into a grand throne for the king to sit on. Each actor performed multiple roles. A pair of nagaras was used–one big and one small. The nagaras were made of leather. Even a hint of moisture was enough to distort the sound they produced. To prevent this, the nagaras had to be warmed. For this purpose, a fire was lit near the stage. If there was a gust of wind, its flames leapt up, throwing shadows onto the stage.

Lighting for the dramas was provided by one or two petromax lamps, which would have to be pumped from time to time.

A Nautanki began with the lighting of a lamp and a prayer to the goddess Saraswati followed by Ganesh worship. Hathras Nautankis were marked by their distinctive music. Actors were trained in classical discipline and struck awe in the audience with their unbroken *taan*.

In the Kanpur style, dialogue delivery, acting, costumes and stagecraft became increasingly refined. The music became less elaborate, its classical base gradually eroding. The opening ceremony got truncated into a simple vandana. The Ranga would sing a dramatic synopsis of the story and usher in the main characters. The play generally started with a scene at a king's court, a robber's den or a queen's palace, providing the occasion for dancing and singing. Suddenly some unusual event would occur, disturbing the colourful scene.

*

Folk influences on Nautanki included the earlier ballads and recitals of bards. When bards or ballad singers sang, stories unfolded. They gesticulated to dramatize the emotions and actions of various characters. Stories of saints, robbers, kings, lovers and knights popular in folklore were carried over into the early Nautankis. Verses from ballads were often used within the plays.

Nautanki had affinity with many popular drama forms like Rajasthani Khayal, Uttar Pradesh's Raas lila and Ram lila, Punjab's Nakal, Maharashtra's Tamasha and Parsi theatre, Bengal's Jatra, Madhya Pradesh's Maanch and Tamil Nadu's Natakam. These were all operatic forms combining elements of music, dance, drama and story in a magical whole.

Often called 'folk' forms, in fact these theatres had multiple origins. Their local roots combined with western melodramatic conventions and stage techniques. These forms have also, therefore, been termed 'hybrid-popular' theatre forms. They developed during the latter half of the nineteenth century and remained the dominant means of entertainment for several decades.[11] Some of these forms were religious in orientation while others, like Nautanki, were secular. In different parts of the country folk-hybrid forms replaced Sanskrit drama, which had stagnated over the past several centuries.

Nautankis clearly revealed a confluence of classical and folk forms and styles. Among classical conventions inherited by Nautanki and its sister forms were those of Sutradhara or stage manager, also called Ranga, Bhagavatha, Vyas or Swami. The Purvaranga, or stage preliminaries, were an essential feature of both Sanskrit and folk theatre. The musicians took their positions on stage, tuned their instruments and played a melody; the dancers performed a few dance numbers; the cast sang mangalacharana—a localized form of the classical invocation. Similar to Sanskrit drama, folk-hybrid theaters employed lavish music, dance, stylization, verse dialogue and exaggerated make-up and masks. Scenes melted into one another. Action continued in spite of changes of locale and scene. Asides, soliloquies and monologues abounded. The Joker—counterpart of the classical Vidushaka—revelled in humour, wit and ribaldry.

Bhagat, a 400-year-old form of operatic drama, was a forerunner of Svang and Nautanki, and is mentioned in *Ain-i-Akbari*, the monumental sixteenth-century record of Akbar's court. At that time it was just dramatized religious singing with a thin storyline, performed by Vaishnava devotees. Later, stories of kings, historical romances and chivalric tales were introduced. Bhagat *akharas* flourished in Mathura, Vrindavan, Agra and other places associated with the worship of Krishna.

In 1827 Ram Prasad of Amroha and Johari Raya of Motikatara produced a legendary folk play, *Roop Basant*, at their akhara in Agra, in the Bhagat form. Several decades later, the same play was produced as a Nautanki, in Hathras, in the akhara run by Indarman.

Most folk-hybrid theatre forms in north India developed within the akhara system—all-male spaces where actors, musicians, poets, writers and teachers spent a considerable part of the day together. A common lifestyle was adopted and members learnt arts and skills under the guidance of a guru. A composite culture was created, marked by physical exercise, nutrition, bodybuilding and spiritual discipline. Theatrical akharas blended seamlessly with wrestlers' practice and performance spaces. Shrikrishna Pehelvan, for instance, ran an akhara where wrestlers, poets and dramatists gathered. His own name—'Pehelwan'—displayed his status as a champion wrestler. His photos on the back covers of Nautanki script books show him as a muscular, moustachioed man wearing briefs, standing tall and proud.

Svangs (which were renamed Nautanki in the early twentieth century in Kanpur) first developed in the late nineteenth century at Hathras in the akhara established by Indarman. Indarman was a poet from the Chhipi (artisans who print cloth) caste. He was a master at poetic improvisation. With his followers Chiranjilal and Govind

Ram, Indarman's akhara began exhibiting Svangs in the 1880s.

Natharam Sharma Gaur was Indarman's most illustrious disciple. The story goes that as a boy he accompanied his blind father who sang for alms. He learnt some haunting melodies from his father. When he joined Indarman's akhara, he began practicing more elaborate singing. He had a melodious voice, and danced and played female parts with flair. When Indarman grew old, he handed over the company to Natharam. In the 1890s Natharam's professional troupe began to travel throughout north India.

At least three other troupes sprang up in Hathras around the turn of the century. Performances often took place in a competitive spirit, or dangal, between the various akharas. After Indarman's akhara, the most famous was that of Muralidhar.

Svang and early Nautanki texts were called 'Saangits'. A number of Saangits were published by each akhara. These booklets were sold during the performances and soon picked up a devoted readership.

*

Hathras Svangs were performed in Kanpur from time to time since the 1890s. One of the best-loved Svangs of the time was *Shehzadi Nautanki* (Princess Nautanki). This Svang was tremendously popular in the Kanpur area. As a result, in Kanpur the form itself began to be identified by the name 'Nautanki'.

Saangits were published in Kanpur, which had a better network of printing presses than Hathras. Kanpur was a fast-growing industrial township with a sizeable cantonment area. Its waterways flourished, with ships travelling on the Ganga all the way to Calcutta. Railways laid in the 1860s connected Kanpur to Lucknow as well as Calcutta. Spinning and tanning were concentrated here, making it a major manufacturing centre.

In 1901 a semi-industrial labour force of some 27,000 people was stationed at Kanpur. This created both audience and commercial structures that could sustain a popular entertainment form like Nautanki. By the 1910s Kanpur became the second major centre for Svang or Nautanki theatre.

Amateurs in and around Kanpur set up a number of small Nautanki companies. Usually it was a group of foppish young men who enjoyed the flavour of Nautankis and fancied themselves as stage actors and singers. The companies were small in terms of financial outlay and talent, but rich in enthusiasm. They would perform plays within a limited geographical area, using barely any props or special costumes.

Lalmani Numberdar, a rich landowner in Mandhana, a village at the outskirts of Kanpur, frequently hosted such Nautanki groups to perform in and around his village. He was on friendly terms with a number of actors and musicians. Once, when a small company broke up, he decided to employ these players to set up a company of his own. He bought new musical instruments, props and sets and got together all the actors and musicians who had been laid off. Lalmani Numberdar's soon became one of the biggest Nautanki companies, thriving during the next many decades. After his death, his sons Jaiprasad Numberdar and Hariprasad Numberdar ran the company.

Shrikrishna Pehelwan's company came up in the 1910s and immediately rose to prominence. He had the advantage of an established base in Kanpur, and set up a regular akhara where wrestling and drama progressed side by side. His plays attracted educated and urbane middle-class patrons. He cultivated his Arya Samaji connections, thus further extending his scope and reach. He was largely responsible for linking Nautanki to the waves of nationalism that swept across the country during the 1920s upto the 1940s.

Srikrishna Pehelwan was an actor, singer and wrestler. He began life as a tailor and is credited with introducing the first proper costumes into Nautanki. He continued running his tailoring shop even after being firmly established in the Nautanki field. In his shop 'every type of tailored clothing [was] sold wholesale, such as coats, shirts, kurtas, women's jackets, waistcoats, three-piece suits, two-piece suits and so on.'[12] Nautanki costumes became increasingly glamorous with specially designed angarkhas, churidars, lehengas and cholis for women, and men's suits and silken robes for kings.

By the 1940s Nautankis adopted a wide spectrum of modern conventions, partly under the influence of Parsi theatre. These conventions included the proscenium stage with painted backdrops, wings and front curtains separating performers from spectators; division of plays into scenes and acts; instruments such as harmonium and clarinet; lavish dresses and modern stagecraft.

*

Tirmohan Ustad belonged to a middle-class family of Kannauj but had neither capital nor a base in Kanpur. His company's achievements were based on Tirmohan's exceptional musical talent as well as a sharp eye for innovation. Not only was he the first to introduce women into Nautanki, he is also reputed to be the first to bring in elaborately painted drop curtains and new instruments such as the clarinet.

Like most other theatrical forms of the time, Nautanki at its inception was associated with systems of feudal patronage. But by the turn of the century it had begun to dissociate from the pre-industrial feudal systems, and develop as a commercial form. It was an important player in the emerging 'performance market'. Nautanki's transition from a non-commercial to a commercial venture was well under way by the 1920s. By the 1930s it had developed its economic dimension, largely on the basis of the new phenomenon of ticket sales. This transition was particularly marked in the Kanpur groups. It was not so prominent in the Hathras area.

In Kanpur in the 1930s and 1940s, the akhara system gave way to companies managed on a professional basis. Staff members were now paid monthly salaries depending on their talent and popularity. This was similar to the pattern prevailing in the 'studio system' of the Bombay film industry of the time. As in Bombay, so also in Nautanki, a company became known by the names of its heroes and heroines, musicians and directors. Box-office earnings were determined by the worth and work of all these, combined together.

10

Kings, Queens and Bandits

Thousands in the audience were left wiping tears from their eyes. Women would be wailing loudly. The crowds would identify with the characters.

—Kailash Gautam

When Harishchandra asks Taramati to pay tax for the cremation of Rohit, believe me people would burst into tears. When Majnu goes mad and meets Laila in Laila Majnu urf Maktab ki Mohabat, *when Farhad beats his head against Shirin's grave in* Shirin Farhad, *when Haadi Rani breaks her bangles in* Amar Singh Rathore, *when Sultana amazes the British police commissioner in* Sultana Daku: *there is emotion created. Nautankis would inspire patriotic fervour and resistance to British injustice. The actors and audience would become one: no artifice on either side.*

—Krishna Raghav

Tirmohan Lalji's shows began taking place all over, at every crossing. Ten to twenty thousand people would gather for each show. They would each give ten to twenty rupees. We were in good form and highly enthusiastic.

—Gulab Bai, 1996

Gulab played the heroine or 'Rani' roles in Tirmohan's plays. By the mid-1930s she was famous as 'Gulab Jaan'. She became in turn brave Rani Durgawati, lovelorn Laila, ill-fated Taramati or Jamal who defended her lover with drawn sword.

Gulab breathed in the flavour and colour of Nautanki dramas, until she became one with the form. They coloured her dreams. They were the fantasies she breathed in, absorbed, and exuded. A young woman with a vivid imagination, her world expanded immeasurably, exploded and sparkled. After all, not every girl is able to live out the roles of powerful queens and passionate lovers, in tragic romances and heart-warming comedies. Not every woman can attract millions of men and sparkle like a star.

The Nautankis she grew to love were picked from a vast treasure trove of medieval romances, royal intrigues and magical tales. Their stories ranged from mythology and legend to realism. People watched intently and absorbed stories interwoven with ideas and ideals. Travelling theatre communicated ancient messages as well as contemporary ones, and helped create a network of shared cultural, political and moral values.

Saintly legends and religious myths were dramatized side by side with Persian romances. In late nineteenth-century Hathras, the earliest Nautankis (then called 'Svang') included *Shravan Kumar, Nala Damayanti, Ram Banvaas, Mordhvaj, Indar Sabha, Puran Bhagat, Roop Basant, Bhakt Prahlad, Shehzadi Nautanki, Heer Ranjha, Raja Harishchandra* and *Laila Majnu*. Around the turn of the century tales based on historical events, featuring characters like Prithviraj Chauhan, Akbar's general Amar Singh Rathore, Tipu Sultan, Rani Durgavati and Panna Dai became popular. Gods and goddesses, wizards and nymphs mingled freely with kings and queens, palace maids and dacoits, landlords and rebels, creating a fanciful world with intense appeal. Noble bandits, brave fighters and truthful lovers emphasized the virtues of valour, honesty and loyalty. Characters were sharply etched, events fast-paced and the ethical intent unambiguous.

Nautankis like *Sultana Daku urf Garibon ka Pyara* or *Virangana Virmati* presented new types of heroes and heroines—outlaws in service of the poor, or women warriors avenging their husbands in battle. Popular social romances included *Triya Charitra* (Wiles of a Woman), *Reshmi Rumal* (Silken Handkerchief), *Shahi Lakarhara* (The Royal Woodcutter), *Siyah Posh* (Man in the Black Mask) and *Sabz Pari Gulfam* (The Heavenly Nymph and Prince Gulfam). Ill-treated daughters and daughters-in-law like *Shrimati Manjari*, *Andhi Dulhin* and *Bekasur Beti* also made their presence felt.

Gulab learnt one part after another. She acted in various Nautankis and became adept at playing diverse roles—romantic or tragic, humorous or comic. As she grew into womanhood, she carried herself like a queen—her magnificent stage persona clinging to her like a second skin. Within a few years, it seemed to be the only skin she had.

*

Gulab Jaan sometimes acted in *Shehzadi Nautanki* (Princess Nautanki). The Nautanki form takes its name from this play.

Princess Nautanki was a famous beauty of Multan. In a neighbouring state lived two brothers, Bhoop Singh and Phool Singh. One day the younger, Phool Singh—handsome, adventurous and rash—returned from hunting and asked his brother's wife to quickly serve him food. She taunted him saying he was behaving as if he were the husband of the beautiful Nautanki. Insulted, he left home, vowing he would not return until he had married Nautanki. His faithful friend Yashwant Singh accompanied him.

On reaching Multan they met the flower woman of the palace and begged her to allow them to stay in her hut. Every day this flower woman carried a garland of fresh flowers to the princess. Phool Singh, an expert in the art of floral decoration, offered to weave a garland for the princess. The flower woman took the garland to the princess, who suspected that someone else had prepared it and flew into a rage. The terrified flower woman explained that her nephew's young wife was on a short visit, and had prepared the garland. The princess ordered her to produce the young woman who wove such beautiful garlands.

The flower woman took Phool Singh, disguised as a beautiful woman, to the princess. The princess fell in love with this beauty. She offered her friendship and insisted that Phool Singh stay in her chamber. He agreed. At night the princess sighed and said that if Phool Singh were a man, she would marry him. Phool Singh asked her to close her eyes, meditate on the household deity and invoke her blessings to turn one of them into a man. The princess did this. When she opened her eyes, she found her friend had turned into a man. A love scene followed. In the morning the palace maid reported the matter to the king, who ordered the young man arrested and killed. Princess Nautanki, carrying a sword and cup of poison, reached the spot where Phool Singh was awaiting death. She drove off the executioners and challenged her father. The king, deeply touched, agreed to her marriage with Phool Singh.

Nautanki and Phool Singh entered the vocabulary of ordinary folk speech. Any beautiful girl dismissing her suitors one after the other became dubbed a Nautanki waiting for her Phool Singh.

The play became very popular. It drew part of its fascination from the deft use of cross-dressing—hero disguised as a beautiful woman, heroine acting as a valiant man. In a society with fixed gender roles, such flexibility displayed on stage tickled the imagination, indicating possibilities that might be impractical, yet attractive. Cross-dressing was common in Nautanki, with male actors regularly playing female parts.

Even after Gulab—and other women—began playing Rani roles, boys continued to be popular as heroines in many Nautanki companies. Not only that, sometimes the women would cross-dress and play the part of heroes! Nautanki aficionados even remember seeing Gulab play the part of Laila, and Krishna Bai the part of Majnu, in the Nautanki *Laila Majnu*.

An important nineteenth century musical drama that continued to be staged well into the twentieth century was *Indar Sabha* (The Court of Indra) written by Agha Hassab Amanat, an Urdu poet of Lucknow. Amanat used traditional melodies, folk tunes and seasonal dances, adding to these his dramatic lyric talent. The operatic play went into many editions. Various Nautanki troupes modified the original to include local myths, characters, situations and melodies. *Indar Sabha* stood between literary drama and folk play. All its action took place in the court of Indra, king of the gods. Its popularity inspired Nautanki writers, who sought to emulate its whimsical and other-worldly atmosphere of fairies, devils, gods, princes, wizards and dancers.

Siyah Posh was another popular tale. Jamal, daughter of the wazir of Syria, was reading the Koran on her palace balcony when handsome young Gabru passed on the street below and pointed out some mistakes in her recital. Jamal invited him to continue correcting her. He scaled the palace wall, and they fell in love. Every night he met her in her chamber. One night he was arrested while scaling the wall. The wazir ordered his execution. Jamal, dressed in a black mask, arrived at the scene. The king, who had overheard their conversation on one of his nightly incognito rounds, recognized the purity of their love and pardoned them. Struck by Jamal's nobility and faithful love, he adopted her as a daughter and married her to Gabru, who was proclaimed heir to the throne.

The sub-genre of dacoit dramas emerged around the 1920s. These plays explored resistance to established power by dacoits and were based on actual figures and events. Here, folklore emerged from people's lives, illustrating a living process of myth-making. These plays, such as *Dayaram Gujar*, *Daku Maan Singh* and *Sultana Daku* had heroes who robbed the rich and generously bestowed bounties on the poor. A complex set of ethical principles including renunciation of wealth, selfless pursuit of truth and, somewhat paradoxically, willingness to submit to higher authority, ran through these narratives.

*

Nautanki writers reinterpreted old legends, Sanskrit dramas, Persian romances and mythological lore for the contemporary era. Over sixty plays, including *Raja Harischandra* and *Siyah Posh*, are ascribed to Natharam though at least half of these were actually written by Indarman and others. A number of plays were published in Kanpur and Kannauj under Tirmohan Lal's name, although Yasin Mian of Kannauj was the actual writer of most of the dramas. Yasin worked as a factory hand in Kanpur.

The name on the cover of a Saangit or Nautanki was not necessarily that of the actual writer. Thus Yasin Mian is not mentioned as a writer on any Nautanki cover, although he is commonly acknowledged as the real writer of most plays formally credited to Tirmohan Ustad. Tirmohan's grand-nephew, Chinha Guru, confirmed this. Chinha Guru had clear memories of Yasin—a tall man in a long white *achkan* who had a marvellous command over language. Tirmohan commissioned him to write, and paid him for each script. He then published the scripts under his own name. Yasin's name is often interwoven in the last verse of the plays that he composed. This is the only evidence left of his authorship. The script books were published with Tirmohan Lal's photo on the title page.

Tirmohan conceived the storylines, while Yasin Mian actually composed the scripts in Nautanki form. Tirmohan directed each new play, and performed the first show at Beeghapur. If this show was successful, Tirmohan got one of his nephews to write out the script in neat calligraphy in an ordinary notebook. Later, Tirmohan would get the script printed, with his own name as writer.

Shrikrishna Pehelwan set up a press and published plays. His photo—clad in briefs, in the proud stance of a master wrestler—adorned the back cover of every Nautanki published in his name, although these plays were actually composed by others writers. The real writers included a poet called Pannalal and another called Lakshmi Narayan. The writers' names were present, if at all, only in the very last stanza of the plays. Copyright was vested with the company owner, while the writers received nothing beyond a small lump-sum payment. The writers, typically indigent and living a hand-to-mouth existence, had no bargaining power, and were forced to be content with the pittance they were paid.

A large measure of Tirmohan's success is traceable to Yasin's brilliant scripts. Yasin Mian was a wizard with words. His grasp of musical metre, rhythm and nuances of Urdu as well as Hindi was truly extraordinary. Yasin died in 1957 while in the midst of writing the Nautanki *Anarkali*. According to Chinha Guru, 'Yasin was a hundred years old when he died.' Yasin's son Aamin completed the writing of this play. He was a good writer, but not outstanding, as Yasin had been.

*

In the 1960s, Tirmohan's fortunes declined, and he sold the rights to publish all his scripts to Shrikrishna Pehelwan for the throwaway price of Rs 2,500. Shrikrishna then published the scripts in his own name, along with all the script books he was already producing, and amassed a sizeable fortune through their combined sales.

11

A Nationalist Streak

Description of a Nautanki performance of *Bahadur Ladki* in Kanpur, 1942: *The British police officer was drinking. A woman was pouring his alcohol, another was dancing, when a junior caught hold of a beautiful woman and brought her in. This girl's lover was a revolutionary. She was abusing the British regime and its rulers, because her lover was in their jail. The police officer says he will release her lover, if she will agree to be his wife for one night. In reply, this courageous girl treats him to a stinging slap. People in the audience spring out of their chairs. In the background an actor claps loudly at the very moment that the girl slaps the police officer. The audience imagines this loud sound to be made by the slap! The officer's reaction is very animated, to further the deception.*

That girl meets the Governor of the area:

Heroine : *Who are you?*
Governor : *The ruler of this country.*
Heroine : *Why have you come here?*
Governor : *To hunt.*
Heroine : *(behere taveel) –*
'*Jab shikari ho khud mulk ka badshah*
Uska haakim bhala shikari kyon na ho?
Daad faryad sunne ke fursat kahan
Kaise barbaad raiyat bechari na ho?'

(When the ruler of the country is a hunter
Won't his officials be hunters too?
Will they pay any attention to complaints and grievances?
Won't the wretched citizens be in distress?)

The British government had long recognized theatre's power and potential to contribute to social unrest. As far back as 1876, it passed the Dramatic Perfomances Act, which gave officials the power to prohibit public performances they considered seditious, defamatory to the government, scandalous, obscene or likely to deprave and corrupt members of the audience.

In 1942, during the Quit India movement, the administration of Kanpur city invoked the Dramatic Performances Act to ban Tirmohan Lal and Company from entering the limits of Kanpur city. It imposed the ban after the company performed *Bahadur Ladki* at Phool Bagh in central Kanpur. The play was popular with audiences across north India. Its conscious intent was to stir nationalist sentiments. Several performances had already been held in Kanpur. It aroused the suspicions of the city police, and they were on the alert.

The repertoire of most Nautanki companies of the time included a number of patriotic dramas promoting resistance against the British regime. Within a framework of pan-Indian nationalism, regional theatres helped generate a consensus to revolt against British domination. Nautanki joined the fray initially with its repertoire of folk warriors, valiant queens and loyal soldiers. Gradually modern patriotic and political themes were staged, portraying leaders and events as well as ordinary freedom-loving citizens. These helped raise issues and consolidate nationalist sentiment.

According to writer-dramatist Vijay Pandit, 'Folk songs, literature and drama inspired ordinary people to oppose their conditions of enslavement. In north India the Nautanki folk theatre was the foremost cultural medium to play a radical role during the national movement. Nautanki fought the battle in its own way: by enacting plays soaked in valour and patriotism throughout the length and breadth of Avadh, Purvanchal and Bundelkhand.'

Shrikrishna Pehelwan's early plays were published under the aegis of the Arya Saangit Samiti of Kanpur—an organization of Arya Samajis. Many of these plays had a nationalist tinge. In 1920 the Great Shrikrishna Saangit Company produced *Khoone Nahak*, a Nautanki based on the Jallianwala Bagh massacre. The Company continued to enact plays on heroic historical figures like Maharani Padmini, Shivaji, Virmati and Hakikat Rai. After 1930, Shrikrishna Pehelwan introduced a number of social-reform dramas like *Aankh ka Jadu*, *Pati Bhakti*, *Vafadar Munim*, *Punjab Mail* and *Bansuri Vali*.

Another Nautanki, written by Manoharlal Shukla in 1922, was *Rashtriya Saangit Julmi Dayar*. It was also about the Jallianwala Bagh massacre. It bore on its cover an image of a whip-flailing policeman labelled 'Martial Law' threatening to disrobe a woman labelled 'Afflicted Punjab'. A sad, contemplative figure resembling Mahatma Gandhi, and labelled 'Satyagraha', sat in a corner. This play reconstructed the Jallianwala massacre from a child's point of view. It ended with wish fulfillment—the collective ghost of murdered citizens came to the evil General Dyer seeking revenge, beat him up and forced him to release all the arrested prisoners.

Shrikrishna Pehelwan's 1931 play *Veer Balak* exhorted youth to join the freedom movement. Lal Babu of Aligarh composed *Gandhi Haran urf Sapne ka Kamaal* in 1932. This inspired people to make common cause with the Civil Disobedience campaigns. Kanhaiyalal Chaturvedi's *Pita-Putra* depicted Prahlad as a Gandhian satyagrahi who makes every sacrifice in order to protect the people against the authority of the Sultanate. *Balia ka Sher* presented the life of the martyr Chittu Pandey and emphasized Hindu-Muslim unity. Munindra Nath Goswami, popularly known as Kakkuji of Lucknow, wrote a similar play called *Balia Balidaan*. Shrikrishna Pehelwan's Nautanki *Shaheed Bhagat Singh* also helped strengthen popular ferment against colonial rule. Roopamji wrote *Bangal ka Sher*, *Jawahar Jeevan*, *Abul Kalam Azad*, *Netaji* and *Rajendra Prasadji* Svangs thus extending the ambit and reach of several significant patriotic figures. *Asahayog Charhni*, *Zulm ki Aag* and *Subhash Chandra Bose* were other Nautankis that contributed to the ferment. *Jhansi ki Rani Lakshmi Bai* was especially instrumental in inspiring women to actively participate in the Gandhian campaigns.

*

Kanpur was an active centre for revolutionary terrorists, trade unions and Civil Disobedience campaigns. During the 1930s the Congress Party spread its tentacles wide and deep into the soil of Uttar Pradesh. In 1942, when nationalist leaders launched the Quit India campaign, the authorities were concerned about an increasingly volatile situation.

When the Nautanki *Bahadur Ladki* was to be performed at Kanpur's Phool Bagh, city authorities posted a posse of policemen at the site to maintain law and order. Earlier shows of the play had created a flurry of interest, and a large crowd was expected to gather. Any crowd was considered cause for concern in those sensitive times. The sprawling public park was known to be a meeting-place for revolutionaries. A thick crowd would render it an ideal venue for distributing leaflets and spreading messages that would inspire or incite people.

The presentation was simple. A wooden stage had been constructed, some chairs laid out for VIPs, benches for other important people, and a rug on which the majority of people could huddle. Spectators had always been enthusiastic participants in Nautanki performances. They cheered, laughed and wept with the mood and action on stage. Their sparks of live interest charged the actors.

In the play *Bahadur Ladki*, a British police officer insulted the heroine Farida, a young flower seller, enacted by Gulab Bai. Farida was a courageous woman with strong nationalist leanings. Her lover was already under arrest. Infuriated by the policeman's abusive insinuations, this courageous girl ('bahadur ladki') dealt him a stinging blow.

The impact on the audience was powerful and palpable. It was, in any case, a volatile crowd, ready to react instantaneously. Anger at British occupation and atrocities was generally at a high. The sight of a British police officer insulting a young Indian woman would have aroused ire. People in the audience would have felt a sense of tremendous relief seeing her react so unambiguously. They empathised with her, and the scene brought out their own suppressed anger. Pent-up indignation found an outlet, and they took to clapping loudly, cheering and screaming.

In the next sequence, Farida told the governor that such misdemeanours were only to be expected from somebody employed by a regime that cared nothing for its citizens. When the rulers themselves were exploiters, their officials and henchmen too were bound to hunt and exploit!

By this time somebody in the audience took the opportunity to raise one or two anti-British slogans. More joined the sloganeering. The police smelt trouble and jumped into action. Scuffles broke out. The police ordered the show closed, and wielded their lathis to disperse the crowd. They were angered by the portrayal of a woman slapping an offensive policeman, and enraged by people's enthusiastic response. Under guise of maintaining law and order, policemen got an opportunity to vent their frustration.

The city administration was wary about the wider impact such a play could have. They therefore decided to ban the show. Not only that; they also decided that the company performing this play would be banned from the city.

Years later, Gulab Bai recalled events and processes that led to the ban: 'Tirmohan Lalji's shows began to take place all over, at every crossing. Ten to twenty thousand people would gather for each show. They would each give ten to twenty rupees. We were also in good form and highly enthusiastic. The city Kotwal called Tirmohan Lal because there were reports of trouble and fights brewing. The Kotwal called me too, wondering, "Who is this girl who is so famous and popular that crowds of ten to twenty thousand gather to see her?" He was a Britisher—Handoo was his name. We presented ourselves before him. Tirmohan Lal asked, "Is the government displeased with us?" The Kotwal ordered, "Leave the city at once!" Tirmohan Lalji had another house in Kannauj. He took all of us there, and began running the party from there.'

Kanpur's prominent HMV dealer Ranvir Singh Bhalla corroborated this account, and added other dimensions to the story: 'It is absolutely correct that the police commissioner told them no programs of theirs would be held in Kanpur. Knives were brandished during a show.'

Big wealthy people all went for these shows. But, they had to leave Kanpur.'

Nautanki artiste Paan Kunwar added, 'Because there were knives flashing at the show, Tirmohan Ustad's Nautanki was banned. He was ordered to leave the city within twelve hours.'

*

Tirmohan Lal was unfazed. He shifted his company to Kannauj. The props and costumes were all shifted there, into Tirmohan's ancestral home.

Nautanki artistes were adventurous people. In the habit of moving from one place to another, they would set up their tents one day and fold them the next. This was an integral part of their profession as travelling theatre people.

Nautankis had always walked a tightrope in the midst of hostile authorities and the law. On various occasions every company faced charges, threats or prosecution. This could be on account of a Nautanki considered obscene, or because it was inspiring people to revolt against the established political order. Quite apart from strictures against a company, specific staff members were sometimes on the wrong side of the law. The artistes were a disorderly lot, more than one committed to drinking, drugs and ribaldry.

Tirmohan's entire company moved with him to Kannauj. He was deeply attached to the members of his staff. They were like family to him. The actors and musicians fanned out into rented tenements in working-class areas near Tirmohan's home in Kannauj. This home became the company's headquarters and the refuge for several down-at-heel artistes. It was the base for rehearsals and management of the affairs of the company.

Gulab shifted to Kannauj with all the rest. She continued as the heroine of *Bahadur Ladki*, and a number of other Nautankis. She later mused, 'In any case work continued in Kannauj. People kept coming to see me as *bahadur ladki*. The days kept passing by.'

12

Rising Prosperity

Our fathers came and took away the money we earned. This was their work. Our work was to earn the money, our fathers' and brothers' work was to take it away back to the village.

—Shaila, Balpurva

On stage I was Shirin and Taramati with heroes like Mehboob and Fazal, Naagar and Moti. But in my personal life there was an eerie silence. Everything was absolutely still.

—Gulab Bai to Suresh Salil

Gulab Bai's parents lived in the haveli. The haveli was magnificent. There were cattle and horses, bullock carts and horse-carts. Tens of labourers looked after the animals. There was the well with sweet water. At Diwali diyas were lit on every floor and ledge so the house looked dazzling and people came from far and near to see the haveli. They came walking from miles away. There was a mango orchard and agricultural land. However, neither her father not her brothers tended the land. They blew up the money she and her sisters earned—on alcohol, meat and lavish hospitality. They sold off the land Gulab had bought for them, and squandered whatever cash they were given. Gulab bought them land thinking they will work and earn something. But they did not do so.

—Ram Prasad

When Gulab became a crowd-puller, a living symbol of Tirmohan Lal and Company's success, other companies too began to vie for her. Gulab was fairly loyal to her mentor Tirmohan, but being in high demand helped push up her price. Numberdar offered her a higher salary to induce her to defect to his company. To keep her, Tirmohan raised the amount he was paying. This happened several times, and was responsible for a dramatic rise in Gulab's income.

When Krishna Bai joined Numberdar's company, competitive dynamics between the two companies intensified rather than weakening. Numberdar still wanted Gulab for his company and made sporadic offers. In retaliation Tirmohan sent across offers to Krishna Bai. This led to an all-round rise in salary for both the actors.

In time the two women became adept at using their piquant position to negotiate a raise. At the smallest opportunity Gulab would threaten to quit Tirmohan and join Numberdar. Similarly Krishna Bai would threaten to quit Numberdar and join Tirmohan. Both company owners were well aware that these were their star attractions. They kept raising their salaries so as to placate and retain them.

By 1942 Gulab Jaan was paid more than anybody else in Tirmohan's troupe. There were some brilliant male actors too, but they could be replaced. Replacing Gulab would not be so easy. Gulab gave all this money to her parental family, feeling duty-bound to support and provide for her younger siblings. At the time of joining Nautanki, she was the sole earning member for her family. Chahetan joined soon after, but her income was a mere fraction of Gulab's. Chathetan played only side-characters, and never attained a status like Gulab's. Whatever she earned was also ploughed back into the parental family. Both sisters contributed to their family's increasingly comfortable lifestyle.

Initially Tirmohan paid Gulab a token amount for personal expenses, but this soon rose to the substantial figure of fifty rupees per month. Multiplying at a dizzy pace, the figure reached well over Rs 1,000 by 1942. Some say it was nearer Rs 2,000. Within the Nautanki world, her reputation was such that many believed Gulab's earnings were more than the district magistrate's income at that time! Quite apart from her salary, people threw 'gifts' onto stage in appreciation of her acting and singing. Well-to-do people would fling silver coins as inaam (reward). Some romantics would throw a purse full of money with their names and addresses on it. The purse would land on the stage with a loud, impressive clang.

When someone offered money to an artiste during a performance, the Ranga announced the donation in an extemporaneous rhyming couplet, often weaving together the names of the donor and the donor's father and grandfather. The artiste accepted the donation with a bow or salaam.

In the 1930s, gold cost twenty-eight rupees per tola, ghee two rupees per seer and mustard oil one rupee for sixteen seers. Thus Gulab's earnings were astronomical. Certainly her rates were higher than what any of the male actors or 'mardanas' earned.

*

Lal Bahadur was unscrupulous: he milked his daughters dry of all their earnings. Despite a decade of hard work and high earnings, Gulab hadn't a penny to her name. Nobody in these circles thought in terms of bank accounts or savings in those days. In any case her family immediately siphoned off all she earned. Young Gulab Jaan did not question this. After all, it was the only system she had ever known. A quintessential 'breadwinner heroine', she accepted her role as natural and god-given.

Gulab's income provided for her brothers' schooling. One brother died young. Three others dropped out of school at different stages. Only one completed high school. Later, her brother Haulu settled in Tera Mallu village, near Balpurva. Gulab bought land for him. She bought land for other brothers too, hoping this would prove to be an independent means of livelihood. But two brothers—Subedar and Gindu—preferred to remain with Gulab in Kanpur. When she was young they were sometimes her escorts and protectors. Later in life she employed them as bouncers, ticket-sellers and general helpers. However, they often helped themselves to her earnings, eating and drinking lavishly and living as parasites.

None of her brothers cared to settle down as agriculturists. From time to time, they gave out land for cultivation to sharecroppers. Often they sold patches of land in return for liquid cash, which was immediately used up in hedonistic pleasures.

Kallu Seth, Krishna Bai's father, siphoned off the best part of his daughter's income. When Krishna Bai's sisters joined the profession, their earnings too went straight back into their parental household. Their father squandered much of this steady flow of cash in wasteful expenses, merry-making and the like.

*

During her first decade in Nautanki, Gulab financed repair and renovation of the old shanty at Balpurva. Krishna Bai did the same for the hut next door, in which she had grown up.

Gulab Bai's haveli, on the spot where the hut in which she was born used to be. Her family continued to live here while she travelled with Tirmohan Lal's Nautanki company. Today the haveli lies empty, while her niece Shaila lives next door.

Drunk on their daughters' success, Lal Bahadur and Kallu Seth hatched a plan to build magnificent havelis to replace their old shanties. This was an ambitious project indeed. It was expensive to carry stone to Balpurva, hire craftsmen skilled in carving stone, and labourers to undertake the hard manual work. Least worried about the financial aspect, they went at it hammer and tongs. They had always nurtured dreams of grandeur, and seized the opportunity to convert these dreams into concrete reality.

Lal Bahadur and Kallu Seth's casual dependence on women's income was part of a pattern. The Bedia social system acknowledged that some women would devote their

Elaborate carvings on the façade of the haveli. Lakshmi, goddess of wealth, wears a 'lehenga' like any dancing girl, and is flanked on either side by a protective elephant and a British officer.

lives to being breadwinners. Marked off as unmarriageable, their primary allegiance was expected to remain with the parental family. They were trained from earliest childhood to believe that they had a moral duty to provide for the entire family. Though they were the main providers, their fathers and brothers controlled the income they earned.

Female breadwinners were held responsible for their siblings' welfare. They paid for the marriage of younger brothers, including bride price if demanded. They bore responsibility for the financial welfare of their brothers' families. Brothers were not expected to earn any income. The only expectation from them was to bring in wives. These wives worked within the household, cooking, cleaning, and taking care of children, the elderly and the sick. The wives also took responsibility for the care of children born to their working sisters-in-law. They took charge of the daily mothering of these children from infancy onwards.

The men became what sociologist Aggrawal calls a 'leisure class'. They spent their days loafing around. They were secure at several levels; their needs were met unconditionally. They firmly believed in their right to survive and thrive on sisters'—and later daughters'—earnings.

The working women slaved away as singers and dancers, and took on wealthy lovers when they could. This took the edge off their poverty, but only so long as it lasted. Sources of income were sporadic and uncertain. At the extreme end, Bedia women worked as prostitutes. Natal families were often the ones to solicit and bargain with customers. They never gave away these women in marriage, but in a sense they gave the women away piecemeal, to a series of customers.

Bedia women were classified into two distinct categories leading very different kinds of lives. One set were the chaste married women—the *byahata*; the other the unmarried unchaste public women, the professionals who worked to earn—the *dhandhewali*. There were clear expectations from each category, with next to no possibility of crossover from one side to the other. Girls were trained from early childhood into the skills required for their future vocation, foreclosing the possibility of making an active choice as adults.

The two categories of women occupied vastly different worlds. Thus while daughters in many Bedia families became public women, daughters-in-law remained in purdah.

Married women were highly valued for their domestic labour, which freed the husband's unmarried sisters and their own daughters to engage in commercial work.

Gulab grew up in this ethos, firmly ensconced as a hardcore professional. When she became well-known and commanded a high salary, she simply turned the amount over to her family.

Gulab knew she would never have the option of a respectable marriage like her mother did. Her fate was sealed. Her life was carved in a different mould. By the time she was an adult, she had seen enough to understand what was expected of her.

Fortuitous in her case was the lucky break into Nautanki—a space where she could earn much better than others of her ilk. There was, moreover, greater artistic challenge, opportunity for learning, security and status in the Nautanki life.

Gulab had four younger sisters, while Krishna had five. All eleven women were trained to sing and dance for a livelihood. Cut off from marriage or other socially accepted lifelong relationships, their allegiance and attachment were bound to remain with their parents and brothers' family units. For their families, each of these women was like the proverbial hen that laid golden eggs. They had a steady inflow of funds without needing to lift a little finger for it.

*

By the time Gulab was twenty years old, she'd matured into a beautiful woman. Brought up like a wild rose in the village, she blossomed in the sophisticated Nautanki world. Attractive and confident, her fame spread throughout north India.

Gulab sang songs full of romantic and sexual innuendo, and revelled in the numerous compliments she received. She sensed lust in the eyes of many men in the audience. She was a 'public' woman, and knew in every fibre of her being that she was somebody men wanted to have.

The very presence of a woman on stage stimulated male fantasy. Gulab—and the other female Nautanki artistes of the time—wore full-length costumes. Yet a woman dancing invariably attracted lewd attention. An uncovered face could be construed as seductive. A bare ankle was taken to imply erotic invitation. In north India's purdah culture respectable women were not supposed to show themselves in public. Victorian prudery reinforced this. Yet on the Nautanki stage, women were on exhibit, public commodities as it were. Male gaze easily classified such a woman as 'available'.

Gulab's father and brothers made it a point to stay with her at all times. They were careful to see to it that she did not form a liaison with any ordinary man. They were not opposed to a relationship as such, but it must be with a wealthy man.

Gulab had crossed the age at which many Bedia girls were given away to a patron for the ceremony of the first night. This was called 'nath utarai'—removal of the nose-ring. Family men kept strict vigil, to maintain control over female sexuality. Wealthy patrons were on the lookout for young virgin women; for the right to her first night, a patron was required to pay a considerable amount to her family. 'Nath utarai' was celebrated as a rite of passage akin to marriage, and publicly acknowledged with dance and feasting. It signaled the woman's new status as 'available' to other patrons.

Bedia families discouraged their breadwinner women from forming long-term stable liaisons. A long-term patron was acceptable only if he was really wealthy and provided for his 'kept' woman's family. As a rule the wealthy man was already married. Yet he might feel involved enough with his mistress to offer marriage. Since polygamy was not illegal, he could openly maintain her as his second wife. Sometimes he would insist that she give up her work. If a woman agreed to give up her career, it was called *ghar baithna*—literally 'sitting at home'.

A subtle ethics and logistics distinguished courtesan or mistress relationships from those set up within prostitution. The patron–mistress relationship emphasized loyalty and mutual attachment. A marriage ceremony may or may not be held, but if there was a sense of mutual commitment, the relationship was referred to as a 'sambandh'. The word was commonly used, with a definite meaning attached to it.

It sometimes happened that a Bedia woman stopped providing for her natal family after she formed a sambandh or entered into marriage. Natal families usually treated this as a breach of trust. They claimed to have been betrayed. They were indignant and resentful, for they saw it as a denial of their 'natural' rights over the woman's earnings.

*

Gulab played the heroine in romantic sagas, singing and emoting—love, longing and desire. Her sweet and powerful voice conveyed mystery and passion. Her name drew people, and her lilting voice and dramatic flair kept them glued to their seats.

Training, travelling and performing soaked up her energies. She was busy absorbing all the colour and rich adventure life offered her. Yet she was still single and independent with no lover, no sambandh, no marriage and no passing affairs.

Years later Gulab Bai recalled: 'On stage I was Shirin and Taramati with heroes like Mehboob and Fazal, Naagar and Moti. But in my personal life there was an eerie silence. Everything was absolutely still.'[13]

13

One Man's Obsession

There was a very famous firm in Kannauj where itr (perfume) was prepared. They printed a calendar every year with the photo of a national leader. The Seth who owned the firm was a restless, romantic sort of person. One day he saw me acting in a drama. He said to me, 'I will make you the queen of my heart. I will bathe you in itr and Gangajal. I will drape you in gold and silver from head to toe… .'
—Gulab Bai, to Suresh Salil

Shiv Chandar, Rai Bahadur of Kannauj, was a very decent man, a very big man. He 'kept' Gulab Bai.
—Shiv Adhar Dube

In the early 1940s, Chandar Seth fell in love with Gulab Bai. Kannauj was famous for its itr (perfumes). Chandar Seth was a leading manufacturer and dealer of perfumes. He was an important personage. Puffed up as Rai Bahadur Shiv Chandar Seth, he served several terms as the chairman of Kannauj municipality. British officials and policemen doffed their caps in deference when they met him. [14]

As a glamorous young heroine, Gulab already received more attention than she could handle. While performing in Moradabad, an influential local man tried to break into her tent. The same night Tirmohan got all the tents packed and the troupe left the area. The infatuated man came to Kannauj to meet Gulab, but she was kept hidden. After a few days he left, frustrated.

Wealthy merchants and zamindars were notorious for their roving eyes. They considered women who sang and danced mujras or acted in Nautankis to be available—potential keeps. Chandar Seth, true to form, set his heart upon having Gulab Jaan, the heart-throb of millions.

He began to pursue Gulab singlemindedly. He entered her inner sanctum with his charm and persistence, wealth and power. In 1942, after she moved to Kannauj with the rest of Tirmohan Lal's troupe, Chandar Seth took to visiting her frequently. He turned up for rehearsals. He would appear at her performances. A police inspector once harrassed Gulab at a mela. Chandar Seth saw to it that the offender was dismissed from his job.

Gulab was flattered by his attentions. He wooed her passionately, and Gulab responded. But then he grew impatient of her other commitments. He became adamant to have Gulab all to himself. The time and energy she spent on her work began to irk him. He asked her to leave her work in the Nautanki—'Why do you want to work when I will look after you? You can relax now. Be comfortable.'

He thought she would be glad for the chance to leave a hard life, and grab what he provided. He promised to provide her a life of luxury—forever. Yet young Gulab Bai declined his offer. She enjoyed her work and was deeply invested in her position as an artiste. Her popularity was at an all-time high. She had no desire to drop it all.

Chandar Seth nurtured a jealous spark. As the months went by, he could no longer bear to have his paramour perform in front of male audiences. Increasingly intolerant of her stage persona, he grew insistent and possessive, and would not let her work unhindered. He resented all the men in the audience. The lust in their eyes infuriated him. It enraged him to think of anybody else possessing even an iota of Gulab's body or as much as its image. He imagined her as exclusively his.

He pursued this dream until he could no longer live without translating it into reality. She haunted him, and he began hunting her. She became the prey he must capture. She would be his trophy, placed within his private home.

*

Chandar Seth's work involved the preparation of khas, kewra and rose itr. These perfumes had a touch of magic to them–romantic, enchanting and strong. They carried the concentrated fragrance of flowers, or of wet mud, evoking the first rains that cooled a parched, dry earth. He also traded in paints and oil. An astute businessman, under his firm hands the family business expanded exponentially. He was accustomed to success.

In his personal life too, he laid detailed plans, working out a multi-pronged strategy. He went to Balpurva to meet Gulab's father. Lal Bahadur had long been waiting for a suitable catch for his talented and incredibly successful daughter. He had nipped in the bud several possible suitors. None had come up to the mark.

Chandar Seth gave in gracefully to all Lal Bahadur's outrageous demands. He agreed to pay a hefty bride price, and look after the family's needs on a regular basis. He also offered to take over the construction of their haveli. These generous promises won Lal Bahadur to his cause.

Chandar Seth was indulgent with Gulab's younger sisters and brothers who floated around the house and came to peep at him with large eyes. They began to dote upon him. He was well aware of Gulab's affection for them. He was affable and kindly with Gulab's mother. Jehangira hoped against hope that her daughter would settle down and have a family. She imagined that with a man like this Gulab would be saved from the continuous indignity of a public life.

Although Gulab had not quite relented, the Seth began to finance the construction of the haveli at Balpurva. He procured the best of craftspersons to carve the stone walls and parapets, designing grand new features. Cost was no consideration. He bought trinkets for Gulab's sisters. He hauled her brothers out of trouble, and managed odd favours for Lal Bahadur.

Her family began to pester Gulab to accede to his demand. She was caught in a double bind. If she abandoned Nautanki, she would leave behind her source of independence and livelihood. On the other hand, Chandar Seth had unlimited wealth. He would give a very handsome dowry to her parents. They would become his dependents. It would not hurt him to add another ten mouths to his retinue.

The promise of a life of leisure, spent in idle pleasures, was not entirely unattractive. Gulab had worked without pause ever since she was a child. She'd devoted every waking minute to her work and couldn't quite imagine life without it. She was addicted to the life of work, acting and applause. She still didn't want to give up singing, dancing or enacting the infinitely varied roles of queens, brave lasses and lovelorn damsels.

Chandar Seth felt frustrated by her resistance. He began creating unpleasant scenes. He would land up with one or two henchmen right in the middle of a show and drag her away. The audience would shout, 'Send Gulab Bai! Send Gulab Bai!' But backstage, Chandar Seth was shouting at her. If she still insisted on acting, he was not above hitting her.

Things came to such a pass that nobody could rely on Gulab's presence. Nobody, least of all Gulab herself, knew when her lover might suddenly arrive and drag her off-stage. Co-artistes in the company observed her plight and sympathized, but were frankly irritated with the situation. It was impossible to find a replacement for a heroine in the middle of a show. If a mardana was at hand who took over Gulab's part, the audience was still unhappy for they had come to see Gulab Jaan. Often the show had to be cancelled. Irate crowds mobbed the company. Its image began to crumble. Gulab's personal crisis threatened to destroy Tirmohan's company.

Gulab was in a tumult. The entire staff was disturbed. Tirmohan was unhappy. The company was being held ransom by the tantrums and tactics of an extremely influential businessman. He was a man of substance who brooked no opposition. Moreover Gulab was emotionally involved with him. She was embroiled in a situation she could no longer control. She had been adamant about staying on with the troupe, but her resolve began to collapse. Matters came to a head. Things could not possibly continue as they were. Something—or somebody—had to give.

Tirmohan realised that Gulab's days in the theatre were coming to an end. She would have to leave the Nautanki. He advised her to submit to her destiny.

Finally Gulab gave in to Chandar Seth's passionate—if violent—pleas to be his and his alone. In 1943, at the age of twenty-three, she bade farewell to the Nautanki world.

*

Chandar Seth duly married Gulab Jaan. The Bedia community adapted its customs to fit the situation of their most famous lady. Garlands were exchanged, a feast held for hundreds of people, and Chandar Seth's dowry prominently displayed.

Chandar Seth was already married but that was irrelevant. Many men married more than once. In fact it was expected of a wealthy man and added to his stature. Among his cronies and associates, marrying such a beautiful and glamorous woman was touted as an additional achievement. As for Gulab, such a marriage was as 'respectable' as she could ever expect. Better a prosperous man who wanted to keep her in comfort, than a procession of poor or middle-class lovers. What more could a woman in her position want?

Years later, Gulab described her new life, saying, 'I let him have his way. He got a bungalow built for me, in his fruit orchard in Kannauj, and spent the evenings there. This went on for several years . . .'

*

Chandar Seth's first wife and children lived with his parents in the ancestral home in a village off Kannauj city. This was his home base. He spent the evenings with Gulab, and returned to the family home by late night.

For Gulab, he built a a spacious bungalow set amid mango groves. Itr was prepared in its vast grounds. Huge mounds of rose petals were crushed to extract heady perfume. These were the desi gulab—red roses with a sweet, wild fragrance.

*

Gulab missed the theatre, tumultuous crowds and adventurous, wandering life. Chandar Seth didn't allow her to meet her old comrades and colleagues. He set the atmosphere and made the rules. Charming on most occasions, he could be autocratic and aggressive. He kept her virtually in purdah, guarding her movements with an iron fist.

He went sometimes to view a Nautanki playing in Kannauj or Makanpur, but did not take Gulab along. If she pined and wept with the desire to see a Nautanki or go out to a mela, he promised to take her 'next time'. The next time never came. The only news Gulab got of her old workplace was from her sister Chahetan, who continued to work with Tirmohan Ustad. News of the national movement filtered in through Chandar Seth himself.

Gulab tried to rest and enjoy the luxuries at her command. For the first time in her life, she had leisure. Servants bustled around doing all the work. She could idle away the hours. She wandered in the grounds, breathing in the intoxicating fragrances. She dozed under the luscious shade of mango trees, drinking in the heavy scent of tiny white blossoms even as summer declared its onset. It was a magical place, set apart from the rest of the world.

She was free to invite her family members to come and share the good life with her. Her sisters and brothers became frequent visitors, often staying over, so she was not lonely.

Chandar Seth ploughed money into the haveli at Balpurva. The excited eyes of several children followed each move. Rooms were built on the ground floor for the family to live. The first floor had a large hall where dance sessions could be held. Atop this, dominating the front facade, an intricate scene was carved. It showed goddess Lakshmi surrounded by two plump elephants and two Britishers wearing suits and topis. Everything was made of solid stone.

Two names were carved on the terrace wall—'Gulab Jaan' and 'Chahetan Jaan'—the two young women whose earnings had laid the foundations of this grand haveli.

Gulab continued to provide for her family even though she had left the stage. Her paramour carried on the covenant. Well aware that a delicate balance would be disturbed if he failed to do so, he shelled out the basic expenses for the family. He paid for Lal Bahadur's alcohol and the many follies her brothers indulged in. He presented clothes and jewellery to Gulab's sisters. The children doted upon their 'jijaji', considering him the most generous of souls. Sukhbadan and Kiran, the youngest, were just three or four years old when Gulab moved in with Chandar Seth.

Chandar Seth tried to be just and generous. He maintained an easy hand when it came to providing for his first wife. She could have whatever she pleased. Deferential to his parents, he loved his children and looked after his employees. He saw to it that the servants and workers in his fields, homes and shops were well cared for.

Yet his wife was distinctly resentful. She wanted her husband to leave Gulab. She tried to influence him by playing the 'good woman'—a wonderful mother, wife and daughter-in-law. She tried to shame him into giving up 'the whore'. Sometimes she let loose, crying and beseeching.

Her husband was moved, yet unmoved. He continued to maintain both households. Inordinately pleased to have a beauty queen all to himself, he bought Gulab clothes more exquisite than any she had ever worn on stage. She received gold and precious jewels. Gulab was fascinated by all this luxury, and equally pleased with all he did for her family.

*

Gulab began enjoying being wife, beloved and lady of the manor. In several Nautankis she'd played the role of a Rani—now, she'd actually become a Rani!

Soon she added another role to her repertoire. She'd played mother on stage hundreds of times. As Taramati she had loved her little Rohit and been heartbroken when he died. But now Gulab became a real mother.

Gulab was delighted with her pregnancy. So was her quiet, careworn mother. Jehangira began coming to Gulab's kothi, sometimes travelling across by bullock-cart, to look after her. She would spent a few hours and return to Balpurva by evening. She cooked special foods, applied oil and soothing lotions. She herself had given birth ten times, and that with next to no resources. During the last month Gulab shifted into the family haveli at Balpurva. Jehangira practised the arts of midwifery, as did most women in the area. She also sent for a dai when the time came.

Gulab walked across every day to Phoolmati Maiya's temple. She sang as she offered flowers. She dreamt and prayed for a beautiful baby.

She gave birth to a baby boy. The child was named Suresh Chandar. She felt, as she held him, that he would follow his father in the perfume business, be prosperous and successful. Gulab loved the idea of bringing up her son in the peaceful bungalow with the sound of koel birds, mangoes lush and abundant and the fragrance of itr. Born with a silver spoon in his mouth, surrounded by solicitous servants, his needs were all provided for. Gulab wanted him educated, like her husband. She saw him growing into the image and likeness of his father. He too would become a man of substance. He would be a big man, an important and influential man. He would earn power and prestige.

As for now, she was absorbed in his small being. She would carry him around the estate, and sing him lullabies and songs. She sang him thumris and dadras, half-forgotten dohas and behere taveels—and the little chap gurgled appreciatively in reply. Sometimes she found herself weeping as she sang.

The gurgles of a baby did not really make up for the loss of enthusiastic, wild applause. A part of her regretted the loss of her artiste self. At the same time she was deeply absorbed in the baby, lost in his insistent, urgent demands.

One or other of her sisters always stayed with her so she had somebody to share the baby with, and take delight in its every movement. Chandar Seth was no longer a daily visitor. One day, as she held and rocked her child, watching him doze off as she sat in the mango orchard, she wondered when he would next come. His visits were now few and far between. Why was that? Was there something wrong?—she wondered.

14

Back On Stage

Nadi naare na jao shyam paiyan padoon . . .
Nadi naare gaye to jaibae karo
Beech dhara na jao shyam paiyan padoon
Nadi naare . . .
Beech dhara gaye to jaibae karo
Us para na jao shyam paiyan padoon
Nadi naare . . .
Us para gaye to gailae karo
Sang sovatiya na lao shyam paiyan padoon
Nadi naare . . .
Sang sovatiya jo laae to laibe karo
Sang sejariya na soyo shyam paiyan padoon
Nadi naare . . .

— Gulab Bai's most popular dadra, sung since the
'30s until her death in 1996

(Do not wander Shyam, to the river's edge
I beg of you, do not!
If you are at the water's edge, so be it
Do not to step into the current my dear, I beg of you
If you've stepped into the current, so be it
But do not cross over to the other side, dear lover, I
beg of you
Well you've crossed over to that shore, so be it
Don't bring the other woman back with you my dear,
I beg of you
You have brought her back, here she is, so be it

Do not sleep on the same bed with her Shyam, I beg of you'
Do not wander Shyam, to the river's edge . . .)

Chandar Seth was no longer the attentive lover he had once been. He said he was busy with work. Distracted and tense, he would shrug off Gulab's questions. He hardly looked at her. In their son, he took no interest at all. Dark forebodings assailed Gulab. Her brothers disclosed rumours floating around about Chandar Seth's pursuit of another woman. She was a young woman who had recently arrived to fill the post of schoolteacher in his village. Chandar Seth dropped by to meet her frequently. He was, in fact, pursuing her zealously.

Gulab found herself weeping—a luxury she barely ever indulged in. Her life had been spent amid practical concerns. The fantasies she'd played out on stage were magic for the audience, but bread and butter for her. She had been contented, earning applause and accolades for the parts she played.

Although she had not wanted to leave the stage, she'd found consolation in her life amid nature, a doting lover, and then the child. She was shattered by the discovery that this haven may not last forever. She felt attached to this home now. Her dreams were entwined with the sap rising in the trees, budding, blossoming and yielding fruit. She was not ready to end this life.

Old dadras and thumris flooded her consciousness and took on new meaning. She sank into their poignant depths. In *Nadi naare* a woman beseeches her lover to stay, not abandon her. Gulab struggled against the pain of betrayal. As she sang, her voice became imbued with feeling.

She determined to win him back. She, with the flashing eyes, dancing until every man's heart was fit to burst—could she not win back her one man?

She tried to please him, deliberately using her charms to woo and seduce. He was entranced, and took pleasure in her again. She felt soothed. But it was momentary, for after spending a rare night with her he would turn away, and fail to show up for several days—even weeks. Gulab was tormented and lonely. She pleaded and fought. But then he came even less.

She grew insecure. She cried, and he was penitent. He told her she would always be his. He would take care of everything, and she was not to worry. But again he did not come for a month. She tried to reason with him. But he refused to reason with her. He was a man, and could do as he wished.

*

Some two or three years went by. Chandar Seth came and went as he pleased. The prevailing arrangements suited him. His wife maintained the family home. Gulab lived in the kothi in Kannauj. He was actively involved with the pretty young schoolmistress. He did not think he was harming anybody. He provided resources and distributed his time evenly between his several women. Society condoned such arrangements: in fact, the big man who could do as he pleased was held in tacit awe.

*

One day a harried-looking older woman stood at Gulab's door. She came quietly, as if she did not want many people to notice her. She wore an expensive sari, and introduced herself as 'his' wife.

Gulab asked her to sit and offered paan and water. She neither touched the paan nor sipped the water. Looking at Gulab nervously, though from a haughty distance, she came straight to the point.

'You are Gulab Bai,' she said. 'Everybody knows you. You are famous and talented. You are young. You can earn. There is so much you can do. Go back to your own life, Gulab Bai. Fame and fortune will be yours again.'

Gulab stared at her fascinated, every word piercing her like an arrow. The woman continued: 'Here you will have nothing. You will sit and wait for this man, but he will never be yours.'

The woman paused, then sighed and said, 'I too wait for his footsteps and watch out for his return home. He treats me as he wants. I am dependent on him. I have no option. I am his wife. I have no way of earning without him. Where would I take my children? How would I survive? But at least I have the status of being his wife. Nobody can take that away from me. I rule over the house, bring up his children and look after his parents. I have a place in society. I have respectability, izzat. You will never have that. You will never enjoy the status of being his wife. Whatever you may do, you will never have izzat.'

She continued, speaking slowly so that each word came out with great force: 'This man will never belong to anybody. Today he is running after a schoolteacher. He is leaving you for her. He will never belong to her either.'

Gulab listened with rapt attention, watching the misery on the face of her co-wife. She felt strangely soothed by this visit. Her mind moved, and quietly a decision was made. Even as her *sautan* spoke to her—words straight from an anguished heart—Gulab felt an echo in her own tortured breast. She listened respectfully and bade farewell with folded hands. The other woman went out after casting a last beseeching look at Gulab.

*

Chandar Seth's wife had made an elaborate plan. She wanted to be rid of Gulab Bai, who still had a powerful hold on her husband. The next step was to arrange a marriage between Chandar Seth and her own younger sister. Well aware that Chandar Seth would never be satisfied with one woman, she reasoned that was the only way to have him under her thumb. She could then rule over the household as benign senior wife. Gulab's brothers heard rumours that Chandar Seth's wife was paying a servant to poison Gulab. The air seethed with intrigues. Gulab felt her dreams turn into a nightmare.

*

Gulab sent a message to Tirmohan Ustad, through her sister Chahetan, expressing her desire to rejoin his company. He replied immediately, in the affirmative. He asked her to come to Kanpur where the group was stationed. Audiences still longed for Gulab Bai. Her charisma would draw the crowds that had been thinning in the absence of a heroine of comparable talent.

Gulab took her mother into confidence. Jehangira knew Gulab was tortured by Chandar Seth's betrayal. With a heavy heart she'd watched her daughter's misery. She accepted Gulab's decision to leave him and return to the stage. Gulab left Suresh—now two or three years old— with Jehangira.

She knew her father, Lal Bahadur, would react violently to her leaving Chandar Seth. Sure enough, he raved and ranted when he got to know. But the die was cast and there was nothing he could do to alter her decision.

Gulab did not breathe a word about her intentions to Chandar Seth, well aware he would try to keep her back. He wanted her to remain his for life, however far he himself might wander. He was unable to understand how deeply Gulab resented and was hurt by the arrangement.

Gulab had been loyal to him. Once she accepted him she had imagined it would be a steady relationship. She'd enjoyed his company and their sexual intimacies. She'd done whatever she could to keep him. Earlier she trusted him implicitly, so much so that even when he began to neglect her she hardly noticed. Later she realized she had failed to fully understand his words and intentions.

She did not want to live with a man who would betray her as a matter of routine. If he considered it his right to do so, she considered it her right to leave him.

*

It was late 1947. The air was thick with the euphoria of Independence, along with the turmoil of a nation divided. Gulab left for Kanpur. After Independence the ban on Tirmohan's company had been lifted. The troupe immediately returned to Kanpur. Tirmohan hired the old house in Cooperganj and held rehearsals there. Most artistes took up residence in Rail Bazaar, a working class colony adjacent to Kanpur Central, the city's main railway station.

Chahetan had worked steadily in the company. Paati Kali joined her and the two sisters rented a room in Rail Bazaar. They welcomed Gulab into this room. Gulab was miserable, but calm. There would be no going back on her decision. She had brought a few simple clothes with her, leaving behind her expensive clothes and piles of jewellery. She was angry enough to reject all he had given her. She wanted none of it. She would earn her living, stand on her own feet.

She plunged once again into the life of rehearsals and shows. It was a mature woman who sang and danced now, playing the parts of queen, warrior, rebel and mother. She entered into the spirit of the show, the skin of the character, and played each role with consummate ease. She looked wonderful in her costumes and danced with the same grace and vigour as she had earlier. Thousands thronged to see her.

Chandar Seth was stunned when he found her gone. Countless affairs were customary for a wealthy dilettante like himself. A woman did not leave her man for such a flimsy reason! He wanted Gulab back. He'd rested easy on the notion that she would always be his. Flustered and angry, his vanity hurt, he sent word to her. His wife watched him closely, observing his reactions and shifting moods. She did not breathe a word to him about her own role in Gulab's departure.

Gulab ignored his summons. He sent another message promising to be faithful to her forever. He came to Kanpur. She met him briefly, but refused to hear of returning to the old life. She told him there was no way she could rebuild her shattered trust. Chandar Seth realized she would not return to him.

Gulab had stored some jewellery belonging to Chahetan and Paati Kali with Chandar Seth. He returned these jewels to them. He wanted Gulab to keep the jewellery he had gifted her, but she said she did not need them: 'Once I have left you I don't want this jewellery either.' He had given her around thirty tolas of gold, but she refused to have any of it. She was too hurt, and too proud. If she ever felt a tinge of desire to return to him, she never showed it.

During the next few years Chandar Seth grew increasingly involved with his own family. His wife succeeded in arranging his marriage with her own younger sister. This strategy succeeded in keeping him at home most of the time.

Gulab said she met him just once, some years later, by chance. She asked him why he had never kept track of his son. He replied with some asperity, 'He has such a famous mother. He doesn't need me.'

*

Gulab stayed firm on her chosen track. Although intensely lonely, she concealed this in the dignity of her bearing. She became absorbed in music. She listened day and night to thumris, ghazals and dadras. She sang dadras and thumris, lavanis and dohas, behere tabeel and chaubolas with style and verve. She practised for hours, accompanied by tabla and sarangi. The sojourn in Kannauj had lent her greater depth. She retained her enchanting looks and slim figure. Her work was now suffused with emotion—be it anger or love, playful romance or high tragedy.

She sang dadras and light thumris in between dramatic acts. The dadra *Nadi naare* became her signature song. She had learnt this folk song as a young girl. Now she plumbed its depths. Tempered by adversity and hardened by betrayal, she sang with every fibre of her being. She herself became the anguished woman beseeching her lover to be faithful. She expressed her own pain and humiliation, and the taste of slow poison that turns trust into mistrust.

The *Nadi naare* song became a hot favourite—a superhit. People wanted her to sing it again and yet again. She acted as she sang—eyes, face and hands together evoking her pain and her strength. It struck a chord with the audience. Many women identified with the emotions expressed. Many men enjoyed the powerful evocation of a woman begging her man to be loyal.

*

At times she missed her life of leisure, but was pragmatic enough to accept the inevitable. She faced the challenge of establishing herself once again as the top actress of the Nautanki world.

Tirmohan and Company's destiny shone bright again. His company had been chugging along; with Gulab back, its popularity soared. Cash flowed into the box office. Gulab's earnings supported her parental family. She sent special gifts for her son, Suresh. Gulab had showered him with attention when he was an infant, and now he missed her sorely. Jehangira and Lal Bahadur provided him a home, and Gulab came every year during the monsoon break. But Suresh grew morose and taciturn as he grew older. He took to wandering aimlessly, walking miles in any direction. One day he had a train accident, suffering injuries from which he never fully recovered.

*

Gulab settled down in Kanpur. Her sisters Chahetan and Paati Kali were delighted to have her. Paati Kali was just a young girl and Gulab enjoyed looking after her. With a flair for the comic side of life, Paati had a talent for bringing humour into the darkest situation. She excelled in comic roles. Tall, slim and dark, she laughed easily, her peals of laughter gladdening her elder sister's heart. Gulab felt her burdens lightening and slipping off as sleep claimed her after a hard day's work.

Gradually her grief lost its intensity. A flash of memory sometimes brought the old life alive. She recalled walking across to the perfumery, observing flower petals being crushed to extract fragrant perfumes. She had revelled in her love life. She had enjoyed unhurried baths, dressing in soft silks, supervising the cooking, and playing with her baby.

But having re-entered the world of stage and song, she felt a sense of belonging. She began to feel whole and herself. Her confidence welled up and her wounds began to heal.

Gulab promised herself she would never again leave this world. As long as she lived, she would remain in Nautanki. It was the primary mooring in her life, and she would not abandon it for the sake of man or marriage. She might set up another liaison: she saw no reason to keep herself from doing so. But whether or not she formed any other attachment, she resolved never to give up her work.

15

Fine-tuning

I heard Gulab Bai sing around fifty years ago. She sang so beautifully, one could not stop listening. Truly she was 'Kalyug ki Saraswati' (goddess of music and learning in the present dark era).

—Chandrika Prasad 'Nidar'

Her voice was pure. Her enunciation was clear. Twenty to twenty-five thousand people would gather, but when Bai got up to sing there would be pin-drop silence.

—Shiv Adhar Dube

Gulab Bai sang full-throated. She did not 'steal' part of her voice, as everybody does today. Even the best singers began doing that after they grew accustomed to microphones and studio recording.

—Jyoti Swaroop Pandey

In the 1940s the nascent records industry began recording popular singers in various parts of the country. Towards the last years of the decade Gulab's songs were recorded. The first time, she sang two songs in the studio, filling both sides of a small record. A 78 RPM record was called a 'tava' in the northern belt—it resembled a tava, the black metal griddle on which women cooked rotis at home. The tavas played dizzily in every shop that could afford to buy a gramophone. After three minutes, the record had to be turned around.

It may now seem to us to be a cumbersome procedure, but at that time it was simply an aid to magic. It helped in the magical spread of the human voice—floating and disembodied. Gulab's voice reached out into an even broader arena than did her Nautankis. The dadras *Moko peehar mein mat chhede balam* and *Nadi naare na jaao* were played loudly at every wedding, mundan and other functions.

Gulab's songs were recorded by HMV, EMI and other music companies as well as All India Radio. Later they blared from every transistor in north India, enlivening the market place.

Of course most of her performances were live. Gulab's voice was unmatched in its timbre, its lilting sweetness. She put all her vital energy into the singing. While the figure of twenty thousand people is undoubtedly an exaggeration, singing to crowds of three to four thousand was a routine matter. Her supple, mellifluous voice carried clearly across wave upon wave of listeners.

Appreciation and applause stirred her to greater effort and achievement. Her emotional range expanded. Her voice took on the slightest hint of pathos or anguish, passion or rage, and expressed it with great intensity. She had always enjoyed singing, but now it became her very life. She spent hours at her riyaz.

She plunged into heroine roles, perfecting what she had begun many years ago. Serious and focussed, she realized just how much she had missed the work during her years of exile from stage. She grew deep roots now into Nautanki soil—roots that nourished her being.

*

In the early years, Hathras Nautankis had concentrated more on singing than acting. The fame and popularity of a Nautanki artiste depended on the power and range of his voice. Boys with melodious high-pitched voices enacted female parts. Dhrupad singing—which Nautankis began with in those days—demanded a highly trained voice grounded in classical music. But in Kanpur-style Nautanki the emphasis shifted to dialogue delivery and facial expression, and actors no longer needed a strong grounding in classical music.

Tirmohan Ustad had originally learnt Nautanki in Hathras. He later added sophisticated dialogue and acting skills to his repertoire, helping develop the Kanpur style. The training he provided within his troupe therefore integrated the best of both styles. Gulab's training was thus broad-based: she was able to learn a wide range of skills, to her great advantage. Acting and dialogue delivery were important to her, as were the finer nuances while singing.

Gulab immersed herself in music. She had developed a fine musical sense in her early years, and was now eager to step further into the depths of music. From Tirmohan Ustad, Mohammad Khan Saheb, Rashid Khan, Gangadin Bhagatiya and Mehboob Master, she kept learning intricate nuances and fine-tuned her singing style.

Kanpur Nautankis were a mix of poetry and prose, folk and classical. *Bhairavi, bilawal, peelu* and *khamaj* were commonly used classical ragas, adapted and rendered with rustic vigour. The poetry was written in various metrical patterns and sung according to special conventions. The basic verse pattern was divided into three portions. The first, doha, was sung free, without any beats. The second, chaubola, formed the main stanza.

Last of all was the daur or chalti, sung at great speed, becoming very slow at the end. The nagara played towards the end of each portion. Other metrical patterns popularly used were behere taveel, sauratha, alha, lavani, jhoolna, dadra, ghazal and qawali.

Lavani was particularly effective in expressing mourning, as with Haadi Rani in *Amar Singh Rathore* after Amar Singh's death and Taramati in *Raja Harishchandra* after Rohit's death. Gulab's performance in these scenes was evocative. Her spirited rendition of lavanis created a highly charged atmosphere.

The lavani style seemed particularly well suited to female singers, perhaps because their roles had a fair share of grief and mourning. Several Nautanki actresses developed into powerful lavani singers. These included Shameem Banu of Lucknow, Nur Jehan Begum of Allahabad, Tara Devi of Hameerpur, Radha Rani of Pilibhit, Kamlesh Lata of Mathura, Bibbo Bai, Mushtari Bai, Chanda and Krishna Kumari.

Behere taveel, a lengthy metrical composition, was suitable for narrative singing. The last half of the concluding line was repeated as a refrain. The singer would go on doubling and quadrupling the tempo, breaking the monotony of the long verse and providing an occasion for dance and drumming.

The harmonium became indispensable for Nautanki singers, since it supplied cues and guided the shifting of scales. Musical scale shifted with the singer.

Language in Nautankis was simple and direct. Nautanki writers cast off heavily padded Hindi vocabulary and employed the more fluid Urdu, which enjoyed court patronage and by the mid-nineteenth century had a well-developed tradition of sophisticated mushairas at which poetry was recited and sung. Only the *mangalacharana* remained in Sanskritized Hindi. The rest of the songs and alliterative dialogue flowed in a hybrid form, including Urdu, Braj, Rajasthani, Hindi and local dialects.

Because of their hybrid language, Nautankis were not generally assessed as literary works. However, due to their musical appeal and dramatic quality, Nautanki scripts sold much better than bestsellers in Hindi or Urdu. Wholesale dealers would weigh the cheaply printed plays in a scale and hand them over to retail shopkeepers, who circulated them among rural folk as well as small-town and city literati. People bought basketloads of Nautanki script books by weight. Thus, a customer might say, 'Give me twenty seers of Nautankis.'

With the advent of cinema, audience tastes began to shift. But Nautanki scripts continued to be popular. Fresh scripts were written, especially satirical plays on social issues such as dowry, conjugal conflicts and poverty. Contemporary film hits were also used as a basis for writing new plays.

*

Gulab was well on her way to becoming a legend, both for her acting style and her singing abilities. Her popularity as a solo singer–performing in-between drama scenes–skyrocketed. She sang rasiyas and dadras such as village women commonly sing—generally in Braj Bhasha, with evergreen themes like Krishna the mischievous son or the dashing lover—

Yasoda tero lala bada utpatiya
Brindaban ki kunj galin mein
Aji daali gale mein bahiyan

Yasoda tero lala bada utpatiya
Raar machave saajan aave

Aji raar machave saajan aave
Natkhat mope teer chalave
Phodi doodh ki matakiya
Hai Ram todi doodh ki matakiya.

Yasoda tero lala bada utpatiya
Chori-chori maakhan khao
Gval-bal ko khoob khilao
Dahi ki taari hanse mori maiya
Hai dahi ki taari hanse mori maiya

Yasoda tero lala bada utpatiya
Brindaban mein raas rachave
Gval-bal ke man ko lubhave
Aisi madhur bansuriya....[15]

(Yasoda your son is full of mischief
He comes up and embraces me
In Brindavan's narrow lanes
Yasoda your son is full of mischief
He creates a scene, my lover
Aims his arrow at me
Shattering my pot of milk

Yasoda your son is full of mischief
He steals and eats butter
Shares it with the cowherd boys
Laughs with cream all over his face

Yasoda your son is full of mischief
He dances with the milkmaids in Brindavan, and
Charms the cowherds with his melodious flute
Yasoda your son is full of mischief.)

Gulab sang uninhibited earthy numbers, originally composed and sung in intimate circles of women. The tunes and sentiments were closely entwined with ordinary women's daily lives and emotional experiences. Gulab's own experiences lent depth to her singing. Through her singing, private female emotions were now expressed in a public space.

Several lyrics were sexually explicit, such as the following:

Akeli dar laage mori Amma
Jab re sipahiya ne ghunghat pat khola
Nayan dono jhuk gaye raat mori Amma

Jab re sipahiya ne choliband kholi
Jovan dono dat gaye raat mori Amma
Jab re sipahiya ne mora lehenga pakdo
Bharatpur lut gayo raat mori Amma
Akeli dar laage raat mori Amma ...

(I feel scared alone, my Mother
Oh when the soldier drew aside my veil,
My eyes were lowered at night, my Mother
When he untied my blouse-strings,
My breasts swung loose at night, my Mother
When he caught hold of my skirt
Bharatpur city was ransacked, at night, my Mother
I feel scared alone, my Mother.)

These were not demure songs. Far from it: they vividly portrayed intimate experiences and emotions, expressed fear, longing and passion –

Aao more sajna milan hui jaae
Machle hai manva, rut hai rangeeli
Tum bhi raseele, main bhi raseeli
Dono ka man lalchaye

Aao mere sajna milan hui jaae
Gaon ki nari, chadar ke peechhe
Ratiyan bitaoon ambva ke neeche
Nainon mein deepak jalaye

Aao mere sajna milan hui jaae
Kaise bataoon hirday ki batiyaan
Dehiyan jalain phagun ki ratiyan
Jajiya pe nindiya na aaye

Aao mere sajna milan hui jaae
Gori kalaiya chikni badaniya
Rahiya nihareen tumhari dulhaniya
Ghuiyan pe chundri bichhaye . . .
Aao mere sajna milan hui jaaye.

(Come my dear, let us meet
My heart is restless
The season romantic
You feel sparks of desire
And so do I
Yearning, longing to be together

Come my dear, let us get together
I a village woman in my veil,
Waiting, sleepless under the mango trees
My eyes light up like diyas to welcome you.

Come my dear, let us make love
How can I express all that's in my heart?
Spring nights set me aflame
And I cannot sleep in my own bed.

Come my dear, let us become one
Fair are my arms, smooth my body
You gaze at your bride
Draped in a pretty chunri
Come my dear, let us make love)

Desires were frankly expressed through the medium of erotic verse. These women were active, flowing with emotion–expressive, not mere oppressed victims. Their experiences emerge as far more complex and diverse than is usually acknowledged. Their voices revealed complex personal and social dynamics.

Ghus aayo mero kamre mein
mera chhota devar mara
Kar gaye kiriya karam raat ko
Tan-tan baaji baarah

Vida hoke jab naihar se
Main balam ke ghar aayi
Paltan ke do randve mar gaye
Subedar sipahi

Gaune vali raat balam ne julam guzaro diya
Upar to chale diesel gaadi, neeche rail ko patariya
Man mein hamare paap lagi jaaye
Rapat likha doongi
Ab ki randvan ko main jail karaye doongi
Ab ki sab randvan ko main jail karaye doongi . . .

(My husband's young brother
Broke into my room, the wretch,
And performed his work at night
The bell rang tan-tan-tan twelve times

When I bade farewell to parents
And came to my husband's house
Two rogues from the army died—an officer and a soldier
The first night with my husband
He took me by storm
Above ran a diesel train, beneath railway tracks

I'm angry, I will take revenge
I will go register a report
This time I will get all the rogue men into jail . . .)

This song speaks of multiple sexual encounters— at least some entered into by choice. There is a transparent relish in sensual pleasure and frank enjoyment of one's own prowess. The singer acknowledges that she broke several hearts when she married. She also expresses anger at being 'taken by storm'. This is a far cry indeed from the notion of passive village women, who accept sex only as a male imposition, taking harassment without demur, as part of the deal.

Women poured their emotions into song and music while going about their daily chores, sharing and expressing anger, unhappiness or enjoyment. As has been discovered in the context of Rajasthani women's songs,[16] in the local UP ethos too women spoke their hearts out through poetry and song. They freely expressed intimate feelings and gave vent to emotions usually locked in, considered indiscreet and unsavoury. Presenting these, as Gulab did, to a wider audience meant shifting registers and moving into thorny terrain. What was quite routine when sung in all-women conclaves could sound explosive when sung in public, by a woman. It could shock and excite, at the same time establishing her reputation as seductive, attractive, desirable, and not quite respectable.

These songs, set to folk tunes, often wove in many easily identifiable local types—characters people could relate to.

> *More panvari re najariya tose laagi*
> *Sona kahe main sabse bada hoon*
> *Aji sona kahe main sabse bada hoon*
> *Ek sunhar se haare*
> *Haai peet-peetke nathuni banai*
> *Aji galva kikar guljaro*
>
> *Re najariya tose laagi*
> *More panvari najariya tose laagi*
> *Phulva kahe main sabse bada hoon*
> *Ek mali se haaro*

Aji goonth goonth ke gajra banayo
Haaigalva kikar guljaro

Re najariya tose laagi
Aji kapda kahe main sabse bada hoon
Ek darji se haaro
Haai kaat koot ke choliya banvai
Aji jubna kikar guljaro

Re najariya tose laagi
Aji loha kahe main sabse bada hoon
Ek angrej se haaro
Haai peet peet ke lineoo banai
Hai jispe chale re railgaadi . . .

Re najariya tose laagi . . .

(My eyes have met yours, my dear panvari,
Gold says, 'I'm the greatest'
But the goldsmith defeats gold
Oh! he beats and beats it and makes a nose-ring
And a string to place around the neck

My eyes have met yours, my dear panvari
The flower says, 'I'm the greatest'
But is defeated by the gardener
Who plucks flowers to weave a garland
To tie around the neck

My eyes have met yours, my dear panvari
Cloth says, 'I'm the greatest'
But is defeated by the tailor
Who cuts it and crops it and stitches a blouse
To tie around the breasts

My eyes have met yours, dear panvari
Iron says, 'I'm the greatest'
But is defeated by the Englishman
Oh! he beats and beats it, and makes tracks
On which run railway trains

My eyes have met yours, dear panvari . . .)

These songs speak of attraction and relationships, with explicit allusion to the play of power between women and men, British and Indian, rich and poor. They reflected sociopolitical hierarchies, and indicated the dilemmas and conflicts women faced living in patriarchal families with intricate taboos and conventions.

> *Moko peehar mein mat chhede balam*
> *Kar le dheer jigariyan mein*
> *Moko peehar mein mat chhede.*
> *Bhari javani dekh ke balam*
> *Haai vo to chhede hai*
> *Haai vo to chhede hai beech bajariya mein*
> *Moko peehar mein mat chhede*
>
> *Tumre sasuro aur maike mero hai*
> *Haai vo to jag rahi*
> *Haai vo to jag rahi raja vo to jag rahi*
> *Nand kothariya mein*
> *Moko peehar mein mat chhede*
> *Bhor ho to sang tere chalungi*
> *Haai tab le leejo raja tab le leejo*
> *Khaat kothariya mein*
>
> *Moko peehar mein mat chhede . . .*

(Do not tease me in my father's home
My dear, be patient, calm your heart
Seeing my youth brim over
Oh! he pesters me in the midst of the bazaar
Do not pester me here in my mother's place, my dear,
Your sasural and my maika

Oh! she is awake, your sister is awake in this tiny room
Do not trouble me in my father's place, my dear
When it is dawn we will leave, yes

Oh! then you can take me
You can lay a bed in our little room
Do not tease me, my dear, in my father's home)

These songs were all sung by Gulab, hundreds of times as part of the 'variety show' before the start of a Nautanki and as item numbers between Nautanki scenes. Gulab steeped herself in these sensuous outpourings, expressions of desire and playfulness, rebellion and mature experience. People wanted her on stage, entertaining them with her songs.

HMV made at least eight records of Gulab Bai's songs during the 1950s and 1960s. Some of these songs were later stolen by the Bombay film industry. Sunil Dutt had Waheeda Rehman sing *Nadi naare* in the film *Mujhe Jeene Do*. He also used the song *Moko peehar mein mat chhede*. For his film *Teesri Kasam*, Raj Kapoor lifted the song *Paan khaye saiyan hamaro* from Gulab Bai's repertoire. None of the films acknowledged their debt to Gulab—or to the anonymous ordinary women of rural Uttar Pradesh.

Many people, including eminent lawyers, urged Gulab to file a case against filmmakers who lifted her songs. HMV too considered filing a case of theft—infringement of copyright. But Gulab Bai asked them not to. She refused to take it up as an issue.[17]

Later she recalled, 'The biggest lawyers of Kannauj came and said to me, "Bai, you won't have to spend one paisa, we will fight the case." I said, "Why should we take on so much trouble?"'

Well-wishers told her that she was losing lakhs of rupees. When songs were lifted from her records for use in films, she should be paid a substantial amount for each song. Gulab Bai's typical reaction was dismissive—'Oho, let it be!' She was comfortable with the flow of music from one place to another, and simply not interested in establishing rights and copyrights over lyrics and tunes.

She admonished those who tried to advise her—'Forget it! These are songs from Braj. Who will compose the music, who can write the words? Women of Braj have been singing these songs since ages—women who beat their dholaks and sing. Oh! what is there to write in these? These are folk songs.'

Even today Gulab's signature songs such as *Nadi naare*, *Moko peehar mein* and *Chandi ka gola* are widely sung in the north Indian countryside. It is impossible to assign authorship for any of the lyrics. A villager from the area says, 'If I heard somebody sing a song, I would think of it while grinding wheat and sing it back, adding some words of my own. Who can say who first thought of which line?'[18]

Gulab always acknowledged her debt to the thousands of village women of Uttar Pradesh who had, collectively, composed these songs. She picked up the tunes and sentiments floating in the air and lent them her voice. By projecting them thus, she provided them currency, made them artifacts to be widely circulated. But she never claimed originality or tried to establish copyright over them.

Bollywood, on the other hand, simply stole, brazenly and with impunity. Bollywood film directors, music directors and singers heard Gulab Bai's records and picked up the words and tunes. They made a fortune. Their growing popularity was partly based on the use of music people already identified with. But this glamorous industry failed to acknowledge the debt it owed to the simple folk in remote villages, or to a professional stage artiste named Gulab Bai.

16

A Rare Balance

Kalakar ki koi jati nahin hoti. (An artist has no caste)
—Nargis

Out of hundred people in a troupe maybe sixty were Muslim and forty Hindu. There were more Muslims among the musicians. Everybody had the same feelings, whether they were Hindu or Musalman.
—Munni Bai

We people may have no caste, but this much I can tell you. There is nothing in marriage if two people are forcibly tied together. A true union is a union of hearts, when two people choose each other.
—Shaila, Balpurva

Gulab Mausi and Raja Master were together. I was eleven or twelve when he died but I remember him clearly. He lived in our midst. There was no attempt to hide anything. If we accept somebody as our partner, it is our own business, not anybody else's. Gulab Mausi was frank and open. Everybody respected her. Mausa was good to us children. We would sit with him and he would teach us singing. He was a great artiste. There was no equal to him in all of Aligarh. He was Mohammedan and from a traditional singing-dancing family–khandani. He was very handsome, like Raj Kapoor. Gulab Mausi never

visited his home in Aligarh. She would say, 'I have been betrayed once. Never again! I will live with my family and my people, I will die with my family and people.'
—Munni Bai, 2002

Women and men lived and travelled together, forming a loose community with its own mores and values. A number of liaisons developed. Many of these were cross-religious–yet acceptable within the community of artistes. They had no strict taboos or moral strictures against such liaisons.

Nautanki actresses of the 1930s, 1940s and 1950s were blazing new trails. Pioneers in a male field, they had no fixed moulds to fit into. They'd moved out of Bedia or tawaif backgrounds, where they were street singers or entertainers in mehfils. They were keen to forge a different identity. They wanted izzat—respectability. After all, they were professionals working for a living in exactly the same way as their male counterparts.

There should have been no reason any more for Nautanki women to seek wealthy patrons or provide sexual services in return for payment, shelter or security. But because of their family backgrounds, the stigma associated with being *female* public entertainers, and their itinerant lifestyle, many could not go in for proper marriages.

These theatre women were usually unmarried. Some entered into a settled relationship over the years, others remained single. Most men were culturally conditioned to interact with women within defined roles—sisters, mother, wives and such-like. They found it uncomfortable to be with a single woman, unable to fully accept her and with no idea how to interact in a normal way. According to prevailing logic, a single woman was 'available', her sexuality uncontained and ill-defined, making her appear vaguely threatening.

*

After Gulab left Chandar Seth and returned to Kanpur, she and her sisters Chahetan and Paati Kali formed a trio of single women, living independently, earning and forging their special identities. The three frequently travelled together, participating in the same Nautankis—Gulab as heroine, Chahetan as side-heroine and Paati as a comic character. Each had her distinct personality. At the same time the three sisters were closely bonded and finely tuned to each other's needs and moods.

Involved with the simple pursuits of daily life, they were equally committed to their demanding professional schedules. There were men enough who wanted and wooed them. They wanted to exercise choice, but they also wanted izzat. They developed a sense of discrimination. Discretion was the name of the game—despite the fact that their lives were like open books, with people milling all around.

Like other women and men in the travelling theatre, Gulab and her sisters faced the challenge of creating new ways of relating. The nature of their work threw women and men into close proximity, giving rise to existential dilemmas. Private space was unheard of. Yet distances had to be maintained.

Compared to mainstream society, with its rigid patriarchal structure and values, the artistes' community was sensitive and open. Living on the fringes of social norms, they were far more liberal than their educated and 'respectable' counterparts. During their wandering lifestyle they shed a great deal of the hypocrisy, and passed few judgments on each other. These were people keen on freedom, savouring the winds that blew in from all sides, more ready than most to acknowledge human needs, including the formation of heterodox relationships.

The three sisters were gracious, keeping an open house in which family, friends and colleagues came and went all day. It was set amidst the hustle and bustle of the Rail Bazaar. People breezed in and out discussing the latest movies, new government policies, goings-on at the Bahraich mela or the price of oil and vegetables. Gulab welcomed everybody with a warm smile and a laughing comment. She mingled with men on an equal plane, and won their respect.

Gulab Bai flirted sometimes, and entertained men at home. Having once burnt her fingers, she had become more circumspect. She was choosy now, and refused to play into the hands of a suitor just because he was wealthy. She was not averse to forging another relationship, but refused to make compromises with her emotions or her work life. She did miss having a steady lover and a mature relationship. But she was not willing to barter away her autonomy for the sake of so-called love.

She was not gullible any more. She could take her own decisions rather than submit to the norms of her family and Bedia society. Her daughter Madhu later commented, '*Ham nachnewaliyon ke paas ya rais aate hain ya sais*' (The men who come to us dancers are either really wealthy or they are working-class). But Gulab wasn't interested in the poorest of the poor either. What she wanted was an equal, somebody who could match her talent, intelligence and professional stature.

*

Gulab fell in love with fellow-actor Raja—and he with her. He often played the hero with Gulab as heroine.

Gulab and Raja began living together towards the start of the 1950s.

Raja had a wife and children in Aligarh. He visited them—and his own parents—during the monsoon break every year. He spent four months there, continuing to participate in the affairs of a rambling joint family. Once the monsoon season was over, he was back in Kanpur.

Gulab never went with him to Aligarh. She had not the least desire to disturb the family there. Nor did she ever want to leave the stage and settle in with Raja as his 'lawfully wedded' wife. She was perfectly content with the relationship they had: comrades, friends and lovers who worked and lived together. Raja was Muslim, but this never became a cause for concern to her. Nor did others in her family or in the Nautanki world think it odd or objectionable for Gulab to live with a Muslim man.

As a Bedia woman, she had few illusions. She knew there was no 'pure' blood in any case. Wealthy upper-caste men slept with poor Dalit women as a matter of right and sired children whom they never acknowledged. In evaluating a prospective partner, a Bedia woman would be interested more in his wealth and circumstances, rather than his religion, race or bloodline.

Gulab chose to be with an artiste who respected her. He was not wealthy. But he worked well, and steadily. They shared a passion for music and a commitment to the stage. He had depth and the concentrated intensity of an artistic mind. She considered all this more important than any caste or religious allegiance he might or might not have.

*

Hindu and Muslim folk cultures blended within the world of popular theatre. Gulab learnt the arts from Khan

Sahebs and Ustads. Nautanki language, music, costumes, themes and characters reflected a mixed social set-up.

Muslims who settled in India from the eleventh century onwards adopted some practices of local Hindus, while Hindus gradually accepted Muslim influences. Dalits who converted to Islam retained large elements of indigenous cultural practices and beliefs. The arts reflected a synthesis of cultures. Classical Kathak dancers were steeped in Radha-Krishna lore but dressed in Persian tunics and girdles. Rajput miniatures of the sixteenth and seventeenth centuries expressed the gilded refinement of Mughal courts as well as Hindu myths and legends. Nautanki too inherited the vitality of both cultural streams.

Nautanki artistes belonged to a wide range of castes and creeds. The women hailed almost exclusively from traditional entertainer-singer backgrounds—either the Bedia caste or deredar Muslims. But male artistes were Muslims, Dalits and middle or upper castes including Brahmans, Kayasths and Khatris. Syncretic traditions flourished within this community of artistes. It was commonly accepted that *kalakar ki jati nahin hoti*— meaning artistes qua artistes are above sectarian affiliations.

Artistes living close together built up an intimate understanding of each other's ways and customs. Sufi traditions wove a web of understanding and an undercurrent of shared beliefs. Nautanki companies performed at dargahs and Hindu shrines, Hindu festivals and Muslim feast-days. Muslims as well as Hindus came thronging to dargahs. Companies always performed at Madar Shah's urs in Makanpur. At Navratri, Nautankis were performed at Devi Patan mela for a whole month. Performers would be in Dargah Sharif, Bahraich, for Gazi Sarkar's urs.

Nautanki troupes would go to Deva Sharif in Barabanki and the Chaumundi mela in Meerut. During the month of Chait they performed in Kashipur. During Shivratri they performed in Beeghapur for three to five days.

Gulab Bai sings to the accompaniment of the 'nagara' or kettledrum on her right. On her left is the harmonium.

Nautankis drew from a mixed heritage, including Persian epic romances and Pauranic stories. The language used had a sprinkling of Persianized Urdu, Hindi and local dialects. Even when the communal rift between Hindus and Muslims deepened all around, local traditions survived. Nautanki-walas were closely integrated within these local traditions.

People in Nautanki developed fluid caste boundaries as compared to mainstream—particularly upper-caste—society. They lived and ate together, sharing their daily lives. This was one reason why the elite looked down upon

Nautanki. In any case, the occupation of singing and dancing was not considered respectable. After women joined Nautanki troupes, the stigma and sense of opprobrium increased.

High-caste families bitterly criticized middle-and upper-caste men who joined Nautanki. They castigated them for betraying caste values. Many artistes could have earned better had they followed traditional caste occupations or taken to education and office jobs. Of course, if they made it big, as did Tirmohan Ustad or Shrikrishna Pehelwan, they gained a new status.

Nautanki troupes were generally mixed. Even as the fire of communal riots raged across the land during 1947, wreaking carnage and destruction, many troupes remained unbroken. Muslim artistes in large numbers chose to stay behind and carry on the lives they were accustomed to. Daily ties and work relations between artistes from different communities provided a feeling of security. Bonds of mutual trust ran deep. With Independence and Partition, change was visible all around. Governments changed. Laws changed. Muslims left India en masse—including large numbers from Uttar Pradesh. But only a sprinkling of Nautanki artistes moved across the borders into Pakistan. Nautanki survived the bloodshed of the times relatively unscathed.

Comradely ties had been fostered within a shared economic universe. The world of travelling theatre encompassed all the artistes in its warm embrace. They might travel at a stretch for six or seven months. They earned from a common source and ate from the same kitchen. Usually a Brahman pandit cooked the common daily meals—dal, roti, rice, vegetables and chutney. Everybody brought their own plates and served themselves food. Hindus and Muslims would sit next to one another and eat. If some staff members felt like eating meat, fish or eggs, they arranged it by pooling money, and buying and cooking the item in one of their own rooms. Most Hindu artistes were from Dalit castes; few were vegetarian. So it was often a mixed group of Hindus and Muslims who cooked and ate meat together, as a special treat.

A Nautanki company would carry along material like stove, utensils, ghee, foodgrains and spices—basic requirements for any household. The cook took charge of all this. Nobody could step into the kitchen tent without his permission.

Hindu and Muslim artistes respected each other's beliefs and customs. Munni Bai recalls, 'We Hindus kept a fast—Brihaspat vrat—on Mondays. During the month of Saavan we kept a fast in which we could eat only fruit—it is like the Karva chauth fast that married women keep. At night after a bath we could have a meal. Muslims kept Roza for a month. They didn't eat all day, but had a meal at night and another early in the morning. I think there was no difference between the customs. Just that they kept their fast during one month, and we kept our fast during another month . . . .

'I couldn't manage the fast—it was difficult while traveling. But the Muslims were very regular. All day they wouldn't take even water. The sehri took place after dusk, before the start of Nautanki at night. They would eat, read namaz, and rest. By midnight their food would be digested and they came on stage to perform. The morning meal was at 4 a.m., before sunrise. We would sing while they went backstage and ate. They had bread and tea or milk, or roti and vegetable, drank water, smoked a bidi, washed and read namaz. By 5 a.m. there would be the morning azan, so they said their prayers. When their turn came they would be on stage again.'

Munni Bai found it really tough keeping the Brihasprat vrat when traveling. During this fast she could eat only a few items and these had to be very clean preparations. Being in out-of-the-way places in a mela atmosphere, it was not possible to ensure cleanliness. That is why she gave up the fast, 'after folding my hands in prayer to Lord Krishna. After that I kept a weekly fast whenever possible. In this I just had one or two cups of tea all day. At night I had a proper meal.' She also made sure she kept the Shivratri vrat, once a year. All the Hindus in the troupe kept that. During that chestnut flour is required, but sometimes this was not available. They would get some milk sweets, jaggery and jau and eat that. In advance they would locate a good sweets shop and order a few kilos of sweetmeats. They would pay for this together, each taking a share.

*

Like Gulab Bai, Raja had come to Kanpur in the 1930s to work in Nautanki, and soon became an established artiste.

When Gulab and Raja began living together, he moved into the tiny house the three sisters had rented. Chahetan and Paati rearranged themselves into one room while Gulab and Raja dwelt in the next.

Raja had earned a reputation as the best singer among male Nautanki artistes of the time. He hailed from a family of musicians. His father and grandfather, and several generations before that, played the sarangi. Raja grew up in an atmosphere where everybody sang, played and was well-versed in ragas and sur-taal. He understood the intricacies of musical forms.

Living and performing with him, Gulab's singing grew increasingly refined. She picked up nuggets of knowledge and absorbed styles of singing and diction. Her singing soared to greater heights.

Gulab neither imagined nor expected that Raja would —or should—leave his wife and children. She didn't conceive of him in terms of the usual notions of matrimony. Nor did he want to persuade her to give up her work and be 'exclusively' his, hidden away from prying male eyes. Their relationship remained vibrant. There was no formal legal tie. Yet it survived better than many relationships that are tracked, pruned, labelled and set into pre-defined moulds.

Raja's quiet and easygoing ways made him likeable. He was dignified, his energies directed towards his art. He suited Gulab. Soul partners, they developed a deep mutual understanding and concern for each other's well-being.

Raja mingled with Gulab's family. Chahetan, Paati, Sukhbadan and Kiran—Gulab's younger sisters—called him 'Jija', the term for elder brother-in-law. He treated them with affection and care, as he would his own younger sisters. He was affectionate to her younger brothers, offering sage advice at points when they seemed to need it.

Gulab's anguish rubbed off, her hard life seemed to soften and mellow. Raja was an entirely different kind of person from Chandar Seth. She could trust this man. Last time, she had been pursued and captured. This time she made a choice, and a wise one at that.

Raja was not wealthy, but Gulab was not seeking wealth. She sought affection, intimacy and the freedom to keep working and earning, travelling and acting. She was determined to keep her self-respect intact.

The Nautanki world accepted Gulab and Raja as a couple. They were often assigned roles opposite one another. A lead pair who worked well together was a tremendous relief for any company manager. Both Raja and Gulab were immensely popular. She was undoubtedly the star of any show, but this never seemed to trouble Raja. He was secure just being himself.

*

Gulab gave birth to a daughter, Asha. Nothing pleased her more than to be with her lovely little daughter, holding the infant in her arms. Looking at the baby Gulab felt this was her heir. Asha truly brought hope into her heart. She imagined teaching this child all she knew. Bright and contented, Asha looked up at her mother with wide, trusting eyes.

Gulab, her sisters and Raja all doted on the fair, plump baby. When Gulab and Raja travelled for performances, the baby went along. But it was difficult. Baby Asha would fall sick, or take to crying the moment her mother left her to go onstage. Gulab left work and lived in Balpurva for a few months. When she returned to Kanpur, she decided to leave Asha behind with her mother, Jehangira.

After a couple of years Gulab gave birth to a baby boy, Rajendra. She left Rajendra too with her mother. Jehangira was happy to take in the children. She now had daughters-in-law who helped with housework.

Jehangira, her pet daughter-in-law Dashrath Devi and others in the Balpurva haveli did not grudge the extra childcare, knowing that this was a fair exchange. After all, Gulab's earnings supported the entire household. Chahetan—who had no children—also sent her earnings to Balpurva. Paati Kali had a daughter, Munni, a year younger than Asha. As an infant, Munni too lived in Balpurva.

The children had many cousins in Balpurva, and led carefree, active lives.

Gulab's eldest son, Suresh, grew into a difficult young man. He wasn't quite able to cope with the many changes he'd experienced early in his life. Of all Gulab's children, he was the only one to whom she gave undivided attention for the first two or three years. Then she had to leave him with Jehangira, so as to be able to pursue her career on the stage. During his initial years at Balpurva he missed Gulab intensely, but later grew indifferent to her. He felt hurt and abandoned, became sullen and resentful. Suresh had no communication with his father. He knew his father Chandar Seth was a big man, a prosperous businessman. Although Balpurva was just a short distance from Kannauj, Chandar Seth never visited his son.

Asha and Rajendra grew up in happier circumstances. They had loving parents, steady and devoted to one another. There were no clashes there. This peacefulness affected both children, and they grew up balanced and easy-tempered.

Asha returned to live with Gulab and Raja when she was four or five years old. She travelled with them when they went for shows. Sometimes she stayed back in Kanpur with her mausi, Paati Kali. Raja taught Asha music. He also taught Paati Kali's daughter, Munni. In another year Rajendra too came from Balpurva to live with them in Kanpur.

With Munni, Asha and Rajendra growing up in Kanpur, it seemed a good idea for one person to be steadily at home. Gulab suggested to Paati Kali, 'Why don't you stay home? I earn enough for all of us. Chahetan is earning well. The children need somebody. Who can look after them better than you?'

Paati agreed. She gave up acting and became a full-fledged homemaker. After Munni, she had another two children—a son and a daugther. Paati looked after all the children in the household. So when Gulab and Raja went out performing in all kinds of distant places, their children's lives carried on undisturbed.

In time the boys were sent to school. The day's rhythm was now dictated not only by rehearsals and Nautanki shows, but also by school timings and breaks, exams and vacations.

Paati Kali was the one to keep the children's clothes clean, and remove the lice from their hair. She tended to their hurts and wounds. A cheerful soul, she enjoyed this life quite as much she had earlier enjoyed her Nautanki days.

Munni Devi remembers that her father, a Bania from western Uttar Pradesh, often visited. He'd stay for a few days, sometimes a few weeks. He was fond of his children—Munni, her sister and brother—and always brought clothes and sweets for them. He made regular contributions to the household expenses. He had another wife and children in his hometown—again, two parallel domestic worlds had been created and were maintained.

The three sisters bought a two-storey house in Rail Bazaar, very close to their earlier quarters. They had more space here, and, what is more, it was their own property. Gulab was away on tour when the offer to buy came their way. Chahetan and Paati took the decision in her absence. The whole family moved in.

Gulab, Raja and their two children were comfortable within the larger family. Their children were well loved. Paati Kali's being a homebody released Gulab from many tensions.

For Gulab and Raja, there was work aplenty. During the early and mid-1950s Tirmohan Lal's troupe travelled the length and breadth of Uttar Pradesh, southwards to Gwalior, Rewa and other sites in Madhya Pradesh, and eastwards to Bihar. Gulab and Raja reigned supreme. They were a star pair. Wherever they toured with the company, they received applause and accolades. The company was doing well. When they returned to their home in Kanpur, a warm welcome always awaited them. Gulab felt her life had finally settled into a comfortable, happy and dependable rhythm.

The Great Gulab Theatre Company

For twenty years, I kept working at one place. My salary went up from fifty rupees to two thousand rupees per month. I called my sisters too, and taught them this work.

Later I started my own company. I located artistes I knew in Kanpur. Together, we would go to wedding baraats and melas. People said that other company owners will get me bumped off. They will not leave me alive. I said, 'One day or the other, I have to die. But I will definitely begin this work in this way.' Then slowly, gradually, we got curtains made, and arrangements for 2000-3000 people to sit. We made tents, shamianas, sets . . . things were cheap at that time. Somehow I kept it going. This was the Gulab Bai Nautanki Company. Bahadur Lakdi kept on being staged.

—Gulab Bai

Earning money is heady. Some can digest it, others can't. Gulab Bai never grew arrogant due to wealth. She never showed off her talent or her money. Any staff member might come and sit next to her. She listened to his troubles. If he were hungry she would offer her thali to him. She would give him fifty rupees and soap for a bath. At the same time the Devi gave Gulab Bai such power that however big a man stood in front of her, she would simply say, 'Sit down, son,' and he would melt. He would be unable to say or do anything against her. No abuses or insults.

—Munni Bai

In 1955 Gulab set up the 'Great Gulab Theatre Company'. She had been considering this for some time, gauging the scenario, playing about with the idea. Once she decided to start her own company, she went about it methodically. She bought sets and costumes. Actors and musicians joined readily. Getting bookings was not at all difficult, since her name carried credibility. She commanded enormous goodwill. Thus her company began putting up shows immediately after it was formed.

It took courage and strength of mind for her to leave Tirmohan's company and set up her own. Later she would often recount how these decisions were sparked off by one unpleasant experience.

One day, in 1954, Gulab was busy at a rehearsal, when a messenger came with the news that her sister Sukhbadan had fallen and was badly wounded. The child had toppled off the first floor of the Balpurva haveli and sustained injuries. A nasty gash on the forehead was bleeding. The family urgently required funds for her treatment. One of Gulab's brothers came post-haste with this message. Gulab was scheduled to perform that very night in Kanpur, but she panicked. At that moment nothing else mattered. She felt she must do all she could for her sister. She went at once to Tirmohan Ustad and requested him for some money and a day's leave. Tirmohan refused.

Gulab was stunned by the refusal. She explained the matter again, emphasizing the urgency. He categorically refused both money and leave. She appealed yet again, for she was desperate. Acting, the stage, singing—none of it made any sense at that moment. What was the use of her fame and wealth if she was unable to help her sister in an emergency?

Gulab was furious. After all she had done for Tirmohan's company, was this to be her reward? Everything she had carefully built up seemed to collapse in a moment. 'Am I nothing,' she asked herself, 'that I am not even given leave to go and visit my sick sister? How dare Tirmohan treat me like this! I have worked for him for more than twenty years, and this is how he treats me!'

She turned around and left him without another word. There and then she decided that she would never again work for his company. She borrowed money from two or three colleagues to tide over the crisis, and set off with her brother for Balpurva. Sukhbadan's wounds were still bleeding. The family took her to Kannauj for treatment. Within a few days the wounds healed.

Sukhbadan's wounds healed, but the wound in Gulab's heart did not. She never forgave Tirmohan for that day's callousness. She never again performed for his company. When he sent word requesting her to come for rehearsals, she sent back a curt reply informing that she would not work with him any more. Once she left his troupe, she never looked back.

Gulab began her career at a time when actors still felt lifelong loyalty to their gurus and akharas. This attitude changed dramatically within the next two and a half decades. Actors were now paid fixed salaries, and freely shifted from one company to another, depending on the payment offered.

Gulab felt the pull of loyalty and gratitude. She always claimed she would not have left Tirmohan had he been sensitive in her hour of need. She said his tyrannical manner at that critical juncture broke her trust in him and his company.

*

Gulab formed deep attachments. She was extremely fond of her sisters, brothers and parents. Gulab was born when Jehangira was just sixteen years old, and they became close confidantes. Though later their daily lives were situated worlds apart, yet mother and daughter retained a strong bond throughout their lives.

Jehangira barely ventured out of Balpurva. The household was a ceaseless whirl of activity. Lal Bahadur and Kallu Seth maintained a lavish lifestyle with plenty of meat, drink and entertainment. A number of servants were appointed to look after the estate. His daughters, of course, financed the entire establishment. It was similar with Kallu Seth's family. All of Kallu's daughters—Krishna, Lallan, Kashi, Shakuntala, Shaila and Munni—went to Kanpur one after the other to join the Nautanki. They worked with Numberdar and other Nautanki companies.

Gulab made her debut in the early 1930s, followed by Chahetan and then Paati Kali. Sukhbadan was their fourth sister, and Kiran the youngest. Sukhbadan was nearly twenty years younger than Gulab. Kiran was a year younger than Sukhbadan.

From time to time Sukhbadan and Kiran came to Kanpur to live with their elder sisters, play with the younger children, and gain familiarity with the Nautanki world. But Kiran hankered for the peace and quiet of the village, its fields and simple walks. A sickly child, she found the noise and routine of Kanpur too demanding. Although Paati Kali ran the household with elan, it was not an easy household to run. Large and noisy, its ranks often swelled with relatives and visitors. Gulab, Raja and Chahetan had rehearsals at odd hours and many tours, planned and unplanned.

Years later, Chahetan Bai commented, 'After Didi, we were four sisters. All four of us lived with Didi. In a way she brought us up. She looked after all five brothers, too. She looked after all of us—and till today she has our best wishes at heart.'

*

Sukhbadan, Gulab's youngest sister, for some years the most popular heroine under the banner of the Great Gulab Theatre Company

Sukhbadan thoroughly enjoyed being in Kanpur. She loved the colour and drama of Nautankis. She sang well, with natural flair. Raja and Gulab began training her seriously. She loved to travel with them and see Nautankis, revelling in the lively action. She memorized some parts and began to look forward to acting and dancing on stage.

While Sukhbadan thrived in the Nautanki atmosphere, Kiran languished. Jehangira missed them when they were away. These were her youngest daughters, and she knew that sooner or later they too would fly the nest. Gulab left the two girls in Balpurva, hoping Kiran would feel stronger in the village air. A few weeks later Kiran contracted high fever. Jehangira looked after her. The rest of the family carried on as usual, Lal Bahadur enjoying his revelries. Not realizing how seriously ill she was, nobody took her for proper treatment. One evening she quietly passed away.

Kiran's death was a cruel blow. Gulab was upset for she knew the family could have taken better care of her. Had Lal Bahadur been less self-absorbed he would have taken her to Kannauj for treatment. The death could probably have been prevented. Kiran's sweet presence was sorely missed.

Sukhbadan was now ready to go to Kanpur but Jehangira was shaken by the tragedy and reluctant to let her out of her sight. So Sukhbadan stayed on in Balpurva. That was when she had the accident, which led to momentous consequences in Gulab's life.

*

A few months after Gulab set up the Great Gulab Theatre Company, Sukhbadan joined. Chahetan and Raja were of course involved in the new venture since its inception. Gulab held methodical rehearsals, perfecting each detail of the productions she put up. She had always been a stickler for quality, and this helped the entire company to reach and maintain a high standard.

Gulab still enacted the role of heroine while Raja usually acted as the hero. People appreciated her shows. Almost overnight, the Great Gulab Theatre Company became an established name in the Nautanki field.

Bigwigs in the field were furious. Tirmohan took Gulab's leaving his company as a personal insult. He never forgave her, nor did his company ever recover its former glory. Shrikrishna Pehelwan's company had almost shut down by the mid-1950s. He was dead-set against women joining Nautanki, and the further step of women becoming company managers was more than he could tolerate. To his mind Nautanki was a masculine world, and should remain so. He believed Nautanki standards and ethos were declining due to the presence of women.

Lalmani Numberdar tried to actively prevent actors and musicians from joining Gulab's company. Despite the hostility of all these seniors, Gulab succeeded in setting up a successful company. Her name in the field began to rival theirs. She knew the craft inside out. Co-workers flocked to her, providing a groundswell of ready support. She had risen from the ranks and had a generous understanding of their needs. Her life was devoted to the art. She gave it all she had.

Raja supported her in this new enterprise. Of the two, she was active and dynamic, while he was quiet and observant. Her brothers, who had spent the better part of their lives in the Nautanki world, helped in the management of the company.

The Great Gulab Theatre Company went from mela to mela and was a roaring success. The box office collected sizeable amounts. Gulab put her brothers in charge of ticket sales and money collection. They were the chief bouncers, managing tumultuous crowds and staving off gatecrashers and hoodlums who tried to break in to create a disturbance.

Gulab's company shone bright. Her personal life was soothing and satisfying. All told, Gulab felt she was in a good place. She thanked Phoolmati Maiya for showering her with such abundance and many blessings. She continued to work very hard. There was a lot she had to do to establish the company and keep it going.

Gulab's energies were now divided between singing and acting on the one hand and running the company on the other. Both jobs were extremely demanding and she found herself frequently feeling drained and exhausted. She needed to concentrate on the logistics of running a company. She knew the quality of her work on stage suffered because she was often tired. She would have to find a way out of this impasse.

Switching Roles: Queen No More

'Why are you crying?' asked Gulab.
'They were so rude to you,' said Sukhbadan, sniffling. 'They made you leave the stage. They should not have done that! I didn't like it.'
'I don't mind,' said Gulab, smiling. 'I'm happy that they liked you. After all you are my sister. I am getting old. How much longer will I act? I am so happy the public likes you, my dear. You can now take over from me.'
—Reconstructed based on Sukhbadan's account, Kanpur

Gulab knew that she could not carry on playing heroine forever. She was nearly forty years old. Sooner or later, audiences would want a younger heroine and she would have to bow out. Since she also shouldered tremendous responsibilities as a company owner, she felt it was time to hand over the mantle of heroine to a younger woman.

She began to train her sister Sukhbadan to play heroine roles. Sukhbadan was a diligent pupil. Under Raja and Gulab's tutelage her talents flowered. Within a year of her training, she was ready to take over.

Sukhbadan adopted a screen name—Nanda Guha. Vivacious and talented, she enjoyed the great advantage of systematic grooming at the hands of masters. Gulab trained her personally, paying attention to every detail, as did Raja.

Sukhbadan stepped gracefully into the role of heroine. For a time both sisters performed 'Rani' roles. Sukhbadan took over the role of Laila, while Gulab still played Taramati. Sukhbadan grew rapidly in confidence and skill.

Gulab focused increasingly on her own singing. As an artiste, she would continue to perform on stage as long as she lived, but as a solo singer rather than dancer or actress. As always, Gulab often sang a rasiya or dadra between drama scenes. Sukhbadan began joining her in some of these items. Gulab took the lead, with Sukhbadan accompanying.

One day both sisters were on stage together at a numaish in Aligarh, singing a dadra. Musicians sat on their left. The small-town audience was entirely male, the majority being young. They whistled when they saw Sukhbadan and made catcalls as she sang. She was glamorous, with her slim figure, delicate features and large eyes. She sang full-throated. Several men sent up sums of money for her. The audience was impatient and irritated when Gulab sang. One man shouted rudely for Sukhbadan—'Sukhbadan chahiye!' Clearly, the audience preferred the younger woman.

For a moment Gulab flinched, hurt at such a rude rejection. But after a minute she felt amused rather than offended. A sense of relief flooded into her. Sukhbadan was now the darling of the crowds! Gulab felt proud of her attractive and talented young sister. Within a short span of time, Sukhbadan had become the centre of attention. Sukhbadan's success was a tribute to Gulab's skills in training the younger woman.

After completing one song, Gulab withdrew from the stage. She indicated that Sukhbadan should carry on singing another number. Sukhbadan felt terrible about the manner in which her sister had been hooted out. Somehow she finished singing another song and then quickly left the stage. Backstage, she burst into tears.

Gulab asked her why she was crying, and Sukhbadan said it was because the audience had behaved so rudely to Gulab. To her surprise, Gulab was smiling, and explained she was happy the audience liked Sukhbadan. It meant that Gulab could now safely retire as heroine.

Sukhbadan looked at her, wondering. She saw her sister was genuinely pleased. She stopped sniffling, and relaxed. All was well, she realized—and began to revel in her new-found glory.

Gulab's popularity as an actress was on the wane, even as Sukhbadan's was on the rise. This meant Gulab could gracefully retire from heroine roles. She had more than enough to do anyway, running the entire company.

*

Gulab's most popular roles as heroine had been in *Bahadur Ladki*, *Harishchandra*, *Pukar* and *Dahiwala*. Sukhbadan took over all these. Gulab's entire body used to express the emotions of the character she was playing. Sukhbadan exuded similar energy and aesthetic sensibility. A younger artiste recalls seeing Gulab in the role of Taramati—'Each action was clear and distinct. As Taramati, when Rohtas dies, she would pull at her hair in grief, and some hair actually came out into her hands and nails.'[19] Sukhbadan was called upon to perform with similar intensity.

Sukhbadan had a natural flair for acting, but suffered from a nervous temperament. Before any stage appearance she would be a bundle of nerves. She was the only one of Gulab's sisters who suffered from stage fright.

Young Sukhbadan needed to have Gulab around whenever she went on stage. Gulab propped up her confidence and gave her last-minute tips. Still Sukhbadan was tense. Before one of her early performances she got so tense that she refused to go on stage. Gulab sent somebody for half a glass of country liquor. Normally she strictly forbade actors from drinking before a performance, but she knew it was needed now. She made Sukhbadan drink the peg, administering it like medicine. Sukhbadan relaxed enough to go on stage, and act well.

Similar fright grabbed her the next time she was to go on stage. Again the same medicine worked. It became a practice, then: before a demanding performance, young Sukhbadan would have a draught of liquor. With a small peg of desi sharab coursing down her veins, she performed wonderfully. The spirit gave her the fillip she required to forget about the crowd, her fears and nerves, and simply swing into action. Particularly when she had an emotional scene to perform— and Nautankis are full of those!—she needed her potent draught. She could then express Taramati's grief upon Rohtas's death with unforgettable power. She had the entire audience in tears, in sympathy with the Rani's grief.

Gulab never allowed anybody else in her staff to drink a drop of alcohol before a performance. A strict manager with inflexible principles, she was known to dismiss actors who imbibed alcohol or smoked tobacco before a performance. But she bent the rules in the case of her kid sister. After all, Sukhbadan had the most challenging task of all—fitting into Gulab's shoes.

Taking over Rani roles from a giant like Gulab was a tall order indeed. It required a great deal of gumption. Sukhbadan needed a little bit of help to rise to the challenge. A small daily 'fix' became a habit with Sukhbadan—a habit that continued well into old age, even when she was no longer performing.

*

In time Asha and Munni were to be groomed as the next line of heroines. The two were the same age, growing up in the same house. From the age of four or five they began watching endless rehearsals and performances. Both were fascinated by the world of Nautanki, and ran around helping the adults—fetching food, combing hair, rubbing oil, passing messages and entertaining with ceaseless chatter. They were asked to come on stage and twirl around in bright little lehengas, as somebody sang a lilting song. They were encouraged to sing. Both girls learnt several Nautankis by heart. They began prompting—providing help for actors from backstage. While their brothers attended school in Kanpur, the two girls were apprenticed directly into the Nautanki trade.

Raja was extremely disciplined about doing his daily riyaz. Often Asha sat by her father as he practised. He would give her tips and encourage her to sing with tabla and harmonium. Paati Kali and Gulab encouraged Munni to join these sessions. Raja enjoyed teaching the girls. Asha showed uncommon promise as a singer, and Munni, too, was talented.

*

By the late 1950s Gulab gave up heroine roles entirely, and concentrated on her work as teacher and company owner.

She continued taking up character roles for some time more. She was a mature singer, and over the next many years audiences expected Gulab Bai to come on stage and sing her patent dadras, rasiyas and thumris. She sang for the public until the end of her life nearly four decades later.

Running the Great Gulab Theatre Company was now her main challenge. She had a head for practical matters, and rather enjoyed organizing everything. These qualities helped her build up the company as a commercial venture.

During the late 1950s and early 1960s the fortunes of the Great Gulab Theatre Company swung high. It performed regularly in Uttar Pradesh and adjacent regions. Along with the old classics new plays were also performed. Some were based on Bollywood cine hits while other Nautankis were written focusing on issues like poverty, dowry and unemployment.

Gulab's unstinting hard work and the painstaking attention she paid to each detail led to immediate success. People flocked to see good Nautankis, though as the years went by they did not want to stay up all night. The dramas were compressed, cut short to three or four hours from the earlier seven or eight. Gulab argued this was because people were too busy now and no longer had the time to sit around watching a show the way people did in the olden days.

Gulab relied on her brothers' help to run the show but they soon began cheating her, helping themselves to huge servings from the box-office. She assigned them odd jobs; they were handy as bouncers and guards. After a few years, she hired a full-time manager—Shiv Adhar Dube.

During the heydays of the Great Gulab Theatre Company, it had around seventy people on its rolls. Running the company naturally involved a great deal of people-management. Actors and musicians were the life-blood of Nautanki, but they were notorious for their moods and tempers. Regular staff was hired, a system lasting well into the 1960s. Many actors, musicians and helpers remained with the company for two or three decades.

Gulab exercised discrimination in the choice of artistes. She was interested in excellence. Several artistes from the Hathras style, such as Master Gulab of Aligarh, joined her company. She invited her old teachers Mohammed Khan Saheb, Rashid Khan Warsi and Mehboob Master to join her company, and kept learning from them. They taught music to other troupe members as well. Gulab often said later, 'All of them taught me, and stayed with me. They were very good people.'

Gulab took the training of young artistes, particularly women, into her own hands. She personally oversaw every aspect of a new artiste's diction and movement, the timbre of her voice and the agility of her steps. Sukhbadan, her first protégé, flourished under Gulab's nurturing eyes. At the same time, Gulab was a hard taskmaster.

She was a perfectionist when it came to work. She refused to tolerate a shoddy performance or a mispronounced word.

Munni Bai recalled, 'If I mispronounced one word, Gulab Mausi would make me repeat the entire part! I had to do it again and again until I got the word absolutely right. Sometimes she would get angry if I kept saying something wrong, and she would hit me. This spurred me on, so I learnt fast. She would make us work for hours. But afterwards, she would say, "Here, come and take your milk, drink it!" There was always one seer of milk boiling on the stove in the kitchen!'

Her artistes and musicians excelled themselves when performing for Gulab. The costumes had to be just right—well-ironed robes, the correct crown or headdress and the proper sword or shield. Sets had to be elaborately arranged and curtains well in place. Before a show began, in the early evening, she would light an agarbatti, asking for divine blessings for her company and that particular performance.

A born leader, Gulab cared deeply for the musicians and actors in her company. She felt concerned about their daily lives, inquired after their families and supplied whatever they required in times of trouble.

At the start of every season she took the entire troupe to Balpurva, where they performed a show in the open space outside Phoolmati Maiya's temple. Gulab sought blessings from Phoolmati Maiya. She felt she was successful only because Maiya accepted her devotion and granted her wishes.

Every year the company stayed at Balpurva for three or four days. People from surrounding villages, and even from Kannauj and Makanpur, flocked to the shows at Balpurva. This was Gulab's unique way of acknowledging her debts to Phoolmati Maiya as well as her beloved family and village.

Gulab's family was delighted with her stature and success. Lal Bahadur would put himself out to entertain the Nautanki company. He kept them in great comfort, catering to their every need. After all, it was their work that paid for his luxurious lifestyle.

*

Everything was going well in Gulab's life. But then, without any warning, tragedy struck. The troupe was out travelling, and had put up at the edge of a small town.

At night, Raja stepped out for a stroll. He was hit by a speeding truck, and died on the spot.

Gulab was devastated. She felt her fine palace, built up lovingly brick by brick, was looted, ransacked and burnt down. Nobody could ever replace Raja. They had built up a rare understanding and companionship. Gulab and Raja had savoured and enjoyed several years together. Death snatched him away, marking an untimely closure to an idyllic relationship. Had he lived, Raja and Gulab would perhaps have remained together, forever.

19

The Show Must Go On

I worked with many companies. I did lots of work with Gulab Bai. She had a different attitude from all others. She respected artistes. She never spoke badly. She was interested in the art. She was truly a 'diamond'. There is nobody who compares with her.

—Paan Kunwar

At that time art was worshipped. The artist was respected. People didn't see whether a person was dark or fair, beautiful or ugly. They saw her art. People were simple and straightforward. Everybody knew what was happening with everybody else, nothing was hidden.

— Shanti

When Raja died, Gulab felt all the joy in her life had passed away. She poured her energies into running the Great Gulab Theatre Company, working tirelessly to maintain high standards.

The company had at least seventy staff members, including actors, musicians, cooks, tailors, painter, prompter, curtain-puller, coolies, helpers and odd-job men. During busy seasons, the number of staff members would swell to 120. They came to Kanpur from various parts of Uttar Pradesh—Etawah, Banaras, Agra, Allahabad, Lakhimpur Kheri, Mathura—and even places as far off as Calcutta.

Gulab selected her staff carefully. She invited accomplished artistes to join, provided appropriate salaries and ensured a satisfactory work ethos. That explains why several staff members stayed on with her company for decades. She had bought elaborate sets, props, musical instruments and glittering costumes—all the paraphernalia required for a good performance. Her company owned tents, chairs, rugs and wooden fencing material. She had talented curtain painters in her troupe—Babban from Lucknow, Nazeer from Agra, and another from Chhapra.

Gulab would rent space at mela grounds, and her stageman and helpers would arrive a few days before the first show. The stageman would make the stage, dig pits and pitched the tents, including a kitchen tent, living quarters for the staff, and an enormous enclosure for the Nautanki performances. Actors showed up a day or two before the show. In the early days actors came by train, covering the last stretch by bullock-cart. By the 1970s they reached the venue by train or bus. Trucks became the chief mode for transporting sets, tents and other heavy stuff.

Seating arrangements were made for four to five thousand people. The helpers put up fences, rows of chairs and large rugs for seating the bulk of spectators. The staff sold tickets—three or four different colours for different classes of spectators. According to actress Paan Kunwar, during the 1960s tickets in a provincial town cost six annas, eight annas, twelve annas and Rs 1.50. Shiv Adhar Dube said tickets in the 1970s cost between Re 1 and Rs 4. He said on an average eight to ten thousand tickets were sold every day, leading to a balance earning of Rs 10,000-20,000 per month. Female artistes were paid between Rs 1,000 and Rs 5,000, and male artistes Rs 400-500.

The troupe performed on a picture-frame stage. Eight petromaxes were fixed to provide lighting from various angles. Seven drop curtains were used, each with a scenery painted on it. Painters specialized in creating curtain paintings. The name of the company was inscribed on each curtain. The play might open onto a royal court, the site of action might move to a garden or a queen's boudoir. Curtains representing a jungle, a bazaar and a war scene might be displayed one after the other. Players entered and exited from the wings.

The costumes used in Gulab's company, as in other Nautanki companies, were eclectic. They rarely belonged to a definite period. King Harischandra might wear a seventeenth-century gilded tunic while Queen Taramati would appear in contemporary sarees. The romantic hero might strut about in a velvet Western-style coat while the heroine flaunted a flowing Persian tunic or silken lehenga.

Actors used bright make-up. They applied face powder and marked cheeks and forehead with red dots and silver moons. Lamp-soot or kohl accentuated their eyes. Nose-rings, earrings, bracelets and ankle bells added glitter and a tinkling sound.

During a performance, Gulab would sit in the wings on a chair, and call each actor before his or her entry. She made sure that the dress and make-up worn were appropriate. She would not tolerate it if an actor had black eyebrows and white moustache! Once she slapped an actor, Pyare from Khurja, for going onto stage with shoddy make-up. Each actor had an elaborate set of costumes when working for a season with Gulab Bai. A stickler for precision, she accepted no shortcuts or compromises.

Local zamindars, seths and policemen often demanded special seats. She seldom acceded to such demands. Even if a DIG arrived she remained seated, attention concentrated on the work at hand.

Once, the company was in Gwalior. The evening performance was to begin soon. Gulab Bai bathed, lit an agarbatti and prayed to Phoolmati Maiya and Lord Krishna for the success of the show. A packed audience filled the shamiana enclosure. Meanwhile the daroga (local police boss) turned up with his mistress and demanded a special seat. Not an inch of space remained for a special seat. The daroga shouted, 'Who is the owner of this company? Call the owner!' Gulab came out saying, 'I will make arrangements for you to sit. Here is a trunk, both of you can sit on it. There is such a crowd it is impossible to give you any other seat.' He grew abusive and shouted, 'I will burn down your company!' Gulab said, 'Light a fire. I will see how you burn down the company.' She called her brothers and commanded, 'What are you waiting for? Put him into the water tub!' In summer, four or five water drums were filled and kept at different places, for dousing any accidental fire. Recalled Munni Bai, 'We picked up that daroga, in his policeman's uniform, and dunked him into the biggest water drum. We all beat him up—we women too. We were not delicate darlings like today's girls!' Next day Gulab went across to the police camp near the mela ground, and registered a complaint about the daroga's misbehaviour the previous evening. He was suspended for several months.

Another time the company was invited by an elderly farmer to perform in his village. After the show the farmer disclosed he had no cash to make payments. His fields had sugarcane standing ripe. He offered them sugarcane in return for the show. But Gulab and her staff found this impractical. Besides, they believed he actually had the cash. They took him along in their truck to Kanpur. They decided to keep him captive until he coughed up the money. The man seemed unperturbed; in fact, he seemed quite happy. After a few days they released him. Recalling the incident, musician Harishchandra said, 'We realized we weren't going to get anything out of him. Moreover, we were spending, on feeding and looking after him. We decided to let him go. We washed our hands off the whole affair, knowing we would get nothing out of him.'

Gulab's company performed at the usual melas in Devi Patan, Makanpur, Kashipur, Meerut, Badaun, Bahraich, Sonepur, Bijnaur, Rajgir and so on. It also went up to Gwalior, Indore, Rewa, Ahmedabad, Calcutta and Asansol.

*

If somebody came onto the stage with a bidi, Gulab was infuriated. Said Munni, 'She wanted everybody to be pure on the stage: no drinking, no smoking. From the time you apply makeup to the time you remove it, you cannot chew tobacco or paan masala or smoke a bidi. That was a rule. Have a bath, do puja and then come on the stage.'

The audience included women and men. Women sat at the front, in a section sometimes separated by a curtain or a partition of tin sheets and wiring. This ensured that no man could jump across and trouble women seated there. Women would come to a mela with children in tow, roam around all day, make purchases, visit the dargah, buy tickets and sit up all night to see a Nautanki. In the morning they folded their sheets, wrapped up their bundles and headed off home. They enjoyed the outing tremendously.

Gulab Bai made sure basic dignity was maintained within her troupe. Male artistes were not allowed into the 'greenroom' tents so long as women artistes were engaged in make-up and dressing. Men began their dress and make-up only after the female artistes were done.

At the same time, Gulab did not believe in moral policing. She knew affairs would take place, for emotions are disorderly and do not fall into straight lines and square frameworks simply to make life easier or a company more disciplined. She thought it entirely natural that persons would be attracted and involved with one another. Sexuality was a part of life, and she accepted it as such. She herself had varied desires, and saw no reason why others would not. The bottomline was clear—there should not be any mess that interfered with the enactment of a Nautanki. The show must go on!

Company members were enthusiastic about their work, and had a great passion for innovation. Sometimes women and girls acted all the parts in a Nautanki. Sukhbadan was famous for her brilliant acting as Majnu. Usually she acted as Laila, but for a change sometimes became Majnu while somebody else became Laila. Cross-dressing was of course an age-old part of Nautanki tradition.

Manager Shiv Adhar Dube, musicians Rashid Khan, Thaan Singh, Ram Prasad, Harishchandra, and actors like Binda Prasad Nigam were assets to Gulab's troupe. Babban and Nazeer painted the drop curtains with fantastic scenery. A number of women—including Sukhbadan, Munni Bai and Asha—acted regularly in Gulab's company while some others joined only for a season or two.

*

Krishna Bai too set up a Nautanki company. So did several other female artistes. Gulab's and Krishna's companies often competed with each other for audience attention.

Tirmohan's company floundered once Gulab left it to set up her own. Nearly seventy years old, he felt resentful and abandoned. He faced stiff competition from Gulab's company. His highly talented scriptwriter Yasin Mian died around the same time. Tirmohan innovated in order to attract the public. It was his idea to introduce the clarinet in Nautanki performances. He traveled to Agra and tracked down Master Gulab on Taj Road. Master Gulab was a well-known clarinet player, and Tirmohan offered him a job in the company. Master Gulab ran a music shop and himself employed a large number of people. While he declined the offer of a job, Master Gulab agreed to play the clarinet for Tirmohan Ustad's company for a month. During that month the company competed with Gulab Bai's new company at the Tikuli mela. According to Tirmohan's grand-nephew Chinha Guru, the clarinet succeeded in drawing a substantial audience towards Tirmohan's shows at the Tikuli mela.

Tirmohan tried to identify leading ladies comparable to Gulab Bai. An actress called Shanti was fairly successful as heroine in his company for several years. But she never became half as popular as Gulab Bai. In the mid-1960s Tirmohan began winding up his work. He was exhausted and depressed. He continued holding a three-day show at Beeghapur during Dussehra every year.

Tirmohan died around 1970, when he well over eighty years old. His wife and three sons had died much earlier. He had no grandchildren. One of his sons had married into a Beeghapur family. Through this relationship Tirmohan had an heir in the family—Chinha Guru. Chinha Guru grew up with the spirit of Nautanki all around, especially at the time of the Dussehra shows. As a young man he helped Tirmohan organize the shows, and later continued the tradition, even after Tirmohan's death. Chinha Guru studied well and spent his life working as a schoolteacher in the government high school in Beeghapur. He remained a connoisseur of good Nautankis, and very knowledgeable.

Shrikrishna Pehelwan's Nautanki company had wound up earlier. After his death his sons and, later, grandsons, continued to publish large numbers of Nautanki scripts. Old scripts continued to sell well, and publishers often commissioned new scripts on contemporary themes such as dowry, love marriage and anti-poverty programs.

Lalmani Numberdar, one of the early giants in Kanpur Nautanki, died in the 1940s. Two sons, Jaiprasad Numberdar and Hariprasad Numberdar, continued running separate Nautanki companies. Ganesh Numberdar, Jaiprasad's son, took over his father's company in 1960, ran it for the next few years, but closed it down in 1984.

Gulab concentrated her energies on the Great Gulab Theatre Company, seeing it through thick and thin, highs and lows. The company touched great heights of popularity during the late 1950s and the 1960s—but the 1970s witnessed a decline in its fortunes.

Coexisting with Cinema

I never left my family. I was always there for them.
—Gulab Bai, 1996

All my life, I breathed Nautanki. If I saw a dream, it was a dream of Nautanki. I lived for Nautanki, and died for Nautanki.
—Gulab Bai, 1990

A couple of years after Raja's death, Gulab met Balbir Singh, the owner of a touring cinema company. They met as professionals whose business lines coincided. Balbir Singh, fascinated with the commercial potential of the film medium, ventured across from Punjab to exhibit 'talkies' in the UP melas. At the melas he saw Gulab Bai's Nautanki. Balbir Singh's work was in competition with Gulab's, since both provided popular entertainment. They vied for the same audience. Though most people still preferred to see a Nautanki, bioscope movies attracted a fair share of attention.

Balbir Singh was a regular on the mela circuit. Gulab Bai and Balbir Singh travelled the same routes within Uttar Pradesh and in time came close to one another. Again there was no concealment. Gulab had always been open and frank about her liaisons. She lived life as it came, with few pretensions. In any case, this time it was a carefully chosen relationship—more a matter of convenience and circumstance than an affair of the heart. Balbir Singh was acceptable as a partner since he had good prospects as a businessman. His family lived far away in the Punjab, so when he came to Uttar Pradesh he could spend substantial time with Gulab.

Balbir Singh had no qualms about setting up a liaison. With Gulab Bai he discovered passion, streaked with the colours of fantasy. He was an English-speaking middle-class man; a liaison with Gulab helped him enter deeper layers of the local culture, which helped him immeasurably in his business. He was able to expand it largely due to the insights and contacts he gained from his association with Gulab Bai.

Both Nautanki and the touring cinema business did well during the 1960s. The Great Gulab Theatre Company was still at a high. Balbir Singh soon purchased another touring cinema and hired people to take it from one venue to another. Within the next few years, he became owner of seven touring cinema companies. Each of these played regularly, at one mela or another. It was the right time for this business, and Balbir Singh was able to cash in.

Balbir visited Gulab frequently over the next couple of decades. It proved to be a stormy, chequered relationship. They had a daughter, Madhu, born in the early 1960s. After each trip to Uttar Pradesh, he returned home to his family in the Punjab.

*

Around the year 1970, Gulab's sister Sukhbadan, who had held forth with aplomb as leading lady in the Ccmpany's productions, left work. She had shone as a star, like Gulab before her. But now she left to live with a wealthy Brahman from Sitapur. She already had two children, but he insisted that she leave her work and settle down with him. Although his wife refused to accept Sukhbadan, she moved into the upper storey of the large house, and stayed there for a good ten years. The wife lived on the ground floor.

Sukhabadan was happy because she felt her 'husband' loved her. She kept busy with her children—five in all. At times, while on a visit to her sisters in Kanpur, she would enact a small part in a Nautanki. One day, a cousin requested her to take up a role in a big mela. Sukhbadan was tempted, and persuaded her husband to let her go. When she returned, she found him in a coma. He died in hospital a few days later. He had made no financial provisions for her. Said Sukhbadan later, 'He died suddenly so he was not able to leave anything for me. His wife stole my jewellery and wouldn't let me into the house.' Gulab sent their brother Subedar to Sitapur to escort Sukhbadan and her children back to the Rail Bazaar house.

In the 1980s Sukhbadan, ensconced in Kanpur, again began earning. But she could never regain her former glory as an actress. In a few years, both her daughters learnt to sing and dance and began earning. None of her three sons took up any steady profession. Sukhbadan moved with her younger daughter into a house in Kanpur, while other children went their separate ways. She took care of the grandchildren, while her daughter went out to work.

*

Paati Kali's daughter Munni Bai joined Gulab Bai's company in the 1960s—soon after Sukhbadan left to go and live in Sitapur. Working under the screen name Nanda Guha or Nanda Devi, Munni Bai proved to be a talented actress, with the gifts of grace, dignity, and a powerful voice. She adored her Gulab Mausi, picking up nuggets of knowledge from her, constantly learning. Munni sometimes played the part of heroine, but more often a character role. She enjoyed her work tremendously, thriving in the Nautanki ethos, though she did resent the fact of being underpaid sometimes. She knew Gulab Bai took her presence for granted, since it was 'all in the family'.

Munni Bai's father was a wealthy Bania from west Uttar Pradesh. He was already married when he first met Paati Kali at a mela, and started visiting her in the Rail Bazaar house. He and Paati Kali had three children—Munni being the eldest, followed several years later by Rani, and then a son. Soon after her son's birth, Paati Kali gave up acting to provide steady care to her own and Gulab's children. Munni joined Nautanki at the age of fifteen or sixteen. Her father, being a respectable businessman, shouted at her when he saw her acting in a mela. Munni challenged him—'You are my father but you have not prepared me for any other kind of work. How else am I to earn? I will earn like this!' Paati Kali found her paramour's objections to Munni's joining Nautanki so intolerable that she broke off her twenty-year relationship with him.

Soon after she started working steadily on the stage, Munni Bai developed an intimate relationship with Kanhaiya Lal, a businessman from Gorakhpur. Though already married, he was keen to have Munni Bai come and live with him in Gorakhpur. She was adamant in her refusal, telling him, 'I will never leave the stage. Remember, it is through this that I met you.' She had children, but continued living in Rail Bazaar with Paati Kali. Her children were well looked after within this family house. Munni Bai's daughter, however, died as an infant. Her three sons attended school. One graduated, got a job in a bank, married and moved away from Rail Bazaar. Two sons continued living in the Rail Bazaar house with Munni Bai and Paati Kali, and in time, their own wives and children. One of her sons prepares and sells spices, while the other dances in stunt shows, for instance, on glass pieces.

Munni never fully recovered from the shock of losing her only daughter. She would say, 'After that whenever I acted as Taramati and Rohtas died, I identified with the scene so intensely that I would really cry. The entire audience would cry with me. I can never forget the grief I felt upon my daughter's death.'

Munni never left the Nautanki stage. Even in old age, she would take up most roles that came her way. She would say, 'The stage is like a place of worship. It is like an akhara. We should be pure when we go onto the stage. We should offer prayers, then go there before the audience.' Through the ups and downs of the fortunes of the Great Gulab Theatre Company, there was never a moment when Munni Bai abandoned it. Gulab could always count upon her.

*

Gulab's elder daughter, Asha, took to the stage like a duck to water. She and Munni Bai were of roughly the same age, and joined Nautanki at around the same time, in the late 1960s. While Munni Bai was pleasing enough, Asha completely captivated the audience with her powerful singing and attractive stage presence. Her voice was sweet and strong. She had inherited Gulab's buxom figure and stunning good looks. Confident and accommodating, she was popular with the all the staff members. In no time at all, Asha had become the major attraction in Gulab's company. She was established as a star. After Gulab,

Sukhbadan had been the major heroine. After Sukhbadan, it was Asha who took over the mantle.

Gulab's daughter Asha performing

The 1970s were not a good time for Nautanki. Crowds were thinning. Cinema lured away many youngsters. Older patronage systems were drying up. The government imposed an entertainment tax on Nautanki shows, sharply cutting into profits.

Gulab Bai refused to compromise on production standards. But she had to grapple with the fact that her company was in a decline. By the start of the 1970s, she could no longer afford to pay staff salaries round the year.

Keeping together a steady staff became a huge challenge. Nautanki artistes were available, but few maintained the high standards Gulab Bai was known for. She wanted to have only the best artistes. They stayed with her because of strong bonds of loyalty, mutual respect and a healthy working environment. Close family members like Asha and Munni Bai of course had even stronger attachments to Gulab's Company. It was a whole world in itself, within which they had grown and learnt, and enjoyed the security of a network of colleagues and co-workers.

*

As a glamorous leading lady, Asha had scores of suitors. She summarily rejected many of them, while Gulab vetoed the rest. In the mid-1970s, Asha allowed one man to come close to her. He was a wealthy young businessman, dealing in metal parts. He approached Gulab Bai for Asha's hand in 'marriage'. Gulab knew he was doing well in his business. Yet she was in a quandary. 'Marriage' usually meant an actress had to give up her career. Giving up Asha as an actress would be a near-fatal blow to the company. On the other hand, she could not keep her daughter tied exclusively to work forever. Gulab agreed to the match, requesting and fervently hoping that he would allow Asha to continue working.

Asha was pliable. She had no special inclination towards this man, nor did she dislike him. She was flattered by his attentions. The fact that he was already married did not bother her. As she remarked, 'I did not expect anything else. This was what I had always seen. I never expected a man who would be devoted only to me. I was happy as I was, acting and singing. When my mother said, "Marry him", I said, "All right." I did not mind doing so. I thought in my mind, "He is keen upon me, and he is an easy-going man. I will convince him to let me continue working after marriage."'

Gulab arranged a grand feast for her entire clan and colleagues. The bride and groom exchanged garlands. The businessman paid a handsome dowry. But after the ceremony, he refused to let Asha work. Whenever she raised the issue he threatened, 'If you go for shows I will leave you.' He set her up in a rented house in a middle-class locality in Kanpur, and visited regularly. Caring and solicitous, he looked after her material needs. He lived in another house in the same city with his first wife and children, but visited Asha daily, and remained devoted to her over the next few decades.

*

Gulab had trained several young women for the stage. Of these, Mangala, daughter of one of Gulab's brothers, married the harmonium player Ram Prasad and settled into domesticity. Suraiya (Krishna Bai's sister Lallan's daughter) acted more in Krishna Bai's company than in Gulab's. She was successful as a heroine, and also took up assignments with various other companies.

With Asha in limbo, Munni once again took over the heroine roles. But despite her grace and talent, she was less acceptable to the audience.

As time went by, Gulab's company had fewer assignments. Box-office earnings plummeted. The future began to look bleak, and Gulab became increasingly anxious.

She began to beg Asha to return to perform in a few shows. Asha was by now sufficiently secure about her husband's affections to take some liberties. 'I would slip out, saying I was visiting my mother,' she explained later. 'I would take up a role and play it at a mela. If I had said I was going for ten days, sometimes I stayed on for fifteen. I didn't mind telling such small lies!' Of course her husband got to know, and sometimes turned up at the venue in his car to drag her away. He forgave her the occasional lapse. Asha would flash her eyes, lower them momentarily and look up with an innocent artful smile to induce him to forgive her. But she knew there were limits to her independence. She risked his ire if she went against his wishes. Keen to keep her marriage going, she agreed to her mother's requests only as a very special concession.

Asha gave birth to a son. This tied her down further. Her husband imposed strictures on her movements. During the next few years, Asha was absent from the stage. Gulab was unable to rely on her, as an actress, at all.

Asha's husband was doing well. He began constructing an independent house for her in a middle-class locality. Gulab meanwhile was engulfed in a crisis of no mean proportions. By the late 1970s her company was in the red. She incurred losses several times in a row.

*

When Balbir Singh expanded his business seven-fold, a large part of the capital was acquired by siphoning off earnings from Gulab's company. Initially she overlooked this pilfering but as her own profits dwindled, it became a major source of conflict. Sometimes he skimmed away the cream even before she had paid her actors and musicians. She was infuriated and demanded that he return what he had taken. But he never did so.

Balbir Singh had been keen that their daughter Madhu should grow up in a middle-class ambience. Gulab too dreamt of educating her children so they could rise higher in life. They sent Madhu to a boarding school. However, by the time the child was ten years old, Gulab began to experience financial difficulties. Balbir Singh was erratic about paying his share of fees. Gulab would somehow pay them herself.

Balbir Singh's fortunes, too, did not endure. Cinema houses having come up in urban and peri-urban centres, people were less interested in touring cinema. Balbir Singh never gave Gulab or her household any money, claiming to have urgent expenses of his own. He spent a packet constructing a house in Delhi, where his wife and children settled.

Gulab was weary, having faced acute disappointments in her work as well as love life. Her relationship with Balbir Singh became increasingly tense, with sporadic outbursts of violence on his part. Several years older than her, he was growing tired of his trips to Uttar Pradesh. The trips yielded hardly any commercial returns, and even less by way of emotional fulfillment.

21

Life Cycle of a Butterfly

In school we studied the life cycle of a butterfly. Insects have a life cycle. In Nautanki too, women have a life cycle.
—Madhu

My mother was different. Everybody knew and respected her. She suffered at the hands of men in her life. For years during her youth she was in the wilderness with Chandar Seth who didn't let her work, and then betrayed her. Yet my mother persevered. She came back to Nautanki and remained devoted to it all her life. Then my father came from Punjab, built his business, bought seven touring cinemas, but the market for Nautanki was disappearing and my mother became financially weak. Yet, she was different. She was Gulab Bai.

—Asha

In 1985 Gulab Bai won a Sangeet Natak Akademi Award for her contribution to folk theatre. This was a highly prestigious award. Not only did it acknowledge Gulab's stature as a performer, it also provided official recognition to the Nautanki form. Through these awards the Indian state formally acknowledged Nautanki as a valuable cultural heritage, and accepted Gulab Bai as its most prominent exponent.

The award gave Gulab Bai a new lease of life. She felt keenly the privilege of being selected for this signal honour.

It brought her into the limelight, and she was able to go on stage and speak for Nautanki. She accepted the award graciously, as her due. She spoke at a couple of important government functions. She received awards at glittering ceremonies. The Sangeet Natak Akademi Awards were presented at a grand hall in Chennai, in the presence of elite art-bureaucrats, celebrities and other awardees from around the country.

Gulab delivers a lecture at the National Theatre Festival in Lucknow in August 1984

At the Ravindralaya in Lucknow, Gulab made a speech to official cultural mandarins, in which she explained that no entertainment tax should be charged for Nautanki performances. As a treasured art form, the state should endeavour to preserve and support Nautanki, rather than strangle it through such measures.

Gulab Bai cut a regal figure. Tall and portly, she still moved with grace and had a commanding presence. She had shifted out of Rail Bazaar and now lived in a middle-class locality. Asha's husband built the two-storey house where Gulab, Asha and Asha's little son dwelt. Gulab might be in indigent circumstances but she lived like a queen. On occasion, a white Ambassador car would drive by to pick her for an official function. She concealed her distressed financial situation, lived regally and exuded hospitality.

After the SNA award, the government began inviting Gulab Bai's company to perform on the proscenium at state functions. These invitations were few and far between. But once Gulab received state patronage, she realized how soothing it was! For a commissioned show, she would receive a lump sum payment, without any of the pressures of a competitive market, box-office losses, or performing to audiences who wanted only cheap entertainment.

Gulab found she preferred doing the occasional proscenium show, with a secure fee paid by the commissioning agency. Her interest in the usual Nautanki circuit flagged, although of course the Great Gulab Theatre Company did keep up a certain number of mandatory performances round the year.

*

Gulab lived in middle-class splendour, but was chronically anxious about the source of funds for this comfortable lifestyle. Her elder son Suresh had moved into an upper-storey room of the house that Asha's husband built. Suresh, his wife and five daughters all had to be supported. Asha had two sons, and no direct financial worries since her husband continued to provide sufficient resources. But she often had to stretch it to include the entire household.

Madhu's school fees had to be paid, a burden her father Balbir Singh had completely withdrawn himself from.

Madhu grew up in the rarefied atmosphere of an elite boarding-school. As a little girl, Madhu had enjoyed the world of melas and Nautankis, lisped the words of songs and twirled around in merry dance. When it was time for school however, Gulab Bai hardened her heart and sent her off to Lucknow to study. She knew the child would be considerably distracted if she stayed home. Madhu proved to be a bright student. Her agile mind and sharp memory stood her in good stead. She picked up English and spoke the language fluently. Her co-students were not really aware of Madhu's family background. She made friends, studied with a will and progressed from one class to the next. She emerged as a natural leader, with a flair for public speaking.

Madhu planned to become a doctor. She enjoyed studying science, and wished to earn status and wealth, as well as be of service to her fellow-beings. Thriving in a totally different environment from home, she developed skills needed for a wider professional world. She loved to read, and didn't mind hard work. During vacations she would return home—earlier in Rail Bazaar, and then the new one in a middle-class Kanpur colony. She enjoyed the time spent with her warm, active and adventurous family.

Madhu passed high school in 1979. Gulab Bai revelled in her daughter's achievement and was keen to support her higher studies. But she was consumed by anxiety regarding the family's finances. Madhu joined a B.Sc. course in Kanpur. Gulab's income was erratic. She asked Asha's husband to support Madhu through college, and he began doing so. But it was not easy for him to cater to an endless set of needs and requirements.

Living in the midst of commotion, confusion and uncertainty, Madhu found it difficult to concentrate on her studies. Her mother was depressed, and drained by the nagging worries occasioned by chronic crises in her emotional and financial life.

The company Gulab had built up over some twenty-five years was in a state of limbo. Trying to keep up appearances and make ends meet, with nearly no income, was driving her crazy. She thought of going to meet Balbir Singh in his Delhi house, to get him to settle some money for their daughter, but knew it was a crazy idea. Confronting him in Kanpur on her own turf was harrowing enough. To confront him in his territory would lead only to melodrama and frustration.

Gulab realized it would be impossible to support Madhu through the long years of study required for a professional degree. She keenly desired a respectable life for her daughter, and set about arranging a proper marriage. Madhu understood her mother's dilemma. Nor was she averse to a good marriage. She adjusted her desires, dreaming now of becoming the respectable wife of a high-status and wealthy man. She imagined an ideal partner, and told herself it would be possible to persuade him to let her study after marriage.

'My mother arranged a match for me with a lawyer,' she recalled years later. 'His family was the same caste as ours, and his grandmother had been a dancer. But they tried to hide this. They claimed to be of respectable descent. The man was bright and an up and coming professional. His father had earned well and the family lived in a plush house in a good colony. I would have a comfortable life if I married him. They liked me and the marriage was fixed. That's when they started making demands!

'They asked for cash and a car. My mother frankly could not afford it. I could understand her situation. She would have given the dowry if she could. So then I approached my father. He had always told me, "Beti, you must study, and marry into a good house. I don't want you to go onto the stage." I wrote a letter to him, informing him of the situation and requesting him to meet the demand for dowry. But my father didn't write back, so I wrote him another letter. Finally, he wrote back saying, "You should stand on your own feet."

'I was furious. That is all he had to say to me! He had three or four other daughters. He was busy marrying them all off with fat dowries. He had agricultural land, orchards and a house in Punjab and another house in Delhi. He gave two or three lakhs for each of his other daughters, but refused to give anything for me. That was the biggest blow he could have dealt me.'

Madhu's marriage plans fell through. The groom's side withdrew, realizing there would be nothing much as dowry. Madhu faced the bitter truth. Her life had proceeded beautifully so far, but now, all of a sudden, it turned ugly. She had no friends to share her sorrows with, since she had never revealed her family background to school friends, and now was doubly ashamed to do so. She sobbed her eyes out. It seemed like the end of the world had come.

One day she decided to take action. Rather than weep endlessly, she would set herself to work. She would earn an income! She could sing and dance, was glamorous and good-looking. She would enter the world of Nautanki.

Visitors from the Nautanki world had been making surreptitious offers that Gulab had not taken up. But now that Madhu expressed readiness, Gulab considered the proposition and could see there was no alternative. She had done all she could to mould Madhu's life in a different direction, but it hadn't worked. Fate willed otherwise.

Gulab's company had ground to a standstill but now she rustled up her contacts and secured a contract for performing immediately at a mela. Madhu took up the challenge. Despite her disciplined studies and exacting school schedules, Madhu sang, dance and acted well. During her school holidays Madhu had dipped into the Nautanki ethos—her home always throbbed with music and dance. She was vivacious, and had all the makings of a star.

Madhu, Gulab's daughter, performing 'Dahiwali', a popular Nautanki, in the Lok Utsav held in New Delhi in 1985

So it was that Madhu saved the day for the Great Gulab Theatre Company. She joined as its new heroine. At the age of seventeen, her life changed dramatically. She never quite forgot how her dearest dreams came crashing down. But she determined to stand on her own feet, and turned to her new profession with a will.

With Madhu by her side, Gulab tried to re-establish the floundering fortunes of the Great Gulab Theatre company. Madhu never went back to college or a white-collar profession. She married an erstwhile classmate of hers— a relationship that went through a familiar pattern of early highs and later, abysmal lows.

*

Twenty-five years later Madhu is articulate about the disappointments in her life. She feels strongly about the disappointments faced by other Nautanki artistes too. She notes that female artistes get a particularly raw deal.

Educated, English-speaking Madhu has one foot in both worlds. This gives her a wider perspective. It also means she frequently feels torn and conflicted, vulnerable to contrary pulls and contradictory desires.

'Our chief drawback is that we are born women,' explains Madhu, expounding a favorite theory. 'Like all women, we too long for somebody to share our lives with. The contradiction is that however hard we try, this doesn't happen. First a woman leaves her work, fooled by a man. When she wakes up to the situation, it is too late. Earlier she earned well but later she is older and doesn't get work. She has to beg, because she does not have even a roti to eat. During her main earning period the poor woman was absorbed in her dreams, in the love of her man, lord and god. But that god looks upon her with the same old idea, that "She is cheap".

My Amma used to say, "*Jab tak gaal pe boti, Tab tak yaar ghar roti* (So long as you are in the bloom of youth, Your lover will provide home and food). Never leave your work. Take a man, try to make the relationship work, but do not give up your work." At that time I would feel, "This isn't relevant for me. She's had it tough because she's not educated... or else nobody was loyal to her. My husband is so wonderful, how well he looks after me!"

'Later when the time for real loyalty comes the man has other systems in place. His other children grow up. The daughters have to be married. His paramour doesn't have the figure she once had – the body he came for so far shows signs of ageing. So why will he come? After all, he has another family, and a home with everything in it. Meanwhile, the woman has been cut off from everything and isolated. She is no longer capable of going into society: where will she go, what will she do? She has nothing and he has everything. He has his business, marriage and children. She has refused him nothing, but he has stopped her from doing everything. She submitted to his wishes, thinking, "Oh, he is my man!"

'In our society when a girl is born her parents rejoice because they see her as an earning member. They are not bothered about her education or putting together a dowry for her marriage. Her exploitation begins in the maika. When she is ten years old, she starts going out to work. The male figure does no work–whether it is a brother or a father. This is my anguish, and it tears me from inside! My mother too began working when she was twelve.

'The system is that if the girl doesn't work how will the family run? It is considered necessary. Younger brothers and sisters are nourished on her earnings. Her mother has grown too old to work. She too didn't ever think that her daughter, born from her own womb, should have a better life. She never saved money for her daughter's future. The same mistake is repeated. Once the girl goes on stage nobody can stop the pattern from repeating itself. It is like the life cycle of a butterfly!

'The money she earns is squandered at once. The girl has never been taught to stitch or knit, study, or be docile and adjusting as required in a sasural. There is no planning about her future. She has only to earn. How the income is spent is in her parents' hands.

'As she grows up, a man comes along who says, "I will provide you a house. I will love you. I will bring down the stars, gift you the moon." Lost in dreams, she leaves her parents to live with her lord god, or he moves in with them. He does no work. He becomes one more person dependent on her income. He drinks and gambles, because she earns Rs 1,500 a night. If he is angry, he beats her. She goes to work at night, comes home in the morning and cooks. There's nobody looking after the children, or sending them to school. She quarrels day and night, thinking, "I earn so much, but nothing is saved." She sees older women crying, with no money, so she realizes she should save for her future. She finds somebody better, leaves the first and takes a second man, but he turns out to be even worse than the first. She catches a third man, a fourth. People think she is characterless: "Why can't she live with one man?" She gets frustrated, thinking, "What am I doing?" Gradually she begins drinking to feel better. She thinks, "If my money is being squandered let me too have some fun..." The children have no source of livelihood to fall back on, so they join the same line. When they grow up they ask her, "What did you do for us?"

'I have seen this with my own eyes, time and again. Where will you find worse exploitation?'

*

Gulab Bai, of course, outgrew Rail Bazaar. She outgrew the confines of provincialism, broke out of the pre-determined 'life cycle' and tried to create a different order. This affected her entire family. Bonds of mutual affection and trust were especially strong between the four sisters Gulab, Chahetan, Paati Kali and Sukhbadan. They grouped together, mitigating the impact of traumatic betrayals and personal tragedies each of them experienced individually.

Chahetan worked steadily, as a side-heroine, for many years. Late in life she adopted a sick orphan girl, who died within a few months. A big-built, tough woman, she lived in the Rail Bazaar house until her death in 1999. She bequeathed her two rooms, on the ground floor of the house, to Gulab's daughter, Madhu.

Paati Kali, tall, slim and jovial, continues to live in the Rail Bazaar house with her daughters Munni and Rani, several grandchildren and great-grandchildren. Paati is nearly eighty, and Munni barely twenty years younger. Mother and daughter live in one room on the top floor of the Rail Bazaar house, spending a lot of time on the terrace outside, especially in the winter sun. They clean spices, chat, cook, entertain or oversee a grandchild. The two lead an active life, part of a busy neighbourhood and lively family. Munni still has professional commitments, and gives her best to each role she performs.

Gulab's daughters proved to be talented artistes. It was difficult for Madhu to reconcile to life as an artiste, since she was groomed for something 'higher'. Nor can Madhu accept the fact that women have a raw deal in personal life—usually as co-wives, with little status and even less security. Gulab's younger son, Rajendra, studied and later joined a bank. A salaried employee, he has a secure world, quite removed from the vagaries of travelling theatre.

Asha and Madhu have two sons each. Muses Madhu wryly, 'Thank god I don't have a daughter. Otherwise she would have come into this same line! At least sons don't have to face the dilemmas we are trapped in! I find it difficult to earn now. Who wants a forty-year-old woman to dance and sing? I have no savings so I am forced to be dependent on "him". Sometimes he is very helpful, when we get government shows in good halls. But he doesn't want me to go on stage at melas. If he doesn't let me perform, I have to submit to his wishes. But I do want to earn and have my own income. Sometimes it tears me apart and I don't know how to pull myself out of this mess.

'Gulab Bai was different. Gulab Bai was my mother. She was the legendary Gulab Bai! In her heydays, she earned more than the district magistrate! Had she saved money, we would have been flush with funds for the next few generations. But she spent it all on her family—mother and father, brothers and sisters, nephews and nieces. Everybody came to her for help, all the time. Nobody spared her. She spent all she earned. When she died, we daughters got nothing. She had nothing left to give us. If she had anything, she would have left it behind for us. All her life, she looked after us, and wanted only the very best for us. But she could not save us from our fate!'

22

A Cultural Icon

If a man is good at singing, he is called an Ustad or a Guru. But if a woman is good at singing, she is called a Bai.
  —Rita Ganguly, musical drama Begum Akhtar, 2001

'*Gulab Bai, the grande dame of Nautanki*'
  —Sibu Sen, 'The Show is Over, The Show Must Go On', *The Hindu*, 9 October 1992

'*Nautanki Ki Bai*'
  —title of article by Nirupama Dutt, the *Indian Express*, 8 July 1999

'*Mrs Gulab Bai*'
  —as named in the list of Padmashree awardees, the *Times of India*, 26 January 1990

One 26 January, the UP jhalki was called 'Nautanki', its queen Gulab Bai sat proudly on the throne. A 'nautanki' scene was enacted to the resounding beat of the nagara. From Indira Gandhi onwards, there was no prime minister, president or vice-president who did not mark their appreciation for Gulab Bai.... She breathed life into various folk art events organised by the government and cultural institutions. She was awarded the Padmashree and Sangeet Natak Akademi awards.
  —Krishna Raghav

Gulab Bai receiving the Padmashree, a national honour, from the then President of India R Venkataraman

In 1990 Gulab Bai won the Padmashree award—a great national honour. This created a flurry of excitement in the Nautanki world. The Padmashree awards were announced on 26 January 1990 over radio and in the national newspapers. A hundred civilian awards—Padma Bhushan, Padma Vibhushan and Padmashrees—were presented that year. The names of the sixty-nine Padmashree awardees listed in the *Times of India* and other national newspapers included 'Mrs Gulab Bai'. She was awarded under the genre 'folk music'.

The Padmashree awards for 1990 were given out on 24 March at a glittering ceremony at Rashtrapati Bhavan, New Delhi. In 1995, just a year before she died, Gulab Bai also received the Yash Bharati award.

Receiving national and regional awards cast a halo around her. Gulab Bai became a cultural icon, a symbol and representative of Nautanki. However, even while she was treated as a celebrity, the theatre form itself was languishing.

The Padmashree came in 1990, by which time Nautanki was clearly a dying art. It continued to decline through the last decade of the twentieth century. The Indian state and its elite cultural institutions did not really do what was required in order to stem the tide.

Gulab Bai sparkled when she received her awards—like a heroine in one of her Nautankis—then returned to her real life. She and her daughters struggled for work, in humiliating personal circumstances. The demand for Nautanki performances kept dwindling. Old-timers committed to Nautanki pined for opportunities to put up good performances, but these were few and far between.

The government claimed to support folk forms, quoting awards to Nautanki artistes like Gulab Bai as a case in point. Government institutions basked in reflected glory—championing locally rooted, accomplished artistes like her. But of course, providing such individual recognition was a token gesture. In fact, it served to divert attention, and the state could conveniently bypass the much larger issue of providing substantial long-term support to help the form to survive.

*

Gulab was delighted to receive the honours she did. She was flattered by all the attention and accolades. Most other Nautanki artistes gazed at her like dwarfs looking up in awe at a giant. She seemed to straddle a different world. She had 'arrived'. From extreme poverty, she now basked in the status of a nationally honoured artiste. Her entire identity was whitewashed to fit into official definitions of an appropriate cultural ambassador. To her, barely literate, the Dalit background an intrinsic part of her, some of the new expectations were confusing.

Insidious processes took place by which Gulab's image was clipped and cropped to fit snugly into elite notions of respectability. She was now projected as 'Mrs Gulab Bai' or 'Shrimati Gulab Bai', her image packaged to meet officially approved standards. Her caste background was deliberately fudged and her marital status carefully obscured. She was presented as properly married, a deliberate distortion of reality. She acquiesced to this manipulation. After all, it bestowed respectability upon her. An accomplished actor, she slid gracefully into the new role.

Gulab Bai always acknowledged herself as Bedia, although the caste was stigmatized as a 'criminal tribe', associated with theft and commercial sex work. She never herself claimed to be legally married, nor concealed her unconventional lifestyle. For India's cultural mandarins, however, such honesty is anathema. They displayed a marked reluctance to acknowledge that an award-winning artiste could hail from such a smudgy background. They prefer to ignore true origins, and pretend that all culture has arisen from 'pure' backgrounds. Hypocrisy in government circles, shining out from official documents, has by now become a convenient routine.

It comes as no surprise, then, that Gulab Bai's Dalit origins were barely mentioned in official documents. The background and contexts of her life were deftly blotted out. At most, her impoverished childhood was mentioned, only to glorify her as a divinely talented little girl—a lotus blossoming in a dark cesspool.

Gulab performing with her daughter Asha at a function organized by the Sangeet Natak Akademi, New Delhi

Photographs in the Sangeet Natak Akademi archives show the elderly Gulab in a pale golden sari, pallu drawn demurely over her head, sitting formally with rows of artistes from across the country. She looks serious, stern and as middle-class as the next person.

Many people from the Bedia caste do try to conceal their caste origins, in a wholly understandable effort to achieve social mobility. Gulab, however, was not really one of these.

*

Having achieved a certain status, Gulab thought she could wield influence in the interests of the Nautanki form. But this proved to be well beyond her reach. Government policies and priorities remained fundamentally insensitive to the plight of Nautanki and its practitioners. Bitter truths were swept under the carpet or driven underground. Nasty caste, gender and cultural politics continued to vitiate the local and regional arts. No effort at all was made to provide centers where the art could be promoted, training conducted and performances rehearsed.

Dramatist Vijay Pandit relates an apocryphal story—revealing some of the dirty underside of glittering award ceremonies. He says that after the Sangeet Natak Awards were given out in a magnificent hall in Chennai in 1985, various cultural groups performed. Gulab's company presented excerpts from a Nautanki. A group from South India, which consisted of Brahman artistes, was to perform after Gulab's company. Before performing they had the entire stage washed with Ganga jal—to purify it!

Whether true or not, this story points to dark undertones lurking beneath the false sparkle of high culture. Stark reality at ground level can be completely at odds with what is projected in public and on stage. Beneath a thin veneer of democracy lurk deeply entrenched notions of caste-class superiority. Ordinary artistes continue to suffer routine humiliation. The roots of such deep disrespect remain strong.

As Vijay Pandit puts it, 'Most Nautanki artistes can never venture through the glass doors of the Akademi's offices. Their clothes are too dirty, their feet too dusty. They are stopped at the reception and allowed no further.'

*

Gulab's status as a national celebrity fanned tensions in the Nautanki world. There were other contenders for national honours. Tirmohan Ustad, Krishna Bai, Sukhbadan, Radharani, Shyama, Anno and several mardanas like

Suhail Baba, Kakooji and Naagar were generally acknowledged to be equally great exponents of Nautanki. While nobody openly contested the selection of Gulab Bai, there were murmurs of discontent and gossip about lobbying with high officials. Her company's manager Shiv Adhar Dube indirectly substantiated this allegation by claiming (when he spoke to us) credit for effective lobbying!

During the last two decades of her life, Gulab Bai was trapped in a financial and professional crisis. Yet at the same time she was honoured and feted, and occasionally invited to sing on television or perform in an auditorium.

Thousands of artistes keen to perform good Nautankis were unable to eke out a livelihood. Their plight was ignored and neglected. What happened with Nautanki is part of a wider politics that affected most folk art, music and theatre forms in twentieth-century India.

The 'revival' of older art forms took a unique turn in independent India. A number of living forms were suffocated at source, and at the same time adopted by others. Torn from their Dalit roots, an elite class established ownership over these forms. The original forms were considered tainted by their Dalit associations, and laundered to wash away elements that bespoke frank sexual expression. The forms themselves changed in the process, losing their earthy vibrancy, ending up as hothouse plants in a rarefied atmosphere. Sometimes they became the material of drawing-room accomplishments, an additional qualification for the marriage market rather than an independent vocation.

Thus the dance form Sadri, performed in Tamil Nadu and Karnataka by devadasis, was transformed into a sanitized version, renamed Bharata Natyam. Cut loose from its origins, it is popular today as a favoured accomplishment of middle-class girls. A few graduate to performing and teaching Bharata Natyam as their profession. The devadasi system that nurtured the form has been discredited and outlawed. Devadasis—ritual dancers consecrated to a temple—were often courtesans to wealthy patrons. Their dance was sensuous and sacred at one and the same time.

Similarly, Orissa's ritual temple dances have virtually died, the form transplanted as 'Odissi'. Beauty queen and danseuse Indrani Rahman, who 'discovered' Odissi, and performed it at national and international forums, first saw it performed by Mahari women in Puri. Her daughter Sukanya Rahman writes that her mother never met the Mahari women because they were not respectable enough to be introduced to her. Indrani learnt from a Guru, and insisted thereafter that Odissi was a classical dance form, with roots in the Natya Shastra. A transnational elite thus transplanted and captured a popular cultural form.

In the arts, opportunities to perform became synonymous with patronage, which got strongly linked to class rather than knowledge and talent. According to musicologist Jyoti Pandey, 'After 1947, the dhrupad was sold as an ideology rather than a species of song. The trick was to link it emphatically yet vaguely to the Sama Veda. This had the effect of inducing veneration and forestalling criticism of what was virtually non-music. All kinds of acoustic outrages are condoned or applauded, under cover of strategically chosen Sanskrit or Persian terms bearing mystical and spiritual connotations. This is truly a brilliant device, which throws up a smoke screen over the listeners' incomprehension and at the same time affords the patron the additional luxury of occupying the moral high ground vis-à-vis the "decadent" west.'

Orthodox Indian upper classes have tried to erase the linkages between cultural forms and the contexts in which they emerged. Suppressing the 'sordid' contexts, the forms are presented as if they arose in a social vacuum. The actual social history of these genres is virtually obliterated. Humiliated and belittled, the highly talented practitioners of the authentic forms have barely been able to survive. This includes Dalit-caste courtesans, ordinary minstrels or dancers from a number of traditional performing castes, Sufi fakirs and bhakti poets. In the process, the elite have heaped scorn on these sections of society.

The original practitioners of Nautanki are mixed in their caste origins, often down-at-heel and flexible as regards sexual norms. This renders them fundamentally unacceptable to the elite who defines what 'culture' is. These people are taken to be obviously 'uncultured', even 'dirty'. Yet most of them are, in fact, highly skilled and talented musicians, singers, actors and dancers.

Middle-class theatre persons and institutions generally ignore the thousands of such down-at-heel but superbly talented practitioners of Nautanki and similar forms. Poverty, lack of schooling and modern sophistication has made it difficult for genuine traditional artistes to compete for a place in the sun. These practitioners are fading into invisibility, the seamy slums they dwell in too far from institutions like the National School of Drama, where a new generation of the elite is trained for the stage.

*

Gulab intuitively understood the larger situation, yet became a pawn in the game played by those more sophisticated in deception. She enjoyed receiving awards, yet realized there was something hollow about the situation.

Her sympathies lay with her brethren, the ordinary Nautanki artistes. She tried to use her position to improve the condition of Nautanki and its naïve practitioners.

Many elderly artistes, particularly women, lived in undignified and indigent circumstances. Gulab articulated the demand for a pension for such artistes. The UP Sangeet Natak Akademi examined the issue and, in time, accepted the demand. This proved to be a lifeline for a few hundred ageing artistes.

Gulab lobbied against entertainment tax levied on Nautanki. She argued that if Nautanki is a cherished folk form, it should be actively promoted by the state, rather than undercut through tax and such-like measures. She took up the cause at official functions: for instance she spoke at the National Theatre festival at Ravindralaya, Lucknow, in August 1984. When Gulab Bai was asked to speak, she was nervous because of the high officials around, but made her points confidently. She spoke of how the police harass her company (and other Nautanki companies) for payment of taxes. Right at the Nautanki venue, if the inspector finds anybody sitting without a ticket, he issues a *chalan* to the company owner. The entertainment tax is exorbitant and neither audience nor companies can afford it.

The debilitating tax was lifted. No doubt Gulab Bai's exhortations contributed to government rethinking on the matter. Yet Nautanki companies continued to run at a loss. Her awards gave the Great Gulab Theatre Company a lease of life, but it was temporary. The work was no longer self-sustaining. A company could no longer afford to commission new scripts or rehearse its plays before a performance. Gulab's company had neither steady staff, nor well-tuned musical instruments nor resplendent costumes. Curtains were frayed, props damaged and audiences aggressive and unruly. Sometimes, when they performed, they ended up with a net loss rather than any profit.

Gulab Bai's life spanned the changing phases of Nautanki. She joined in the days of open shows and then, in the golden era of Nautanki, performed in tents with ticket lines and a picture-frame stage. Much later, she gave up commercial performances. During the last decade of her life, her company performed sporadically, and that too, only commissioned shows.

For most Nautanki companies, the 1980s brought complete collapse. Nautanki company owners lacked the capital to usher in new technologies and innovations. Companies either shut down or were forced to submit to the market trend of replacing authentic drama with salacious dancing.

*

During the last decade of her life Gulab accepted only sponsored shows. Government bodies invited her company to perform. The invitations were few and far between, so there was no regular source of income. But at least, in such a performance, there was no risk involved. The government would pay a lump sum, so the company never had to deal with the vagaries of the market. It was flattering to be invited to perform by governmental agencies, since it was a marker of status. Besides, it was satisfying to keep up the tradition of performing good drama.

In a way, the glory she won during her twilight years was a fitting tribute to a lifetime of sheer hard work. She sparkled like the diamonds in her nose-stud, as she sang full-throated, in the limelight one last time.

During the 1980s the company performed *Bahadur Ladki* on television and for a distinguished audience at New Delhi's Mavalankar auditorium. Asha appeared as the leading lady. The group performed *Dahiwali* at the 'Apna Utsav' in New Delhi, with Madhu in the lead role. 'Apna Utsav' was a festival for the traditional performing arts, organized by the Sangeet Natak Akademi. SNA made recordings and these are today available as archival material.

Gulab did not act in these Nautankis, but invariably sang some of her most famous numbers, especially *Nadi naare*. Her voice still conveyed power and pathos, her facial and hand gestures were expressive, and the lyrics haunting.

The Yash Bharati award Gulab received in 1995 carried a cash prize of Rs 1 lakh. She was able to repay some debts, and meet various obligations with dignity. However, she was in no position to save any of the cash.

In 1996 Gulab arranged a Nautanki performance for the Vishwa Hindi Sammelan held in Trinidad and Tobago. Her group performed *Amar Singh Rathore*. Asha and Madhu, Binda Prasad Nigam and music director Ram Prasad were included. Gulab traveled to Delhi with her group and spoke to the media. She returned to Kanpur when the company left for Trinidad and Tobago where they performed at the conference, and outside. Audiences were reportedly thrilled with the shows.

*

Gulab took part in melas very selectively. A fan, Chandrika Prasad 'Nidar', recalls her appearance at the Takiya mela during the 1990s. She was too unwell to walk unaided. But the audience was screaming for a song from her.

She came on stage leaning against somebody, another person holding her hand. She sat on a chair, and began to sing. The audience became silent. Then came the thunderous clapping, and demand for encores! Gulab Bai was still the darling of the masses.

Gulab's success notwithstanding, she was unable to save Nautanki. Many talented performers had little option but to flow with the market, that reduced Nautanki to titillating dance numbers. Hardly anybody was prepared to shoulder the rich heritage, which had become a burden rather than a badge of honour.

Gulab Bai died sad and bewildered, for the form she had devoted her life to crumbled to dust under her very eyes. Nautanki fell into a state of irretrievable decay, and nothing she did could save it.

23

Into Other Worlds

'Antim kshanon tak gulab si mehekti raheen Gulab Bai'
(Up to the last moment Gulab Bai was fragrant like a rose.)
—A newspaper headline, 14 July 2006

The empress of Nautanki lay on her death-bed saying, 'I have thought, and said to several journalists—"Take this news to Delhi that a Nautanki Kala Kendra should be opened in Kanpur. I will teach in it so long as I am alive. We will invite people to learn, then this world will move forward. Otherwise it is already sunk. If small and big people learn, and carry my name forward, then I will be happy even when I die."'

—Krishna Raghav

Ab vo murki kahan se laayen? (Where can we get that turn of voice now? From where can we bring it?)
—Harishchandra

Besood hai tumhara ro-ro ke dil jalana
Duniya mein jo hai aaya, usko adam hai jaana
Jaata hai jo yahan se, vaapas na koi aata
Hota hai jeete-ji ka bhai-behen ka naata
Nahin baap hai kisi ka, koi nahin hai mata
Khali ye tan hai apna aur sir pe hai vidhata
Jaari yoon he rahega, duniya ka karkhana'

(What use is your weeping,
Each one will die
Never to return,
Relationships–sister or brother, mother or father,
Last merely as long as we live,
Only this body is one's own, and the Maker above,
That's how the world is,
And will continue to be)

—A 'nauha' Gulab used to sing

Gulab Bai died on 13 July 1996. She had lived three-quarters of a century–a colourful, tumultuous journey.

As one muses over Gulab's life, imagining her persona and experiences, cinema, paradoxically enough, supplies valuable clues. The classic *Teesri Kasam* has an uncanny resonance with her life.

The film, made in 1966, shows a Nautanki company performing over several nights at a village fair in Bihar. The ethos of village melas is recreated on screen. Heera Bai's role portrays the self-respecting Nautanki actress who desires love and a settled marriage, but knows she will not get these. Waheeda Rehman's tragic figure reflects some of the real-life pain experienced by a Gulab Bai. Like Heera Bai, Gulab forged more than one tragic attachment. Aborted affairs behind her, Heera Bai is on the roads once again, working for her bread.

Her work involves dealing with lust and unwanted attention. The local zamindar considers Heera Bai, the beautiful and alluring young Nautanki heroine, as 'available'. His lascivious gaze dwells on her physique and features as she cavorts and pirouettes on stage, sings and expresses emotions appropriate to her varied roles.

Heera Bai is wistful and deeply sensitive. She resents her position as a woman who can never marry for she is not considered respectable enough. She is attracted to the warm-hearted simplicity of Hiraman who sings haunting local melodies. She is the lone passenger in Hiraman's bullock-cart, travelling several kilometres from the railway junction to the mela venue. He considers her to be simple, guileless and innocent. The local zamindar on the other hand tries to buy her sexual favours. When she refuses to go along with his desires he threatens to take revenge. The company manager is frightened, for the zamindar could wreak vengeance on the entire company. In danger of being kidnapped and violated, Heera Bai flees the area. She decides to leave the company, and go join another group back in Kanpur.

The story is not so far from the reality of Gulab Bai's life. As in *Teesri Kasam*, the Nautankis of the time prominently advertised their leading ladies. Huge posters and placards were put up advertising shows, sketches or colourful paintings of the heroine being the star attraction. Messages were shouted out to the accompaniment of dholaks. These women were responsible for ensuring box-office success, yet their lives were fraught with danger and any number of existential dilemmas.

The performances in a tent-theatre erected on the street of a dusty provincial town evoked the magic of vaudeville, grand opera and cinema rolled into one. Heera Bai performs an excerpt from *Laila Majnu* and four song items on successive evenings, all of which play exquisitely on the fluctuating hopes, desires and inevitable loss she and Hiraman share. As in the earlier sequences on the road, the camerawork slowly pulls us into the constrained yet complex world of travelling theatre, revealing glamour, glitter and sparkling talent. Scenes painted on drop curtains evoke the ambience of different locales, and the lyrics and rhythms carry authentic flavour and depth.

Heera Bai's terse speeches effectively communicate her dilemma as a professional woman: love of her craft versus her longing for home, family and respectability. Like Hiraman—and in this again like Gulab Bai—Heera Bai is in love with her work. She says with rare honesty, 'I get the same intoxication from dancing under the lights that you get from driving your cart.'

The complexity of her sexual and personal identity is succinctly conveyed when she tells the lascivious zamindar, 'You think I'm a prostitute, he [Hiraman] thinks I'm a goddess. You're both wrong.' Whether or not she prefers one projection to the other, she doesn't really have a choice.

We catch a last glimpse of Heera Bai leaving in a train, forlorn and grimly determined. She leaves behind Hiraman and the promise of warmth and companionship. She goes ahead to meet her destiny—dancing in the bright lights: pretending to be a fairy, a harlot or a queen... concealing her real self.

*

In June 1996, just days before her death, Gulab Bai delved into her past in the course of the filming of a biographical documentary.[20]

She was ill throughout the shooting. Earlier in the year she'd fallen and fractured a hipbone. She was treated in hospital, then laid up at home. She insisted on her lifelong routine of waking at 4 a.m. and having a bath. Madhu attended to her baths while Asha saw to her food.

Gulab sang a dadra, accompanied by Asha: *More maro na tirchhi najariya balam* . . . (Do not gaze at me with those flashing eyes, darling). Despite her grave illness, Gulab Bai was alive to each note on the harmonium. She frowned if the bajawala played a false note. She roundly scolded the dholakwala when he increased the beat. When he corrected the tempo, she expressed her appreciation, saying, 'Fine'. She took the notes up to the highest—the taar saptak. That was the last time she sang the taar saptak.

When asked how she learnt to enunciate so well she replied, 'By listening. I listened when the big teachers of the time spoke, like Shrikrishna Pehelwan. Once at a mela I came onto the stage and spoke one word—"malka". The Seths sitting in the front row scoffed—"Ha, big name, but not worthy in person." I heard this and went offstage. I felt so ashamed that I didn't come out again. You see, I had pronounced the word in a different way.'

Gulab's artistes and daughters sang various types of verse, for instance dedh tuki, behere taveel and chaubola. She had trained all these singers. She said, 'It takes quite a long time to learn Nautanki singing, dance, acting—it takes several years. Those whom I taught were the children of musicians and actors, otherwise I could not have taught them to sing so well.'

Said Gulab's niece Munni Bai, 'Bai was a wonderful teacher. She loved to teach—from the smallest detail to the biggest lessons of life. She taught many of us. We would like to carry forward what we learnt from her.'

When asked whether she had to struggle to bring up her children, she replied, 'Nobody stays with one forever. In these forty years nobody came to stay with me forever.

I brought up my children by dancing and dancing . . . singing and singing. None of the men stayed on. I could not put pressure on anybody. Nobody had married me, brought a baraat for me, so what could I say to anybody? All I can say is that the real man is the one who respects the "other woman" as much as he respects his wife. Understand? He has enjoyed her too, lived with her for years on end. Now, more than this I cannot say.'

Gulab Bai wanted to lie down. The film crew and her daughters helped her lie down and drink a few spoonfuls of water. Then her large eyes gleamed, she smiled and said, 'I told my daughters, "Do not depend on anybody. If somebody comes, he comes. In any case, you have your feet, your body. Rely on yourself." These girls are like me.'

Said her son Rajendra, 'Our mother is an ideal mother. There would be few mothers in the world like her, who have struggled to make their children so capable that they can today raise their heads high and walk in society.'

Paati Kali said, 'By singing and dancing, she educated everyone.'

Questioned about the secret of her success, Gulab said, 'God's grace, and everybody's good wishes. Those who appreciated me can tell whether they saw beauty—what can I say? The listeners can tell you whether my singing was powerful—how can I tell?'

When asked to comment on contemporary Nautanki, Gulab grew angry. She said, 'Today there is nude dancing!— all for money. In our times such things never happened.'

Her daughter Asha brought a young girl, barely fifteen years old, to demonstrate 'Nai Nautanki'. The girl danced to a film song, wearing a translucent white sari clinging to her body. Said Gulab, 'I want this kind of work to stop. It should be banned. These girls and boys have spoiled the name of Nautanki. Such obscene work should not be allowed. If we sing good songs, dance properly, we could hold our heads high. If you sing and dance well, your name will be remembered—just like mine.'

After lying down Gulab asked Asha to sing, saying 'Asha sings well. Sometimes I learn from her.' She listened with total absorption, and joined in too, as Asha sang Jigar Moradabadi's ghazal:

> *Yahan insaf kis se maangne aaye ho 'jigar'*
> *Chalo yahan se ye andhon ki rajdhani hai*
> (You appeal for justice, but who will give you justice here? Come let us leave this place where nobody has eyes to see).

*

What she left behind was a heritage—the strong, heady fragrance of a desi rose. The flower wilted, the petals dropped off. They grew brittle and were swept away by the wind. It is a complex legacy: of honesty, unconventionality, hard work, sheer talent and commitment to aesthetic excellence.

Gulab Bai was larger than life. She surged out of the set moulds. She didn't fit the set frames—yet those frames remained. She couldn't quite break them.

PART III
NAUTANKI TODAY

Unemployed Heroes and Musicians

Nobody looks at us. Everybody looks at the actors. But we play throughout a performance. What is a Nautanki without music?
  —Ram Prasad, music director and harmonium player

Earlier there was izzat in Nautanki: now there is none.
  —Amarnath, nagara and dholak player

I have lost only a few teeth, I still have some intact. I have not dyed my hair because then company people would come and take me to act as Majnu! I will dye my hair and act as hero. . . . after all I still have my body and my voice!
  —Binda Prasad Nigam 'Sherdil', Nautanki actor

After women joined Nautanki, Nautanki declined. If they hadn't joined, we could have maintained high standards. With women, filth came in.
  —Common sentiment among male Nautanki professionals

While Nautanki is being hailed as a folk art, its 'folk' are not being valued. . . .They have carried on the art for centuries, yet they remain poor. They should be provided means to keep the art alive. Economic means and status are connected to the survival of Nautanki and its artistes.
  —Vijay Pandit, dramatist, Unnao

Originally an all-male genre, from the 1930s Nautankis grew increasingly woman dominated. Over the next couple of decades, not only did women take over all the female roles in Kanpur Nautankis, they were also paid better than men. A number of women set up and ran Nautanki companies. They usually hired one or two men as company managers. Instrumental music remained in exclusively male hands—a bastion women were unable to storm. Male roles continued to be enacted by men, called 'mardanas'.

The men today are a disgruntled lot. Each is a unique character; collectively they present a picture of sullen resentment. Though largely unemployed now, they live by memories of grandeur. Many have led colourful lives—colours that seem even more vivid when compared with the dull present.

*

Cool, capable Ram Prasad plays the foot-pedal harmonium, and coordinates an entire orchestra. He was Gulab Bai's music director, and fulfils the same responsibility when her daughters organize a show. Throughout rehearsals and shows of *Teen Betiyan*, enacted by the Great Gulab Theatre Company in 1997, Ram Prasad was quietly in charge. Neat and dapper, he seemed a man of few words, yet carried authority. But in 2003, when I meet him in his tiny house in Rail Bazaar, his wife Mangala, Gulab's niece, can barely get a word in edgeways, for Ram Prasad has so much to say!

'There is no demand for Nautankis any more,' he fumes, 'nor for good clean music. We are paid 200 or 300 rupees and made to play for hours on end. Young good-looking girls are paid 1,000 to 2,000 rupees for two hours of dancing.

I refuse to compromise and play for vulgar programmes. Naturally my earnings have dipped drastically.'

He avers that Nautanki today requires a leader who can lobby for the form, and win appropriate patronage. 'Gulab's daughter Madhu tried to form a union,' he says. 'But there is ignorance, infighting and filth in the Nautanki world, so she found it difficult to carry on with it. If somebody makes an effort to fight for our cause, I will join at once.'

A Brahman who left devotional music to join Gulab's company some four decades ago, Ram Prasad abandoned his upper-caste legacy and became one with the demanding ethos of a Dalit caste and travelling-theatre lifestyle. He regrets this sometimes, but is aware that the choice was entirely his own. As music director, he has gained wide experience, status and authority, and continues to enjoy the role whenever he gets a chance to perform in a 'good Nautanki'. Unfortunately such chances are rare today.

*

Harishchandra played the dholak, then learnt to play the nagara from Ustad Rashid Khan Warsi, who worked with Gulab Bai. Rashid Khan's father Bashir Khan was a famous nagara player with Tirmohan Ustad. Harishchandra played in Gulab's company until her death, and her daughters still call upon him when required.

Soon after Rashid Khan's death in 1991, Harishchandra set up a school providing training in Nautanki style music, the 'Nautanki Prashikshan Kendra'. Keen to maintain Nautanki as a dignified form, he notes, 'Some schools and colleges teach Nautanki today, and girls from good families learn. Of course they cannot sing as well as those who devoted their lives to Nautanki. Still, it is good that somebody is learning.'

Harishchandra feels some Nautanki old-timers have grown greedy: 'They exhibit girls on stage semi-nude so that a crowd gathers. We send our own daughters to exhibit on stage. Making money is the sole concern. Art has vanished. The world may do anything. The main question is, what am I doing? I have resisted joining "variety programmes". Since last year however, I have done some: how else can I earn? Yet I am dying to do good Nautankis. If I had the power I would design programmes in which the main part is Nautanki. Today nobody can sit and see serious drama for several hours, so I would keep a few breaks for "variety" items.'

Harishchandra says Nautanki rests on collective endeavour: cooperation between actors produces the best results. Internal competition is disastrous to a show. But today each artiste tries to prove he is better than the rest, which spoils the effect of the show as a whole.

He rues the fact that now nobody wants their children to become musicians. He himself would have earned better had he gone into another job like his brothers have. A nagara player has no future, security of employment or income. He suggests that the government should consider schemes for employment of good musicians. Only by this means can the arts—and traditional artistes—be kept alive.

He notes governmental apathy and prejudice as evidenced by a recent experience: 'I went to a senior bureaucrat for his signature on a form, but he said, "Why do you want to ruin people by doing Nautankis?" I said, "Many Scheduled Caste people are connected with Nautanki." Then he said, "Do you want to ruin the SCs too?" I said, "There is nothing bad about learning Nautanki, Saab." But he refused to sign the paper.'

*

Tracking down a clan of nagara players, we reach them in a run-down shanty set amid open drains and piles of garbage in a labour colony.

Brothers Master Amarnath and Master Prabhu Dayal wear a permanently stressed look. Both played the dholak and nagara in Shrikrishna Pehelwan's company. A garlanded photo of their father, Moolchand, who was a nagara player in the same company, hangs on the wall. Moolchand's father Maibu Pehelwan was a nagara player with Lalmani Numberdar and Shrikrishna Pehelwan's companies.

Amarnath, who is the younger of the two brothers, recalls, 'I filled in for a dholak player who was missing one night, at a programme in Sanni Sarai, Unnao. I was nervous but my father encouraged me. It went off fine.' That was in the early 1970s. His father earned Rs 5 per show at that time, while young Amarnath was paid Rs 3. Later Amarnath and Prabhu Dayal worked with Gulab Bai, Krishna Bai and several other companies. Others in their family—Lalji, Totaram, Rajendra and Munnilal—have also been nagara players in Nautanki.

Amarnath notes, 'Earlier there was izzat in Nautanki: now there is none. We were comfortably off with steady employment for nine months right from Janamashtmi up to Holi. There was so much work that we didn't have time to eat! Today my brother and I are offered barely twenty to twenty-five programmes a year. If a mardana or musician is taken for a programme he is paid Rs 400–500 out of which he has to travel, eat and arrange for costumes. Company owners and contractors pay as little as possible, that too after a long delay. Their instruments are badly tuned, torn and in need of repairs.'

Prabhu Dayal's son Robert played the dholak with his father for six years but we meet him sitting at the family's paan shop. He explains, 'My father has a rich knowledge of ragas and taals. I am interested, but there is very little demand for this music so I do not spend much time learning. I play at some programmes. Rest of the time I sit at our paan shop.'

Prabhu Dayal too sits at the paan shop. He reminisces, 'Earlier our family owned four small houses in Coolie Bazaar, but we had to sell our property. We somehow survive in this Harijan labour colony.'

The family belongs to the Dhanuk caste, traditionally concerned with curing leather and making percussion instruments. This family was 'Bajaniya Dhanuk', which means they played the shehnai. Maibu Pehelwan's father, Dalla Dada, switched to nagara playing. Dalla Dada's father Bakhtiar played both shehnai and nagara. The family prided itself on making fine percussion instruments. People came to their shops in Nagare-wali Gali, Coolie Bazaar, from as far as Jaipur and Gwalior, to buy the best nagaras and dholaks. In the hoary past their family traded in camels, and played several instruments including a heavy metal flute. Until several generations ago the women too sang and danced, but with prosperity they withdrew into the household. They are known to be good midwives, a skill they still practice.

Amarnath and Prabhu Dayal learnt to play the nagara from their father Moolchand and grandfather Maibu Pehelwan, dholak from Sarnayan Guruji and music from Pandit Satya Narain and Rajdev Guru Mishra of Banaras. Later Rashid Khan also taught them.

Says Amarnath, 'Nautanki crashed because of the presence of women in it. When women first joined, its popularity rose. But whatever rises to the sky has to fall down. It fell, crashing to its death.'

*

We meet actor Hafiz in Bakarganj, a dilapidated slum area. He grew up in Aligarh district and came to Kanpur in 1977 to work with Gulab Bai. He claims that, like other Nautanki artistes from Aligarh, he combines the best of Hathras and Kanpur styles. He explains, 'The Hathras style is sweet like laddus. The Kanpur style tastes sharp and bitter. Some like sweet, others bitter. We combine both.' He notes that innumerable actors and musicians from Aligarh have come to work in Kanpur Nautankis.

Hafiz worked as hero in *Sultana Daku*, *Harishchandra*, *Bhakt Prahlada*, *Srimati Manjari*, *Shirin Farhad*, *Indarharan*, *Satyavan Savitri* and other dramas—at least forty to fifty of them. He still acts whenever offered a role. He has worked in Numberdar's, Gulab Bai's, Krishna Bai's, Shanti Varma's, Radharani's and Chanchala-Mala's companies.

He reflects, 'There was nobody like Gulab Bai. She was very particular. I was careful to make no errors when performing for her.' He became well known while working in her company. Recently, he accompanied Gulab Bai's daughters for a Nautanki and variety performance in Bombay.

*

White-haired Binda Prasad Nigam 'Sherdil' lives in his family home in a middle-class locality. Upper-caste (a Kayasth), he was a college student when the Nautanki bug bit him. 'I kept Nautanki scripts in between textbooks, and read the scripts while the teacher thought I'm reading textbooks. In this way I learnt ten scripts by heart,' he reveals with an impish grin.

Binda Prasad still likes to act, but confides, 'Two daughters are to be married. I am arranging this. Once they are married, I will act again. After all, I have lost only a few teeth, I still have some intact. I have not dyed my hair because then company people would come and take me to act as Majnu! I will dye my hair and act as hero . . . after all I still have my body and my voice!'

When young, Binda Prasad sang kirtans and performed in Ramlilas with Shankarlal Rasdhaari's party in Mathura. His first Nautanki show was with Gulab's company in the early 1960s. He had gone to see *Laila Majnu* at a mela, but the hero fell ill. Binda Prasad volunteered to act, and was given one day to learn the part. He had never read the play, but set to the task with a will. Next night he played Majnu. At one point in the play, Laila—played by young Sukhbadan—slapped him. Binda Prasad did not know about this the scene, so he grew furious. She had slapped him hard: her fingers left a mark on his cheek. In reaction, he gave her a push, so she stumbled and fell. Later that night, Sukhbadan upbraided Gulab Bai for hiring such an uncouth man, who misbehaved with her on stage!

He once played Harishchandra, to Gulab Bai's Taramati. In subsequent years, Binda Prasad frequently played hero opposite Sukhbadan as heroine, whom he greatly admired for her acting and singing.

Later Binda Prasad stood up for the rights of Nautanki employees, taking up cudgels on their behalf when they had a problem, such as under-payment by company owners.

*

Octogenarian Shiv Adhar Dube was Gulab's company manager for several decades. He enjoys rambling through memory lane.

Dube hails from village Thathiya, next to Balpurva, and saw Gulab and her sister Chahetan dancing when little girls of ten or twelve. He was about the same age. Much later he developed a serious interest in Nautanki, set up a group and ran it for a while, then closed it down to join Gulab's company as manager.

Soon after his school days he joined Indian Railways as a ticket checker, but resigned due to ill health. His wife died within a few years of marriage, and Dube married Shanti, a Nautanki actress and the main heroine in his company. When Shanti was ageing, she retired and her younger sister Neelam began playing heroine roles. Neelam and Dube had an affair and they too married. Recalls Dube, 'Shanti and Neelam were wonderful. Whatever I could do was because of them. They lived together amicably and affectionately. With Shanti I had a son and two daughters. Neelam died young, in 1973, within a few years of our marriage.' Dube called his company Neelam Sandhya Theatre—Sandhya being his and Shanti's elder daughter.

His children are educated and respectably married. Sandhya, is now a post-graduate who 'abhors Nautanki and dance'. The younger daughter holds a police job. His son is well settled. Dube is contented enough with his daily life—he is loved and well looked after—but misses the colour and adventure of his earlier years.

As manager of the Great Gulab Theatre Company, Dube played a pivotal role in managing the affairs of the company and liaising with concerned authorities. He says,

'Gulab adopted me like a brother. She wouldn't go anywhere without me. She would say, "You can talk. You have experience." She was illiterate. I did all her paperwork. I had no fixed salary; sometimes she would hand me a thousand rupees, sometimes five hundred.'

'I located and hired artistes and musicians, got dresses made, directed dramas. I located many girls—Nurjahan from Punjab, Rajeshwari from Kashmir, Maina from Nadgaon in Etawah district—she sang ghazals. There was a lot of cut-throat competition. We would hire six nagara players: four would have to just sit with us, so that they could not play in any other company.'

Dube says, 'From 1960 onwards Nautanki became "theatre". There were eight purdahs, with sceneries of jungle, palace, garden, bazaar . . . . Most managers were cheats and drunkards. I drank, but never when a show was on, or when I had to meet an artiste. I met Dev Anand in Rajgir—he was making a film with Hema Malini. I knew Meena Kumari well.'

'I met a lot of the officials when Bai won the Sangeet Natak Akademi and Padmashree awards. I went with her to Lucknow, Delhi, Chennai, and looked after everything.'

*

Chandrika Prasad 'Nidar' runs a paan shop in Sukulganj. We drive past melons and cucumbers growing by the banks of the river Ganga, to reach this Kanpur suburb. Winding our way past ramshackle shops and homes, we find his neat little shop. The distinguished-looking man at the counter is delighted to have visitors and an opportunity to talk about Nautanki.

Chandrika Prasad began acting as a child—as Rachna in *Pati Bhakt* and Rohit in *Harishchandra*. He graduated to playing hero roles, including Majnu in *Laila Majnu* and Feroz in *Mohabbat ki Putli*.

Chandrika Prasad's family was Dalit but quite well off. In 1960, when he was fourteen, Chandrika Prasad and his friends bought a tent for Rs 1200 and launched their own company. They hired Jaikunwar and Ramrati, both popular dancers from Kanpur. They themselves—eight to ten mardanas—played most of the roles. They put up their tent at the Takiya mela. However they knew nothing about entertainment tax. They had three classes of tickets—red stamp for Class 3, green for Class 2 and yellow for Class 1. Class 1 cost Re 1 while the others cost a few annas each. But, 'the tax people came snooping around and said we must sell tickets for 7 paise only, or wind up. Other companies knew how to get around the rules, but we were stumped. Our staff was shattered, because we couldn't pay them the settled rates of Rs 50, Rs 100 and so on, if we sold tickets at such a low price. The harmonium player started demanding his payment, the nagara player his. Everybody got up, took some props and ran off. The company folded up right there!'

He laughed, and continued on a philosophical note, 'Anyway we wouldn't have survived the competition. Naagar Master—Uttar Pradesh's champion singer—was there, and Savitri from Calcutta, Ladli, Radharani, Sitarani, Krishna Bai, Gulab Bai and Rajshree. Nautankis at that time were so popular that people queued up in ticket lines for tickets costing up to two rupees—more than it cost to see the talkies. Costumes were dazzling, and sets grand. An actor like Vishvambhar looked like a king if enacting the king's part. Cattle traders came from as far as Sultanpur and Pratapgarh to the Takiya mela.'

Chandrika's father disapproved of his son's obsession with Nautanki. At night Chandrika would lie awake, then stealthily place a pillow under the sheet and run off to the mela. Sometimes he took his mother's white cotton kitchen sari, and went off to perform a role, wearing this as a dhoti. He would return late next morning.

Chandrika says that during a scuffle in his village, he unintentionally murdered a man. He fled to Kanpur to escape the law. There he found a small-time job. The government had banned Nautankis in Kanpur, so he fulfilled his passion for singing by joining a kirtan party. He sang kirtans for the next twenty-five years. Nautanki became like a dream. He missed the beat of the nagara. He notes wistfully, 'Sometimes I still see a good Nautanki, in Beeghapur or Takiya. Small Nautanki parties still perform at weddings in Unnao district. But there is nothing like this in Kanpur any more.'

He built a house and opened his paan shop at Sukulganj in 1983. His wife, children and grandchildren live here with him. Earlier he lived in Sirki Mohal, Kanpur, with seniors like Naagar Master and Lakshmi Master as neighbours. They were Marwaris. When Nautankis declined Naagar Master went off to Nagpur and became a pujari in a temple.

Chandrika Prasad still sings at kirtans. When a tooth became loose he got it tied up so he could still sing. He teaches his grandchildren to sing and play various instruments.

*

In a Nautanki programme, jokers provided humour, which was often risque. We track down elderly Rashid Joker—a wee bit drunk, even though it is morning, yet coherent and expansive. His wife looks in, makes a few comments, and goes off.

Rashid relates, 'As a child I loved singing. We lived in Gwalior, which had the biggest music training institute in India—Maharaja Sangeet Vidyalaya. I was poor so I couldn't reach there. But I dreamt many dreams. I had an excellent voice and people said I would be a success if I went to Bombay. Well, I never reached Bombay but came into Nautanki!'

Young Rashid joined qawali parties with whom he traveled to Agra and Mathura. He trained under Umrao Master of Agra, who taught him Nautanki singing. Rashid acted female and male parts, often playing the hero. He joined Lalmani Numberdar's company in Kanpur at a monthly salary of Rs 30. Later he worked with Krishna Bai's, Mannu Dada's and Gulab Bai's companies.

Rashid took up comedy roles like the gardener in *Raja Harishchandra*, Ragoomal in *Sultana Daku* or Anwar Harami in *Laila Majnu*, and began developing humorous slapstick items in between drama scenes. These won appreciation and he became popular as Joker for the next twenty years. He notes, 'Jokery requires a face so mobile you can make the audience laugh as soon as you enter. There's no need to paint the face yellow and red. One must talk in a certain style. It should have some meaning. It can be healthy, or dirty. Amusing the audience by twirling a donkey's tail, or wearing a little skirt–that is not jokery, it is just deception. Jokery draws upon natural talent. People stop in their tracks and begin to laugh.'

Initially there was no joker in Nautankis. Later it became a tradition. The joker was also called Munshiji, Khissu or Pissu. In Ramlilas the comedian was called Vidushak. The word joker came into Nautanki from the circus.

He recalls, 'People were crazy about my jokery. Big men like T.P. Saxena, who was the district collector of Hamirpur, would wait for my part, and laugh uproariously at the funny places. He wanted to promote me as a film comedian through his friend, a director in Bombay. The director sent for me, sending a Bombay ticket to my Kanpur address. But I never got that ticket, because the house was locked since my family and I were travelling. Years later I chanced upon the same officer in Hamirpur and he cursed the fate that prevented me from going to Bombay at the right time!'

Rashid Joker directed a few Nautankis in his time. He asserts, 'Fifty years ago Nautanki was so popular that cinema houses had to close down in towns like Vidisha, Gauna, Sikri. Just one cinema show could be held—from 6 p.m. to 9 p.m—when there was a Nautanki in town. The 9 p.m. to 12 midnight shows were cancelled because nobody would come for it. The entire public ran off to see Nautanki. The cinema owner, his operators and workers would also go off to see the Nautanki!'

Of late, Rashid hardly leaves Kanpur. He hasn't even visited Gwalior for years. His wife intervenes spiritedly, 'He ran away from home, so they don't care about him. If you fight with everybody why should they be concerned whether you are alive or dead?'

Rashid Joker explains, 'My father, Meherbaan Khan, fought in the Maharaja's army. My brothers joined the Indian army. My father objected to my singing, saying this is not the family profession. I ran away to sing and dance. Our ancestors came into India with Mahmud Ghazni. They wandered through thick forests. Sometimes they were arrested.'

Rashid married in Kanpur and the couple have a son and three daughters. The entire family would travel along with Rashid during the Nautanki season. Their son is unemployed but daugher Shahbano works as a dancer. At present her income supports the entire family.

*

We meet Ganesh Numberdar at Mandhana, a suburb of Kanpur. His grandfather Lalmani Numberdar, one of the early giants in Kanpur Nautanki, died in the 1940s. Two sons, Jaiprasad Numberdar and Hariprasad Numberdar, continued running separate Nautanki companies. Ganesh Numberdar, Jaiprasad's son, took over his father's company in 1960. The company had magnificent sets including a marvellous carved gate for the entrance, grand drop curtains, chairs and props. Several trucks were required for carrying the sets. During its best years the company had a staff of up to 120 people. Shyama-Anno, Rashid Joker and many other talented artistes worked here for long stretches of time.

The Numberdars were Brahman zamindars, owning land and property in Mandhana. They regularly hosted a large number of actors and musicians, allowing them to hold rehearsals on the family estate. In the 1970s after the market for Nautankis declined, Ganesh Numberdar no longer found it profitable to keep a regular staff. He shut down the company in 1984.

He analyzes changing audience tastes, saying, 'Earlier people came to see Nautanki for its art and singing. Then they began coming to see its women—attractive and seductive women. Today the art is degraded. Now women are everywhere in public, attractive and semi-clad. If people come for a Nautanki now, they want to "buy" the women. Earlier, we never allowed anybody to come and meet the women.

'My father began the modernization of Nautanki—gates, sets, loudspeaker, orchestra. This was 1960 onwards. Around the same time the craze for women in Nautanki began. Along with Nautanki, we had songs, cabaret, ghazal, qawwali and jokery—for variety. Rehearsals were held for four hours daily, to prepare for the night show.

'The government patronized B.N. Sarkar for his magic shows, at melas. I remember once the district magistrate inaugurated Sarkar's magic show, but then left it and came to see our Nautanki! He saw our plays daily. People turn up their noses at Nautanki, yet they enjoy seeing it.

'Eighty per cent of the old artistes worked with us. My signature is sufficient for an artiste to get a government pension. Artistes have not been able to maintain themselves. And the art has disappeared. Both my sons are in the steel business. What would they do in Nautanki now?'

*

Chinha Guru and his family live close to the main bus-stand in Beeghapur village—a couple of hours from Kanpur. Chinha Guru has a fund of Nautanki-related stories. He still organizes good Nautankis during Dussehra every year, a tradition set up by Tirmohan Lal in 1928. This is one of the rare sites where talented Nautanki artistes still congregate.

However, he says, 'Now we have Nautanki for one night and orchestra-dancing the other night. Older people, women and children gather for the Nautanki. For the dance-night, the shamiana is over-packed with young men. We can't avoid it!' Chinha Guru seeks out good artistes, wherever they are. 'Every year one or two die. They are all getting old. Hardly anybody in the new generation is learning', he laments.

Chinha Guru enjoyed Nautankis since childhood. Tirmohan Lal's daughter was married in Beeghapur, to Chinha Guru's uncle. Tirmohan's wife and small sons all died within a few years. Chinha Guru would sit with Ustad Tirmohan Lal and learn all he could about Nautankis. Thus, although he isn't a practising artiste, he is an expert on Nautanki music, costumes, scripts and indeed history.

Chinha Guru recently retired from the post of schoolteacher in the Beeghapur high school. His children, nephews, nieces and grandchildren are all studying. The family is Kurmi by caste. Chinha Guru explains that Tirmohan would often organise the first show of a new play in Beeghapur. If it was successful, Tirmohan got the script copied in beautiful long-hand by Chinha Guru's brothers. He showed us one specimen, carefully preserved in a greasy polythene bag—the original manuscript of the play *Bahadur Ladki urf Aurat ka Pyar*. The writing is indeed beautiful, each character neatly formed.

Chinha Guru thunders on about Shrikrishna Pehelwan cheating Tirmohan out of all his copyrights, and making untold money by publishing and selling Tirmohan's scripts—including the script of *Bahadur Ladki urf Aurat ka Pyar*. Chinha Guru had carefully kept a set of all Tirmohan's own publications, but somebody took it away. 'I have all the stuff but people come and just take away things,' he sniffs. A kindly, affable old man, with a passion for drama and history, Chinha Guru notes in a stoic, matter-of-fact way, 'The time for Nautanki is over.'

*

We climb several steep flights of stairs to reach drama expert Siddheshwar Awasthi's room in an old building near Kanpur's main market. Awasthi has written and directed some 200 to 250 plays, including a number of Nautankis. He wrote the Nautanki script *Teen Betiyan* that Gulab's daughters performed in 1996-97. Associated with the Sangeet Natak Akademi, he frequently works with school and college students in Kanpur, training them to act, sing and produce plays.

He reminisces, 'My childhood was spent in Nautanki. Many Nautankis were performed in Arauli, where I was born, and Kanpur, where I moved as a child. At night I would place a pillow under the blanket, and slip out to go see the Nautanki. Boys from upper-caste families were not allowed to see Nautankis. But they would go off like this!'

Awasthi shares some of his experiences as a Nautanki director: 'In 1960 I was asked to prepare and present a Nautanki, to be performed in Delhi within three days! I took up the challenge, conceived a story, and gathered together seasoned artistes and musicians. I took them to Delhi, installed them in a couple of rooms. They weren't used to rehearsing since usually they knew plays by heart. They were more concerned about their tobacco, bidi-cigarette and alcohol. I cajoled and scolded, persuaded and pushed. Once they got into the act they were brilliant! These are adept actors and singer. The play took shape —although it took its toll on me! We performed at Mavalankar Auditorium. The critic Charles Fabri appreciated the show in next day's newspaper!

'Another time I wrote and directed a Nautanki in Delhi for "Apna Utsav". It was performed at Ferozeshah Kotla Maidan. Munni Chakoowali played the leading role, while Paan Kunwar was the side-heroine. Munni Chakoowali was a great actress but at the rehearsal she wasn't exhibiting anger strongly enough. Before the final show, I refused to provide her a meal. And just before she went on stage, I told her that Paan Kunwar's acting was excellent. Munni Chakoowali did the scene brilliantly! She was red in the face and shaking with anger. Afterwards, I explained my strategy, appreciated her acting, and sent for some good food!'

During the 1980s, Awasthi went on tour to several places with the Great Gulab Theatre Company. His room is crammed with books, statues he's carved from coconut shells, and little green boxes of churan and tooth powder that he prepares to a secret formula and sells informally. Twinkling eyes and a stream of anecdotes keep visitors engaged. Grandchildren with large bright eyes peer in and are treated to a pinch of churan on their open palms.

Awasthi has resisted bureaucratization, and remained true to his creative urges. A votary of Nautanki, he declares dramatically, 'If Uttar Pradesh doesn't have Nautanki, what will it have?'

*

I meet dramatist and writer Vijay Pandit in Unnao, some two hours from Kanpur—in the city library. He reminisces, 'As a Brahmin child, I learnt chanting. But I began singing in a different direction from my family pandits. I gravitated towards drama. Here there is no caste taboo! I sit and eat with many artistes. I have worked quite a lot with Nautanki, and its Dalit artistes. They are experts in singing and acting. I'm keen that the form revives. But it will not be easy.'

Pandit notes that Nautankis were very popular in Kanpur, including in labour colonies. Arrangements had to be made for safety, especially for protecting the women. Nautankis filled a cultural vacuum. 'But,' he rues, 'while Nautanki is being hailed as a folk art, its "folk" are not being valued. The form is still looked down upon, and not respected enough. Nautanki artistes have remained cut off from social approval. Social attitudes towards women are cheap, intolerant and stereotyped. Gulab Bai became a celebrity so there was a better attitude towards her. But it was never generalized.

'Nautanki is degenerating because it does not have due recognition or status. The Uttar Pradesh state government calls actors from Bombay to perform at functions, but not a Nautanki troupe. With globalization, we no longer care to know our own culture. Where do we begin putting things right? What is the right point to begin? The artistes are poor Dalits, so they are treated as second-class citizens, put up in dormitories or green rooms rather than in hotels. They feel hesitant about entering elite cultural organizations.

'Nautanki is the most powerful medium in the world . . . and it has all but vanished today. It was a part of education. Nobody read *Raja Harishchandra* but everybody knew it. In every village at harvest time, a Nautanki was performed at the temple.

'Today Nautanki actors don't want to learn new roles. In Unnao there are still several Nautanki companies. In Bangarpur, Unnao, we have sixteen good Nautanki performances over three days. These are by all-male troupes.

'Educated classes should take initiative to resurrect Nautanki, but let it remain in the hands of Dalit artistes.

It should not slip out of their hands. They have carried on the art for centuries, yet they remain poor. They should be provided means to keep the art alive. Economic means and status are connected to the survival of Nautanki and its artistes. People should start a movement to bring more and more Nautankis onto stage, TV and various functions. Training should be systematically taken up: in schools, colleges, gurukuls, workshops, whatever. Cooperation between Nautanki artistes and new theatre-persons can be fruitful. Nautanki too will have to change, to draw more people towards it.'

25

Side-heroines and Bar-girls

Art never dies. I have grown old, but art is still alive within me. It will be in me till my dying breath. I still have dreams. I feel suffocated, I want a chance to sing, act and show people what is possible. We are artistes. We want an opportunity to display what we know, what we can do, what we are. But where can we do this? An entire world has disappeared into thin air. Our art is dying with us.

—Nargis

I have not taught my daughters Nautanki. I have acted in Nautankis and won a name for myself. But today the line has deteriorated and women in it are considered cheap. We sent them to school and arranged their marriages.

—Suraiya

Why should girls today learn Nautanki? Girls earn just by moving to music on stage, wearing 'short-cuts'. If a Nautanki is done, we perform: we are all fifty to sixty years old. What future does Nautanki have?

—Kamlesh Lata

Where will you see worse exploitation of girls? It starts in the girls' own families.

—Madhu

Women from Bedia and deredar Muslim communities came into Nautanki, carrying on a tradition of women performers, earning for the parental family and remaining excluded from conventional marriage. Many tried to break out of the pre-ordained 'life cycle' but only a few succeeded. As they guided their lives through the bumpy terrain of professional touring theatre, financial autonomy went hand in hand with a sense of responsibility for expanding circles of relatives, with overblown expectations.

These women walked a tightrope between making independent sexual choices on the one hand and the notion of being 'available' on the other. They earned respect for their work, carving out a sense of identity that was exciting and new. They also faced frustrating denials, loss and loneliness. Whether on stage or off, their lives were turbulent, dramatic and full of unexpected twists. Sometimes it seems as if the romance and magic of Nautanki spilt over and blurred into their lives. Their own stories are poignant, many-layered and multifaceted.

*

Kamlesh Lata, a well-known Nautanki actress, lives in a two-room tenement on the second floor of a run-down building in Bakarganj. Peeling paint on the staircase walls —but her smile is warm and welcoming. This ageing beauty has an expressive, mobile face.

A cooler makes a thunderous noise in the small, bare room. We enjoy the cool air, but have to shout to be heard. Her son sits with us—an amiable young man. Kamlesh speaks of her sisters Mala, Chanchala and Allo, all well known for their work in Nautanki. Kamlesh's real name is Quraishi, and Mala's is Mallika. They grew up in Nadgaon village, Etawah district. Mala, the eldest, first joined a

Nautanki company in Mathura. Krishna Bai's husband Hamid Bhai saw the four sisters on stage, and went to their village to offer them work in Krishna Bai's company. 'We didn't want to go,' recalls Kamlesh. 'We had heard Kanpur women are too bold. But when we went, we found they were the same as us.'

Kamlesh acted as heroine for a number of companies, including Gulab Bai's. After Gulab's death, Kamlesh acted in a Nautanki directed by Madhu and Asha, for a government function in Lucknow. Every year she still acts in the Nautanki festival at Beeghapur during Dussehra. Dabboo Master, her long-time paramour from Mathura, who lives with her in Kanpur, goes to Beeghapur to play the harmonium. The two share a comfortable companionship, and often take up work together.

Kamlesh describes the high level of skill required for Nautanki: 'You have to sing, dance and express emotions—all at the same time. Imagine that! Yet, now there is no demand for us. Young girls dress in "short-cuts" and earn a thousand rupees a night for moving on the stage. They have no knowledge of singing or acting. Yet the public wants them! In our time, there was no obscenity. We wore full costumes. Only the face and hands could be seen.'

Her nephew, Chanchala's son, works in Balaji Productions, Mumbai, as an editor. Over the telephone, Kamlesh Lata provides him a detailed critique of acting, costumes and enunciation in Balaji serials. 'I can act much better than the actresses in the serials,' she says with simple confidence. 'I wish I could reach Ekta Kapoor to let her know. My nephew is too scared of her to tell her about us. Shall I write a letter to her—what do you think?'

She continues spiritedly, 'Today people say Nautanki is bad. If it is bad, why were we given hundreds of certificates and testimonials? Do people give testimonials for doing something bad?' Her son fetches a thick wad of papers: indeed, these documents testify to Kamlesh Lata's rich contribution to Nautanki over the years.

Mala and Chanchala ran their own Nautanki company for several years. Kamlesh would act for them. She says, 'My sister Chanchala was a famous heroine. She ran her own company. Now she has fully retired. I am the only one still carrying on!'

We meet Chanchala briefly. She returned from Etawah just that morning – a plump, middle-aged lady sleepily rubbing her eyes on the landing: she lives next door. She talks animatedly about her children and grandchildren, rather than about Nautanki – a world she hopes to have left firmly behind.

*

Nargis lives in Bakarganj, in a building opposite Kamlesh's. Gracious in middle age, elegant even in her faded home clothes, she is happy to talk: 'It is our good fortune if you write about us. We are artistes but have no opportunity to perform. I feel suffocated. My heart is wilting.'

Nargis is well known professionally for her work, under the stage names 'Saira Banu' as well as 'Chhoti Helen'. She acted in Nautankis under the stage name Saira Banu, whom she resembles. She would watch Helen's cabaret numbers in Hindi films, and adapt the steps to dance as 'fillers' between Nautanki scenes: thus earning the sobriquet 'Chhoti Helen'.

Nargis reminisces, 'My nani and par-nani (grandmother and great-grandmother) were tawaifs from deredar Muslim stock. My mother came into Nautanki. She supported my nani and nana with her earnings. She looked after me. Then she fell ill and died, at the age of twenty-six. I was just a baby then.

'For five generations just one girl was born in each generation of our family: me, my mother, her mother, her mother and her mother—each an only child. Amongst us the mother brings up her child. Fathers are missing. I am the first to have a son. I have no father, chacha, tau. My nani taught me to sing and dance, and appointed Gurus to provide more intensive training—Afzal Hussain and Azhar Hussain. I had to leave my studies at the age of ten, and enter the Nautanki line.'

She explains, 'Among us, women have always earned. Tawaifs were talented artistes. Nowadays people do not understand culture. We lived independently, performed mujras at mehfils, to just ten or twelve people who appreciated music. Nawabs would bring their sons to us so we could teach them tehzeeb. You understand? Nawabs' sons learnt from us!'

Daughters learnt singing and dancing from mothers. They absorbed detailed knowledge into the very pores of their bodies. Nargis values the legacy: 'We are khandani. So we know the haav-bhaav, the nuances. We kept thumri alive. We sang and charmed our listeners.'

Nargis' mother, Munni Fatehgarhwali, left work as a tawaif, and came into Nautanki. Nargis never re-entered the world of mujras. She made her mark in Nautankis.

Nargis fell in love with a young photographer from Punjab, who had a studio in Kanpur. It was a grand romance. They lived together, had children, then shifted to Ambala, his family home. His parents insisted he marry again. Three years after the other woman came into his life, Nargis returned to Kanpur. The children came with her.

'I washed dishes in people's homes to earn,' she recalls bitterly. 'Finally I came back to Nautanki and dancing. I tried to change the world, but was defeated. My children still attach his surname to their names, but we have not seen him for the past thirteen years. I have brought up the children entirely on my own. Artistes live hand to mouth. Every day we dig a well and drink the water. God gives to everybody.'

Nargis has a son and three daughters. She sighs as she relates: 'In our families women could not marry. Nobody knew who the father was unless we said, "So-and-so is the father." I thought I would change all that. But I couldn't! I wanted to keep my children away from this line. I have managed to educate them. But my son doesn't work. My two elder daughters finished high school and began earning. They dance and sing at functions in Kanpur, Mumbai and Dubai. They say to me, "Ma you rest, we will take care of you." Bless them, they are wonderful children! My youngest daughter is still in school. Perhaps she will be able to study further and lead a different kind of life. I pray for this.'

Her family hails from Pinahat, a small town near Agra. Famous Nautanki artistes Shyama and Anno, both related to her, hail from Pinahat and have returned to live there. Saira Banu, the famous film actress, hails from the same area. So does Nimi, a well-known screen heroine of yesteryear. In her youth several people advised Nargis to try her luck in the Bombay film industry, but she couldn't because she was under tremendous pressure to earn for sheer survival.

*

Beena, who is from a Bedia family, joined Nautanki as a young girl. A few years later, a wealthy patron built a bungalow in Kanpur and kept her there on condition that she leaves Nautanki. He lived with his wife and children in a village in east Uttar Pradesh, and frequently visited Beena. Beena gave birth to a daughter and two sons. After he died, leaving the bungalow in her name, Beena began a Nautanki company and ran it fairly successfully. When she fell ill and couldn't run it any more, her fifteen-year-old daughter Babita began dancing to support the family.

Babita earned for the family, and continued studying. A bright student, she proved to be a talented performer. Her quicksilver steps and come-hither fluttering eyelashes attracted crowds of men. She began to receive endless offers for dance shows. Babita got the opportunity to act in a couple of good Nautankis, which she did well. However, these opportunities were so rare that it was impossible to make any income from Nautanki acting. In the late 1990s, she travelled to Mumbai and joined the ranks of bar-girls. Bars employ some 75,000 women in Mumbai. Most hail from erstwhile nomadic and entertainer communities.

Says Babita, 'I heard about the Mumbai beer-bars from other girls in Kanpur. They said we can earn really well there, because the rates are high. They said that it is safe. I went only after making sure it was a good option.

'I like my work. I want to save money for my future. I know many women who earned well when they were young, but didn't save anything. They supported brothers, parents, and husbands or lovers. When they grew old, the men abandoned them. My mother had no savings, so I had to start working. Still she was better off than others—at least she had a house. I would like to study but then how will this house run? Both my brothers have studied because of my earning.'

Babita's brothers are both graduates, yet both continue to live off her. One brother has married and has a child. He doesn't want his wife to know the nature of Babita's work. Others in their neighbourhood too are kept in the dark about this. Says Babita with asperity, 'I have told my brothers they should start earning soon. I won't support them forever. Why should I? I save some of my earnings now. Nor will I tie myself down to a man who will one day exploit me. When I have my own car and bank balance, twenty men will line up to marry me!'

Babita can sing well, act, is talented and ambitious. Though hard-working, she has the airs of a star—turning up late for rehearsals and shows. As a dancer in Kanpur, a bar-girl in Mumbai, and occasionally an entertainer in Dubai, Babita has worked hard and earned well. Though there is a hard edge to her personality, there is also self-confidence and an air of great satisfaction.

*

Beena's younger sister Mona joined Nautanki as a young girl and worked with a company in east UP and Bihar. She 'married' a zamindar from a village near Rajgir, who looked after her well. He made a house in the city for her, and lived there for long stretches of time. They had a son, whom they sent to a boarding school. The zamindar's village family accepted Mona, and she often visited them.

Mona and her husband set up a company and produced Nautankis for several decades. She was a well-known heroine, acting as Anarkali, Laila, and even Phoolan Devi. 'As Phoolan Devi I made my entry on stage on a horse,' she recalls, laughing. 'Old-timers still remember the dramatic entry.' The mela at Rajgir was a fair for horse-trading, so it was easy to get a suitable horse!

After her husband died, Mona moved to Kanpur to live with Beena. Mona's son is a doctor in Bombay and does not like to acknowledge that his mother was once a Nautanki heroine. He would be ashamed if his wife were to learn of this. Mona is happy her son is doing well, but frustrated about concealing her professional identity even within her own family.

In her own home, Mona seems to be just an ordinary woman, a little cranky in old age. Beneath the outer appearance, her dramatic past lurks, barely suspected by others in her family or neighbourhood. She says, 'Take me anywhere else and I will sing a whole Nautanki for you. I will sing all the parts. Be prepared: it will take several hours!'

*

Aged Hiramani lives in Rail Bazaar with her middle-aged son Saajan. Hiramani, when young, came from Banaras to sing and act in Kanpur Nautankis. She worked with Gulab Bai, Numberdar, Mala-Chanchala and Krishna Bai's companies. For a brief while she set up her own company but couldn't sustain it. Hiramani grumbles, 'I still want to act but Saajan doesn't let me. He stands in my way. I just run the house now!' Saajan explains, 'Nautanki isn't what it used to be. There are no good dramas any more. There is only vulgarity. I cannot act in these, much less Hiramani!'

Hiramani recalls, 'I played heroines—Laila, Taramati. I remember these plays by heart. Often, I became the vamp. Gulab Bai would say, "Oho, this one is a born villain—she has to play the part." I didn't need to be told what to do. It came naturally to me!' Jokes Saajan, 'Her name itself is dangerous—Hiramani!'

Hiramani still acts occasionally, in mother roles. Recently she played Mangal Singh's mother in *Pukar*, and Jodhabai in *Anarkali*. Hiramani had a daughter, Rani, whom she trained in singing. Rani sang old film songs and ghazals particularly well, and gave solo programmes. She sang in Hindi, Punjabi and Urdu, under the stage name Sandhya Rani.

Gulab liked Rani's voice and encouraged her, calling her on numerous occasions and paying two rupees for a song. Says Saajan, 'Gulab Bai would say, "Rani will become a great artiste. She will win fame in India and abroad." But my sister died. All our dreams are unfulfilled.' Sighs Hiramani, 'Had Rani been alive today I would not have been in this condition.' Hiramani would love to train younger women to sing and act, but there is no framework within which she can do so.

*

Paan Kunwar, a gifted ghazal singer and Nautanki actress, is about eighty years old and lives in Sirki Mohal, Kanpur.

Exuding an air of contentment, she relates stories from her colourful past. Her mother's name was Tulsa. Her father Gajraj Singh was a Thakur zamindar in Nawada, Bihar. Her mother was in the line of singing and dancing. Tulsa's mother Hansmat was also a professional singer and dancer. Hansmat's mother had been a grihastha, or housewife.

Tulsa came away from Nawada with her children— two daughters and a son—to join Shrikrishna Pehelwan's company in Kanpur. Paan Kunwar recalls her mother Tulsa singing brilliantly without any microphone. Paan Kunwar's elder sister joined their mother on the stage. Tulsa's sisters also came to live with them. Tulsa was weak and often ill.

Paan Kunwar has strong feelings about her matrilineage. She says, 'I had a dream that I should build a samadhi—a memorial for my mother, in Bihar. Recently I have done so. I built a temple, and installed the deity. I hosted a feast and performed rites for her soul.'

Paan Kunwar came onto the stage when she was ten years old: 'There were fifteen people at home—my mother, two mausis, and all their children. We had to work and earn. I worked in Pehelwan's company, and for many years in Numberdar's.' Later she worked in Krishna's and Gulab's companies.

She relates, 'When a new play was to be rehearsed, after the night show all the actors would have dinner and then gather together. Roles would be distributed. The prompter would read out all the roles. Everybody would get a copy of the drama to learn the part by heart. By next evening we were ready to perform!' She adds, 'Today nobody can learn a part so quickly. We put up whole plays like this. We did so many plays—*Mohabbat ki Putli, Gulbadan, Harishchandra, Pati Bhakt, Maya Machhander, Laila Majnu, Veermati, Pukar, Amar Singh Rathore, Aurat ka Pyar, Sikandar, Garib ki Duniya, Sultana Daku* . . . .'

Several people had mentioned that Paan Kunwar, when young, had an affair with Gulab's brother Haulu, which carried on for several years. Paan Kunwar herself avoids this theme, preferring to talk about her husband Rama Babu (Ram Kishore Vajpeyi). They have been married for many years now. Rama Babu first saw Paan Kunwar perform at a mela in Bhind, Morena. He met her a few months later at a numaish in Gwalior. He was manager with Krishna Bai's company at that point, while Paan Kunwar was with Pinahat-vali Shyama's company.

Rama Babu hails from Beeghapur where he worked in his family's printing press. Crazy about Nautanki, he joined Tirmohan Ustad's company as actor, and later manager. Afterwards he was manager in Krishna Bai's company, and for some time in Numberdar's company.

Paan Kunwar and Rama Babu live in a house that they rented from a Muslim lady. She went for Haj and died on the way, leaving no heirs, so by default the house became theirs. Paan Kunwar's mother Tulsa had made a house in Bakarganj and another in Phulaganj. When dying Tulsa gifted one house to her son, who promptly sold it, and the other to Paan Kunwar. Paan Kunwar gifted the house to her adopted daughter.

Paan Kunwar and Rama Babu had a daughter who died when four months old. They then adopted Paan Kunwar's brother's daughter. She studied up to Class 10, married and now has two daughters of her own, both educated, and one married in Calcutta. Paan Kunwar's nephew used to run a Nautanki company, Manohar Nautanki. Rama Babu had a daughter and a son from his first marriage. He met and married Paan Kunwar after his first wife's death.

Paan Kunwar describes a memorable performance in Delhi many years ago, in the Nautanki directed by Siddheshwar Awasthi. The troupe stayed in Delhi for six days and performed in an open ground as well as a huge auditorium, to an audience of highfalutin bureaucrats and art-lovers. The play got rave reviews and so did the female characters Munni Chakoovali and Paan Kunwar. A lady from London was keen to take Paan Kunwar to England, promising her riches galore is she agreed to perform there. Paan Kunwar says she declined the offer, because she would have to go 'so far away'.

*

Septuagenarian Hasina Banu Lucknowvali has enjoyed performing in Nautankis, usually as heroine. But today she doesn't feel like venturing near a Nautanki. She says she cries her heart out when she sees the state of affairs today.

Of her marriage to Abid Hussain, she says, 'We were both artistes. He was hero, I heroine. That's how we met and a feeling developed between us. We married. It's forty years since that day.'

Their one regret is that they have no children. 'If we had children we would have trained them and put them into the Nautanki line,' says Hasina Banu wistfully.

*

With Munni Bai, Rashmi, and Feroz the taxi driver, I set off one morning to Balpurva and Tera Mallu villages. Feroz is a sympathetic presence—a little nervous, since he feels it incumbent upon him to protect us from any mishap. A rainstorm felled hundreds of trees the previous night, so thousands of trucks are lined up in a massive road jam. Honking, disorderly vehicles surround and dwarf our Maruti van for well over an hour. Munni Bai sings for us: ghazal after evocative ghazal flows, its liquid beauty captivating the already captive audience. I record her voice, though the orchestra of blaring horns forms a poor accompaniment to her inspired singing.

She reminisces about her days in Nautanki: 'We did puja before wearing our makeup and costumes. Today nobody even recalls this. Now people first drink a shot of liquor, then begin their makeup. Girls come on stage wearing skimpy clothes. This was not possible in those days! They earn Rs 1,500 a night for dancing two hours. That time we saw Rs 600 or 700 in a whole month! Gulab Bai took Nautanki so high it touched the sky. Why is it falling so low today?'

At Tera Mallu we meet a number of Gulab's relatives. Two of Gulab's brothers settled here, upon land she bought for them. Both have passed away, but Haulu's wife, Dashrath Devi—a little old lady living in a tiny mud house—is alive. A guava tree stands in the centre of a neatly swept courtyard. Her house is bare. She despairs of her son, who is sitting on a string cot, staring vacantly. We are told he has drunk himself silly.

Dashrath Devi is sunk in her own grinding misery. She volunteers, 'My nanad was very good. She never let me remain in want. I did not go to see Nautankis. She used to come here.' Munni Devi pipes up, 'Her husband, my Haulu Mama, went off with Gulab Mausi's company. He had an affair with a well-known actress. The walls of this house were covered with photos. He stuck so many photos—all with his mistress!' I look at Dashrath Devi, who appears unperturbed. Gingerly, I explore this explosive theme, asking hesitantly, 'He brought her to the village?'

Munni Bai is expansive. 'Yes, Haulu Mama once brought her here. She was a Nautanki actress. He would go away for months at a stretch.'

'How did you feel about that?' I ventured to ask Dashrath Devi.

She was unexpectedly forthright. 'I didn't like it,' she said firmly. 'I didn't like her coming into my home, and I told him so. After that he never brought her here.' She sounded satisfied with this triumph, though her lips were set in a thin line, and she sniffed disapprovingly. A touch of pain gleamed in her eyes, despite the passage of years.

*

Asha of Terra Mallu, the daughter of one of Gulab's cousins, makes tea for us in her house, a short distance from Dashrath Devi's. Her husband stands about idle. He is Sukhbadan's son. In Bedia families it is common to find double or triple connections between people, since marriage alliances are loose, and there is frequent intermarriage between cousins or other close relatives.

Asha prepares tea on a kerosene stove, fumbles about in a cupboard and brings out a packet of glucose biscuits. Her husband hovers around in a nervous, shifty way, then leaves. Asha is bristling with tension and unhappiness, but doesn't say much. Munni Bai confides that Asha worked for years in Nautankis to earn and bring up her son and daughter, while the husband sat around, drank and abused her. He squandered the larger part of her earnings. When Asha became too ill to earn, on the verge of collapse, the family moved to Tera Mallu. Their daughter Neetu was about fifteen years old then. She began dancing and providing for her parents and siblings. But recently she started living with a man and no longer sends money home. At present the family has no source of income.

I recall seeing Neetu act in *Teen Betiyaan* in 1997. She was seventeen years old, soft-spoken, shy, her eyes invariably lowered. She was unlettered, so somebody read the script out to her. She danced with orchestra music for a living, and I remember asking her how it felt. Looking up momentarily, her eyes flashing saucily, she remarked, 'I like it if the men in the audience shout and whistle at me. It means they like my work.'

Seductive dancing and wolf-whistles moulded Neetu's growing sense of self. This is a sad commentary indeed, on the degeneration within the Nautanki genre. From a family of talented performers, Neetu can sing, dance and deliver dialogue with aplomb. However she has had little opportunity to act in Nautanki dramas, while cheap dancing is very much in vogue.

Since her 'marriage', Neetu decided to withdraw financial support to her parental family, and has not visited Tera Mallu since. Her mother Asha is too unwell to return to the stage.

Munni Bai comments, 'Gulab Bai bought land for her brothers and cousins, but they sold most of it. The men prefer to sit idle rather than toil on the land.' Two ageing men—Gulab's nephews—are silent. Gulab's grand-nephew Ravi, who studied up to Class 3, says, 'I don't have a job, nor do we work in the fields. If we grow something, we hire labour to do the work.'

Ravi volunteers to come with us to Balpurva to show the way. En route a fallen tree blocks the mud track. It is being cleared painstakingly by a very old man. So we take a much longer route, and it is late afternoon by the time we reach Balpurva.

*

In Balpurva, we see Phoolmati Maiya's temple, its graceful dome sparkling white in the summer sun. A kindly pujari greets us and asks after Gulab's daughters Asha and Madhu. Gulab built this temple, its boundary wall and pujari's rooms—upgrading the little stone shrine of her girlhood days. Munni Devi pays obeisance to the devi inside the shrine. From the temple two havelis are visible, and further off a cluster of houses that constitute the main village. The sky is a bewitching powder blue. We walk through green fields towards the havelis. As we stand uncertainly outside, a young woman rushes out, overjoyed to have visitors. Few outsiders come to this lonely spot. Exuberant, she embraces Munni Devi, Rashmi and myself, and leads us in to her mother, Shaila. Shaila and her children live in the haveli built by Krishna Bai. Next to it is Gulab Bai's more elaborate haveli, lying empty since many years.

Shaila is warm and dignified. We sit on a string cot in a huge room with high ceilings and carved walls—the main hall in the haveli built by Krishna Bai.

Krishna joined Nautanki soon after Gulab. In a few years Krishna's sisters Lallan and Kashi joined Nautanki, both proving successful as side-heroines. In due course, their younger stepsisters Shakuntala, Shaila and Munni also joined.

Shaila talks of Krishna Bai's marriage (or 'sambandh') with Hamid, a wealthy patron from Kayamganj in western Uttar Pradesh. Around 1960, Krishna Bai and Hamid set up the Krishna Nautanki Company. The company became very popular. Krishna Bai accompanied Hamid to his ancestral home in Kayamganj, converted to Islam and read the Quran daily. Their daughter Pappu grew up in the joint family there. Krishna withdrew entirely from Balpurva. She was angry with her father, Kallu Seth, for appropriating and misusing his daughters' hard-earned money.

Krishna's daughter Pappu—her screen name was Rita Lakshmi—became the star heroine in Krishna's company. When Pappu married and retired from pubic life, Krishna Bai closed down the company. Hamid died in the late 1970s. After that Krishna lived in Rail Bazaar, Kanpur, next door to her niece Suraiya (Lallan's daughter). Krishna Bai kept an open house, providing shelter to a motley crew of Nautanki old-timers, some of whom earned by driving rikshaws. Everybody called her 'Bari Ma' (elder mother). She kept a bhandari to cook the meals. She still sang in Nautanki programmes, and sometimes put up a special show.

At the time of her death in the late 1980s, the government was considering her for a Padmashree award.

Shakuntala, Shaila and Munni—all much younger than Krishna Bai—performed in Krishna's company and other companies like Sita's company that toured eastern Uttar Pradesh and Bihar. Munni married, left the stage and settled in Kanpur with her husband and children. Shakuntala gave birth to three children, while continuing on the stage. She died of a sudden illness, and Shaila adopted her children. In Balpurva, I meet Shakuntala's grown-up sons, a daughter-in-law and grandchildren, as well as Shaila's two children–a son and a daughter.

Shaila gave up acting in the early 1980s, after the birth of her daughter, and settled in Balpurva. She has maintained a steady relationship with a Yadav landowner from a nearby village. She says this has been a stable, supportive relationship. He continues to live in his family home, with his wife and 'legitimate' children, but visits Shaila regularly, cares for the children and supports the household financially.

Says Shaila with rare conviction, 'We had a love marriage. We people may have no caste, but this much I can tell you. There is nothing in marriage if two people are forcibly tied together. A true union is a union of hearts, when two people choose each other. Why, we may not be married in the eyes of the world but he has been faithful to me for the past forty years.'

Life is not easy in this isolated outpost. Out tumbles her litany of woes: 'This place is in ruins now. It was full of life when we were children! Some years ago the well dried up, so we dug a tubewell. We can't operate it because we seldom have power. Somehow last year we had a bumper potato crop. But so did other farmers; the government set the procurement price low and we incurred a huge loss. My nephew Ashok took a loan and bought a cow but it died, so he is running from pillar to post to get the loan commuted. Just now he has taken documents to the bank.'

Shaila didn't train her daughter to sing and dance, because 'Nautanki is not the honourable profession it used to be in my time. I want to get her properly married, but boys' families ask for one or two lakh as dowry. It's a marriage, not a business deal! I will spend forty to fifty thousand but more than that I can't afford.'

A practical and wonderfully frank woman, her list of troubles is indeed daunting.

Shaila's daughter bustles off to the main village to buy milk. 'Our cow gives milk in the mornings, and the children drink it there and then,' says Shaila in a satisfied tone. 'Later if we want to make tea we go buy milk from the village. We are stuck quite far from the village, in the middle of nowhere. Even if we need a matchstick somebody has to go there to buy it.'

Smiling wryly, she says, 'I have become fearless. Living in this wilderness, I have become wild. People who come and stay with us get scared. At night if they have to go out to relieve themselves they wake me up. As for me, I can walk in the middle of the night all the way to the next village. I am not afraid!'

Munni Devi has a fit of sneezing immediately after drinking tea, which diverts everybody's attention. She lies down for a while, then springs up and begins an animated discussion on prospective bridegrooms for Shaila's daughter. It is evening, and we have the journey to Kanpur ahead of us. Shaila and her daughter press us to stay the night, and indeed I am tempted to do so, but Rashmi (my research assistant) needs to get back to her children. The goodbyes are strange and sad: Shaila's daughter is disconsolate at our departure.

*

Back in Kanpur, we meet Suraiya, Lallan's daughter. Lallan, just younger than Krishna Bai, was well-known as a side-heroine. Lallan married fellow-actor Master Nishar. He had come to Kanpur from Mathura, where his brother Fazal Baba and nephew Master Kallu worked as actors. Lallan often accompanied Master Nishar to Mathura. They had two daughters, Pauva and Suraiya, and three sons.

The elder daughter, Pauva, shot into prominence as a heroine at the age of fourteen or fifteen. Suraiya says Bollywood director B. Shantaram once came to Kanpur to offer Pauva a job. Lallan and Nishar demurred, saying, 'What will happen to our daughter if she goes so far away?' Pauva's stage name was Kamini Kaushal. When she moved about on a tonga she created a stir on the streets of Kanpur. She had long hair, large eyes and a sultry complexion. Pauva died at the age of sixteen in mysterious circumstances. Her family believes rivals in the Nautanki field poisoned her. She was found dead with blood spurting from her mouth.

Suraiya began acting at the age of four or five. Her screen name was Neelam Suraiya. She worked by and large in Krishna Bai's company, and various companies based in Mathura. She was a popular heroine. For years she became the main provider for her parents and three brothers. The boys were encouraged to study, but they failed in school and began doing odd jobs instead.

Suraiya's father forbade her from performing in Kanpur city. Once, however, she acted in a Nautanki in

Aalu Mandi, Kanpur. The unruly crowd started fighting, pulling the microphone and misbehaving. Suraiya was whisked away for safety's sake, escaping from the 'shringar room'—an improvised greenroom—via lanes and bylanes to ensure her safety. She never again performed in the city.

Suraiya married 'Darji Master' Ram Raj, who specialized in stitching Nautanki costumes. Leading ladies including Rita Lakshmi and Suraiya, Asha and Madhu went to Master Azam's in Lucknow to get their dance costumes tailored. One day, Rita Lakshmi was furious because Master Azam had not prepared her dress on time. She went to Ram Raj and told him she wanted a dress exactly like the one in the new film *Sajna*. She gave him money to buy a ticket to see the film. At that time Ram Raj was an apprentice with Azad Master of Pakeeza Tailors, Kanpur. Ram Raj stitched the dress as desired, earning a hundred rupees for the work. Rita Lakshmi and Suraiya appointed him their tailor. Says Ram Raj, 'Wealthy men come to see Nautanki and gaze at the leading ladies. I fell in love with Suraiya, and it is her personal feeling within the heart that she liked me.'

After marriage, Suraiya cut down on her acting commitments. She has not taught her four daughters Nautanki singing or dancing. She knows this line has deteriorated and women in it are considered cheap. She is glad her daughters are educated and married into conventional households. Ironically, to break the exploitative cycle endemic in Nautanki families, women prefer to send their daughters into the patriarchal family system with arranged marriages, dowry and no opportunities for independent earning.

Suraiya still acts if offered a good role. She says, 'I don't go for programmes, because company owners just want to do "variety" programmes. In Bhagwant Nagar, Unnao, they said they would do Nautanki, but the variety went on and on. The public wanted a Nautanki. So the company sent somebody to Kanpur, saying, "Come with us immediately." I went, and we did a Nautanki. If I perform on stage you think the public will not watch? If I agree to go somewhere, I write on my letter pad, "I will do the Nautanki at such-and-such time."'

*

One evening I meet Moonga at Rail Bazaar. I gather she is Subedar's daughter from an earlier Nautanki actress, who died young, and Subedar and Shanti took her in as a little girl. She is one of the best singers in Gulab's extended family, especially talented in ghazal singing.

Moonga married a photographer from Bihar and the two set up house in Patna. They have three daughters. Her husband's forefathers were musicians at the court of the Maharaja of Darbhanga. He is a skilled sarangi player. The two put up shows together. 'But,' they say dolefully, 'nobody wants classical music nowadays. Everybody says it is wonderful, but only girls from high-class families get shows. There are hardly any shows for us now.'

Several aficionados tell me how good Moonga's singing is. She is disciplined about her riyaaz and performs with finesse. She sings solo at Nautanki programmes, as in Beeghapur village, her husband providing musical accompaniment. They have educated their daughters and hope the girls will take up professional courses and secure mainstream jobs. Their eldest daughter is married. All three daughters learnt classical music and sing well. Moonga and her husband are frustrated because there is very little scope for girls from ordinary families making it in today's classical music circuit. And they will certainly not put them into cheap dancing.

Moonga and her husband are visiting Kanpur for a show, staying at the ground floor of the Rail Bazaar house where Paati Kali and Munni Bai live. They come across as dignified, honest people. Tragically, their arts are likely to die out with them.

*

Next to Nargis's house in Bakarganj, across the first-floor landing, is Shilpa's home. She is a modern-style dancing girl rather than a Nautanki artiste. Shilpa's living room is sophisticated, with sofa sets and a glass centre-table, lush natural scenery across one wall, and an aquarium with large fish and water plants. A maid serves Pepsi in crystal glasses. A few potted plants, leaves glossy and freshly washed, complete a picture of tasteful prosperity, though set in a seedy locality.

Shilpa has visitors, but greets us warmly too. Pappuji, a portly figure, is there to invite her to work for an orchestra programme, but she has declined since she is leaving for Dubai the next day. She will perform in a hotel in Dubai for three months. Her husband hovers around, shifty-eyed and unkempt.

Pappuji mentions his own marriage to an actress, acknowledging that he doesn't like her to dance or act now. 'Men are like that,' he explains. 'A man likes to see other women dancing but doesn't like it if one's own wife dances. Because then other men will see her!'

Impeccable logic—to which Shilpa listens politely, without comment. She begins describing her work: 'I dance simply because I have a flair for it. Nobody in my family danced. My husband's family has been in this line for a long time. He is the one who runs my company.' She brings out a large poster of a programme she has recently done in Bombay. A young woman in shimmering blue sings, microphone in hand. Huge lettering announces a Nautanki on the occasion of Ram Navami at Thakre Rangmanch, Shivdi, by Dreamgirl Shilpa Theatre. It says Dreamgirl Shilpa will bring six selected, best 'lady dancers' with her, to meet the heavy demand for such entertainment, felt by Mumbai's north Indians.

Shilpa is one of the highest-paid dancers in the profession today, earning three to four thousand a night for two or three hours of performing solo item numbers. She performs in and around Kanpur, in Bombay and Dubai. Despite her success, she appears troubled. There is a simple dignity in her bearing. Soft-spoken and sensitive, she listens carefully, and relates warmly to us. Dressed in a plain salwar kameez, she barely resembles the shimmering, alluring figure on the poster.

Kamlesh Lata, who lives across the road, says Shilpa really respects genuine Nautanki artistes. Shilpa tries to take Kamlesh Lata and other artistes along when she organizes a programme in Bombay, and they put up at least one or two proper Nautanki scenes. Shilpa herself has no pretensions to being an actress. Yet, she performs under the sobriquet 'Nautanki'.

Nautanki seems to have come around full circle—the genre and its protagonists a completely transformed lot. Its humble origins in the akharas of Hathras, with disciplined body culture and classical ragas, are lost in the mists of time.

Dhrupad to Disco

If Uttar Pradesh doesn't have Nautanki, what will it have?
—Siddheshwar Awasthi

Nautanki is the most powerful medium in the world . . . and it has all but vanished today.

—Vijay Pandit

We have to learn from them and set up theatrical troupes based on folk arts at various places, in each region, with these people—whatever is the local art of the area. So by learning from them rather than teaching them, we have to turn them towards a new direction. This is the challenge, and we ought to accept it.

—Mohan Upreti

The government should discriminate between real and spurious Nautankis. Chaff is being sold as wheat—and at a higher price! The government should stop this. Spurious Nautankis should be banned, but the real Nautankis should be promoted . . . . If the government provides us some help, we will open Gulab Bai Nautanki Kala Kendra, and teach in the way our Amma wanted us to teach.

—Madhu

Will Nautanki survive? Perhaps it is time to accept that like other genres Nautanki has an origin, rise, decline and natural end. Yet if the end is inevitable, at least an ageing form can receive appropriate care and attention so that it lives out its last years with dignity.

*

Born in a feudal ethos, nurtured in akharas and performed in the open air, Nautankis burgeoned into one of our most successful cultural forms. It moved to tents and then halls, tickets were sold and box-office earnings totted up. By the middle of the twentieth century, Kanpur Nautanki adopted the picture-frame stage with painted scenery and elaborate costumes, and established itself as a commercially viable form. During the last quarter of the twentieth century, however, Nautanki began to lose its grip.

Folk theatre forms declined in other parts of India as well. The reasons for their widespread decline include changing popular taste, competition from electronic mass media, disintegration of older sources of patronage and absence of critical state support. The context and environment in which Nautanki and similar forms flourished changed dramatically, irreversibly.

The government imposed entertainment tax on Nautanki shows, but later withdrew the tax on the ground that Nautanki was a folk heritage that should be promoted. This withdrawal led to an unintended consequence. A number of companies sprouted calling themselves Nautanki parties although they have little or no connection with the original drama form. Their output is restricted to salacious female dancing with orchestra and recorded music. Earlier most Nautankis were family fare, but 'new' Nautankis serve exclusively male audiences. Demand for titillating song-and-dance shows grew while 'good' Nautankis became increasingly rare. Minimal investment is required for salacious dancing as compared to the substantial inputs required for producing an authentic Nautanki.

Nautanki drama companies became trapped in a vicious circle. Demand fell, income and profit margins dwindled, leading to slackening standards of production. Actors began to perform multiple roles so as to minimize staff strength. Rehearsals are barely ever held. Younger people are reluctant to learn the complex singing required. Ageing actors continue playing hero and heroine roles. Falling production standards led to further decline in audience interest.

*

The links between gender and genre are complex indeed, in the case of Nautanki. Although Nautankis became more popular after the entry of women, most people trace the decline of Nautanki to this very presence of women. Women performers have been strongly associated with sexual availability. The performance space was considered pure if men performed, but polluted the moment women stepped onto it. There is a long history to such associations.

As far back as 1790, Khanum Jaan, in the novel *Nashtar* written by Hasan Shah, was a dancing girl performing in Kanpur for officers of the East India Company. Kallan Saheb, a British officer, kept Gulbadan, a dancing girl, as his mistress, paying her Rs 300 a month. Kallan Saheb also paid fifty rupees to Khanum Jaan, and thirty rupees to the troupe, for a weekly mujra performance. At that time, 'Even dargahs had become places where nautch girls pitched their tents and held their dancing sessions. After the death of Aurangzeb, as a reaction to his austere puritanism, Mohammed Shah Rangile (1719-48) had made Delhi the musical capital of the East. The institution of mujras and tawaifs had come into being. Many tawaifs came from Punjab, Rajasthan and Kashmir . . .'[1]

Dancer-singers spread out in search of employment, which many found in Kanpur city. Khanum Jaan was part of a such a troupe, but she dreamt of settling down in marriage. Her grandmother Chameli Jaan was from a caste of dancing-girls, and trained Khanum to entertain British officers. A British officer had a mistress from Farrukhabad, but asked Khanum Jaan to be his mistress as well. She refused. Khanum, her relatives and co-dancers all said their prayers five times a day and observed other religious rites, yet Shah wrote, 'They are utterly immoral. They believe it is pre-ordained that they be born as procurers and courtesans.'

Khanum Jaan thought differently and tried desperately to escape. As we see with several Nautanki women, she wanted to move out of the systems she was born into. Khanum was unsuccessful in her efforts to step out. She secretly married Hasan Shah, but he neglected her. She thought that he had abandoned her and fell ill, wasted away and died.

*

Unlike the popular notion associating dancers with sex work, women often exercised divergent options. In 1857, the dancer Mastani, who sang for British soldiers in Kanpur, passed on information to Indian rebels. Thus, she played an important role in the 1857 nationalist movement. The story goes that the British offered her full pardon if she would agree to apologize and grant sexual favours to British officers. Mastani declined, and was sentenced to death.

*

Singing and dancing were often the means by which women supported entire clans. They remained unmarried, engaging in unconventional sexual arrangements, interpreted as sexual availability. This interpretation clung to women performers well into the twentieth century.

Singer-danseuse Malka Pukhraj rebelled against this stereotype. In the 1930s, from the age of twelve onwards, she was paid to entertain at the royal court of Jammu and Kashmir. When she and her family moved to Lahore in the 1940s, Pukhraj was already well known, and invited to sing at musical soirees. Her family—mother, aunt, uncle, cousins and motley relatives—mopped up all her earnings. Her mother did not let her go out with men. She kept a tight hold on this daughter who was the proverbial *sone ki murgi*—the hen that lays golden eggs. Pukhraj eloped with her friend Shabbir who had wooed her for several years. Though she continued to sing, marriage brought respectability with it, and the association with sexual availability gradually faded.

*

Binodini Dasi came into Bengali theatre because her mother, a prostitute, thought acting would ensure better income, and a modicum of respectability. This was in the late nineteenth century. Binodini Dasi won laurels as an actress, but respectability was another matter. After a few years she agreed to be the second wife of a wealthy patron. She lived in an outhouse, on sufferance, and gave up acting on his insistence. She had a daughter who died as a young child. After her patron died, Binodini had to leave her dwelling place and survive somehow.

*

Bedia and deredar Muslim families sent young daughters into Nautanki in pursuit of good income and respectability. Later, girls and women from other Dalit castes joined, especially after the Suppression of Immoral Traffic Act, 1959. This Act compelled a number of sex workers and nautch girls to leave their professions. Some shifted to the Nautanki stage.

*

During the 1920s and 1930s a number of women joined cinema as actresses. Respectable families wouldn't dream of allowing their daughters to act in public. Several early actresses were from performing castes. Nargis, Meena Kumari, Naaz and Madhubala were among those placed in film studios as young girls—the sole earners supporting entire families. Some, like Nargis, were able to move into respectability and marriage, shedding the legacy of a tawaif background. Others, like Madhubala, were kept on a tight leash by avaricious parents. Madhubala's autocratic father refused to let her marry, leading to trauma, which was partly responsible for her early and tragic death.

Exploitation of female performers has thus been common in India, whether in Nautanki or other theatrical forms, music, dance or popular cinema.

*

The term 'Nautanki' today is associated with female dancers performing item numbers for the masses. But in fact, it is sizzling sexual images on screen that have fueled a change in audience tastes, leading to a demand for similar 'live' (i.e. stage) performances. Female catering to male pleasure has become normalized, a routine part of daily media entertainment. Item girls are enormously popular. Contemporary 'Nautanki' dancers ape item girls and dance numbers popularized by well-known heroines–providing local substitutes for big names like Karishma Kapoor and Shilpa Shetty, just as 'Chhoti Helen' did in the previous generation. Shedding its classical elements, this vulgarized version of Nautanki presents women as seductive and sexually available; it has little pretension to being a form of art or drama.

Stereotypical male gaze defines such dancing. Sometimes mistakenly conflated with female liberation, such male-oriented body-show is in fact one of the few lucrative professions open to women who lack education and vocational training. A woman can earn quick fame and money, within a media industry that commodifies female sexuality. Projected as erotic items for mass consumption, aiming at male pleasure and gratification, women's bodies are manipulated and objectified.

Definitions of erotica, obscenity and permissible intimacy have changed over the decades. Body-show is now considered au courant, though an aura of non-respectability still clings to women who project themselves within these frames. They earn well and command high status, yet their image is never quite 'clean'. They remain vulnerable to the charge of indecency. Their status and income is partly at the expense of dignity and social respectability.

Women are using whatever performance space they have—strategizing to gain status and wield power even within starkly male-defined frameworks. Of course, through the centuries women have composed and sung, danced and acted, partly for their own pleasure. The sheer pleasure of singing shines through the voices of Naina Devi or Begum Akhtar, Malka Pukhraj or Siddheshwari Devi, or for that matter, Gulab Bai. At some point in her life each of these artistes decided to commit herself to her art, consciously making it her own—thus challenging fate. Striving to achieve perfection, their lives became lives of struggle, leavened by courage.

Women, including tawaifs and devadasis, contributed to the development of poetry, song and dance. For instance Vidya Rao, a contemporary singer and scholar, interprets 'thumri' as a women's genre. She explores thumri as a singing style through which women have expressed and expanded their worlds, in nuanced and sensitive ways.

Nautanki was a male genre that women entered, contributing to its spectacular success. Women, who entered Kanpur Nautanki in such a big way that it began to be labeled a 'woman-dominated form', transformed the genre in positive ways but also led to its degeneration. The old association between women performers with sexual availability continued, dovetailing with modern consumerist commodification of the female body by the mass media. In time, the demand for titillating entertainment has overtaken and overwhelmed the desire for good theatre. It is interesting that in Hathras and Unnao, a number of all-male Nautanki troupes still exist, perform 'good' Nautanki plays in the countryside, and have a devoted audience.

*

Performers like Gulab Bai and Krishna Bai led exceptionally eventful lives. They achieved unprecedented success. Though exploited by families and plagued by the taint of non-respectability, these women set up their own companies— a unique achievement, set within the very centre of a chronically patriarchal culture.

It was, of course, a precarious balance. These women's achievements were born of persistent struggle within male-defined caste-class contexts. Given the wider arena of culture and gender politics, the victories these women won were fragile. They leave a lingering memory of inherent possibilities, but for subsequent generations of Nautanki women, similar significant levels of achievement are an unattainable dream.

A number of girls from Nautanki families today earn by dancing in spurious 'Nautankis', and at hotels and bars. The bar-girls of Bombay—recently at the centre of a controversy over government moves to ban bar-dancing—are generally from traditional performer castes—Nats, Bedias, Kalbeliyas, Tamasha artistes and the like. Women's groups have supported the bar-girls' right to work. Some 75,000 bar-girls are struggling to survive, in the context of mass unemployment and grinding poverty. If denied opportunities to work as bar-girls, many will be sucked into sex work. Some say they will commit suicide if bar-dancing is abolished.

The feminist struggle to preserve male-oriented female dancing represents a painful and bewildering dilemma. It is paradoxical and self-contradictory: yet choices have to be made. In these harsh times, making the best of a bad deal might be as much as we can aspire towards.

*

Is real Nautanki a vanishing act? Most 'Nautankis' today bears little resemblance to the actual Nautanki—the grand, operatic form of yesteryear. Can real Nautanki be revived? Is it possible for surviving musicians and actors to work out a fresh lease of life?

Elderly artistes are keen to pass on their skills, but lack the requisite infrastructure. The Sangeet Natak Akademis provide marginal support through token awards, pensions to ageing artistes, and occasional sponsored shows. But talented elderly artistes are too poor, with neither savings nor income, to transmit skills free of cost. Surely the state ought to step in to create an institutional framework within which talented elders can train the younger generation.

Aged Sukhbadan, once a popular heroine, yearns to teach—pass her skills on to others. Kamlesh Lata longs to perform on TV. With styles of acting that have mesmerized large audiences in live shows, these artistes are quite capable of teaching, as well as putting up fine performances in television soap operas. But they lack the confidence and cultural capital to reach out and approach 'big people'.

Madhu and Asha want to set up a centre for teaching authentic Nautanki skills. At present they are hard put to produce any 'good' Nautankis. In the summer of 2003 they were lobbying to persuade the state government to lift a ban on Nautankis at the Bahraich mela. This ban was imposed a few years ago after several groups performed vulgar and titillating dances that they called 'Nautankis', at which lumpen crowds gathered, fights ensued and knives were flashed. Madhu emphasizes that the government should ban spurious, and promote real, Nautankis.

*

Madhu tried unionizing Nautanki artistes in a bid to protect their right to work. However, she admits it is an uphill task with not much hope of success. Krishna Mohan Saxena has set up the Nautanki Kala Kendra (NKK) in Banda, which performs good Nautankis and provides support to practitioners. In 2003, the NKK put up a play, *Nartaki ki Peeda*, that voiced the concerns of local dancing women. The play was performed in several villages including Mehndipur, a village in Fatehgarh district. Kiran Bharti, a persuasive activist from the Bedia caste, played the lead role. The play depicted the plight of women who perform mujras—including abuse by families, customers and policemen.

Urmil Thapliyal wrote a satirical column, 'Aaj ki Nautanki' in a leading Hindi newspaper for twenty-eight consecutive years. His group 'Darpan' produced some fine theatre, including several 'Navya Nautankis'. Vijay Pandit, Siddheshwar Awasthi and some other modern dramatists are making similar experiments—incorporating elements of Nautanki style into modern Hindi productions. Sarveshwar Dayal Saxena's *Bakri*, a blistering social satire in Nautanki style, has been very popular and successful.

*

Traditonal Nautanki drama today survives at a few select places like Hathras, Singahi and Beeghapur. 'Good' Nautanki still retains a devoted following, because many older people prefer its familiar charms.

Srikrishna Pehelwan's printing press, Shrikrishna Pustakalaya, which sold an estimated 75 million copies of Nautanki script books up to 1971, continues to do. roaring business. The Pustakalaya still publishes and sells hundreds of script books, several claiming to be in their sixtieth or sixty-second edition!

The popularity of script books would suggest interest in Nautanki drama, yet authentic performances are rare. Spurious Nautankis dominate the scene, even in traditional venues like Bahraich, Takiya, Makanpur and Devi Patan melas. Just as hand crafted village goods have given way to mass-produced tawdry plastic and synthetics, local performing arts are reeling under the assault of mass-produced aggressively advertised slick fare. Films manufactured in Mumbai, 'globally' produced television programmes, and live 'item numbers' have become the favoured modes of entertainment.

In variety programmes such as 'Dream Girl' Shilpa's shows in Mumbai, a smattering of Nautanki drama is provided. Shilpa concentrates on fast-paced item dances as the staple fare, but short excerpts from Nautankis like *Laila Majnu* and *Amar Singh Rathore* are also performed. She takes a few aged Nautanki actors from Kanpur to enact these excerpts.

*

Some Nautankis have been aired over television, produced for radio and performed in proscenium theatre as part of national or state-level cultural fests.

Thus in March 2001, Andhra Pradesh's Sangeet Natak Akademi held a weeklong festival of theatre arts in Hyderabad, in 'an attempt to revive the eventually declining Theatre Arts, a colourful and aggressively loud traditional form of entertainment.' The festival included a Nautanki by 'Gulab Theatre of Kanpur', a tamasha by Kalasagaram, Pune and Kutiyattam by Smaraka Gurukulam of Trichur, Kerala.

In March 2004, the Hindi Akademi invited Krishna Kumari Mathur and Company from Shikohabad to perform at Delhi's Triveni Chamber Theatre. Krishna Kumari Mathur travelled to Delhi in her chauffeur-driven car. Her husband is a politician, her sons own trucks, and she, at the age of sixty, continues playing heroine roles with great gusto and charm. The group gave a marvellous performance of *Amar Singh Rathore* in a hall packed to overflowing, the aisles filled choc-a-block, with more people pouring in all the time. Old-timers in the audience recalled seeing the same Nautanki decades ago in their villages, with barely any props or special costumes, actors walking freely amid rows of spectators. The company performs in the Hathras style, its music elaborate, with a classical grounding. Heavy costumes and refined dialogue add flavour and popular appeal.

*

Indian cinema bears a debt to Nautanki and other theatre forms. In a way, Nautanki has been absorbed into cinema. The first Hindi film, made in 1913, was *Raja Harishchandra*. The Nautanki by this name had already been performed thousands of times. The film was released in Coronation Theatre, Bombay: 'The live band has struck up a tune and now the screen flickers alive. For the next half-hour, cinemagic envelops the audience. The tale of the truth-obsessed king is declared a hit, and runs for a record twenty-three days!'[2]

Dadasaheb Phalke's silent film borrowed from folk theatre—a trend the cinema industry maintained. Films borrowed plots, styles of song, dance and characterization from Nautanki, Parsi theatre, Tamasha and other popular genres. Melodrama, tension between evil and good, royal courts, bandits and jokers were imported straight from stage to screen. Initially cinema coexisted comfortably with folk-hybrid theatre. They were evenly matched in terms of popularity and borrowed freely from one another. But by the late 1950s the tide started turning, and cinema became dominant. Now it was time for Nautanki to re-model itself on the screen.

Cine material was used to create new Nautankis. Thus Yasin Mian scripted the Nautanki *Jehangir ka Insaf* on the basis of the film *Mughal-e-Azam*. The Nautankis *Pukar*, *Sholay* and *Nagin* were directly inspired by the films bearing the same names. Nautankis borrowed costumes, dialogue, songs and plots, and actors modelled themselves on well-known heroes, heroines and character artistes.

A number of well-known cine artistes, such as director Ranjit Kapoor, actor Raghuvir Yadav and qawwali singers Shankar and Shambhu hail from Nautanki families.[3] They were able to make the transition from local artistes to big-time celebrities. Many other Nautanki artistes continue to dream of such great good fortune.

*

Just as Nautanki survives within the folds of Indian cinema, is it being reborn in other guises, in different parts of the world?

Searching the Internet for material on Nautanki, I find the following advertisement for a documentary film:

AJUBA DANCE AND DRAMA COMPANY (twenty minutes, 1979) ... introduces a troupe of popular entertainers in North India. Performing in private compounds, factory yards, and mango groves, they stage a type of theatre known as Nautanki, an amalgam of music, dance, comedy routines, and drama. Nautanki draws as easily from the arts of the royal courts as it does from the latest Bombay feature films. The film allows viewers to see the performers in their everyday lives, meet Bhaggal, the director, travel with his Ajuba troupe, watch them rehearse their lines and put on their make-up, and finally, under the stars, witness a Nautanki performance itself, with dance, song, color, and romance.

*

In a globalized cultural ethos, perhaps Nautanki will survive in different garb—dressed up as modern theatre, sparkling in a documentary film, or imported into completely different contexts. Like a museum piece or an exported cultural artefact, it might well attract new admirers in foreign lands. Will the nagara continue to beat, in different cultural contexts but still pulsating, vibrant? Will Nautanki migrate to other lands—reborn?

An intriguing answer to this tantalizing question is another treasure from the Internet. This is about an event in Singapore in February 2003:

> Nautanki 2003 was presented by the 'Society of Indian Scholars' in Singapore on 7 and 8 February 2003 at the University Cultural Centre Theatre, National University of Singapore. Its advertisement blurb reads: 'After the wildly successful Nautanki 2001, the Society of Indian Scholars proudly presents Nautanki 2003, an evening of quality theatre. The plays include the first ever production of *The Mirror Has Two Hands* written by Mohit Sindhwani and featuring the music of Levee.
>
> A handful of NUS students put together this show in less than a month. Mohit Sindhwani wrote the script, conceptualized the music video, created the website, sold tickets, paid for the venue and publicized the drama to uncharted corners of patronage. He managed to do all this despite his job and coursework. Golam Ashraf, also in a full-time job, directed the play, shaping amateur actors into distinct characters, striving to bring professionalism into their acting. A 'world premiere' was held at the University Cultural Centre Theatre, University of Singapore, with an audience of over six hundred people watching.
>
> The 'awesome show' became 'a huge success'. It reflected enormous dedication to Nautanki and proved that that

'passion can sustain our myriad constraints and create something beautiful'.

*

Back in India, some imaginative attempts are being made to bring forms like Nautanki to a wider audience. In 2004, Nehru Centre, Mumbai, presented an innovative research-based musical programme, *Indradhanush—The Rainbow of Indian Folk Arts*. The idea was 'to trace the evolution and development of various Indian folk arts and to understand why some folk arts stayed frozen in their original nascent form, while others graduated to become more classical.' Apart from audio-visuals, live performances were presented by a galaxy of accomplished artistes.

The programme on 16 July 2004, at the Nehru Centre Auditorium featured Nautanki by Madhu Agarwal, Murali by Kamlabai Shinde, Lavani by Rajashri Shekhar Jamkhedkar and D.V. Utpat, Kathak by Madhurita Sarang, Bharat Natyam by Sandhya Purecha and Gotipua Odissi by Jhelum Paranjape.

The Nehru Centre website advertised the programme thus: 'Seen in action on stage in a rare sangam of the folk and classical will be a Nautanki by Madhu Agarwal from Kanpur, daughter of the legendary Gulab Bai . . . .'[4]

Gulab Bai's legacy might yet survive!

List of Interviews

1. Asha (Gulab Bai's daughter), Kanpur, 1997, Dec 2002 and May 2003
2. Asha, Tera Mallu, May 2003
3. Babita, Kanpur, 1997, May 2003
4. Beena, Kanpur, May 2003
5. Billoo, Kanpur, May 2003
6. Binda Prasad Nigam 'Sherdil', Kanpur, June 2003
7. Chanchala, Kanpur, May 2003
8. Chandrika Prasad 'Nidar', Kanpur, May 2003
9. Chetan Bai, Delhi, Jun 2003
10. Chinha Guru, Beeghapur, May 2003
11. Daddu Pehelwan, Kanpur, Jun 2003
12. Dashrath Devi, Tera Mallu, May 2003
13. Ganesh Numberdar, Mandhana, 2003
14. Harishchandra, Kanpur, Jun 2003
15. Hasina Banu Lucknowvali, Kanpur, 2003
16. Hiramani, Kanpur, Mar 2003
17. Jai Kunwar, Mehndipur, May 2003
18. Jijji, Kanpur, 1997
19. Kamlesh Lata, Kanpur, May 2003
20. Kiran Bharti, Mehndipur, May 2003
21. Krishna Kumari Mathur, N Delhi, 1996
22. Krishna Mohan Saxena, Mehndipur, May 2003
23. Lallan Pehelwan, Kanpur, Jun 2003
24. Madhu (Gulab Bai's daughter), 1997, Dec 2002 and May 2003
25. Mangala, Kanpur, May 2003
26. Meenu, Kanpur, May 2003

27. Mona, Kanpur, May 2003
28. Munni Bai (nee Nanda Devi), Kanpur, Tera Mallu-Balpurva, 1997, Dec 2002 and May 2003
29. Nargis (nee Saira Banu nee Chhoti Helen), Kanpur, May 2003
30. Neetu, Kanpur, 1997
31. Paati Kali, Kanpur, Dec 2002
32. Rajkumar, Kanpur, May 2003
33. Ram Prasad, Kanpur, 1997, May 2003
34. Rashid Joker, Kanpur, Jun 2003
35. Ravi, Tera Mallu, May 2003
36. Saajan, Kanpur, Apr 2003
37. Shaila, Balpurva, May 2003
38. Shiv Adhar Dube, Kanpur, Jul 2003
39. Shanti, Kanpur, Jun 2003
40. Shilpa, Kanpur, May 2003
41. Siddheshwar Awasthi, 1997, Dec 2002
42. Sukhbadan, Kanpur, 1997, May 2003
43. Suraiya, Kanpur, Jun 2003
44. Tilak Raj, Kanpur, 1997
45. Vijay Pandit, Unnao, May 2003

Notes

Part I: Setting the Stage

1. Rashid Khan Warsi, in U.P. Sahitya Natak Akademi Archives, cassette no. 476
2. Interview with K.M. Saxena, Mehndipur, district Fatehgarh, May 2003
3. Interview with Saajan, Kanpur, April 2003
4. Raheja, Dinesh and Kothari, Jitendra, *100 Luminaries of Indian Cinema*, India Book House, Bombay, 1996
5. The Great Gulab Theatre Company collaborated with the NGOs Alaripu and Mahila Manch to produce the play.
6. Interview with Chandrika Prasad 'Nidar', Kanpur, May 2003
7. Numaish—literally, exhibition. Numaishes were like fairs held in different parts of U.P. with craftspeople selling their wares and entertainers performing
8. Bahore, Ravindra Nath, 'Ye Parampara Hamesha Chalti Rahe!: Padmashree Gulab Bai' in Bahore, Ravindra Nath and Pandit, Vijay, eds, *Loknatya Nautanki: Kuchh Prashna*, U.P. Sangeet Natak Akademi, Lucknow, 2000, pp 140-45. The article is based on an interview conducted by Ashok Banerji on 22 December 1986 in the SNA studio, Kaisarbagh, as part of a series of recordings of prominent singers. Gulab Bai also sang a few numbers, accompanied on the nagara by Rashid Khan Warsi, on the harmonium by Ram Prasad and on dholak by Mahesh Prasad. The entire interview is available at the SNA archives, cassette no. 476.

Part II: Gulab's Story

1. See Pushpa, Maitreyi, *Alma Kabutari*, Rajkamal, 2000, pp 126-33 for 'our very own history' recounted by Ram Singh of the Kabutari tribe, M.P. He heard the stories from his mother who heard them from her grandmother who heard them from hers . . .
Alauddin Khilji captured Raja Ratansen of Chittorgarh and threatened to kill him unless his wife Rani Padmini surrendered herself. Rani Padmini and her men engaged in battle with Khilji's soldiers, defeated them and freed Ratansen. However Ratansen was killed in the battle. History books say Padmini committed jauhar—burnt herself at her husband's pyre—but the insiders' history is that she escaped. With a band of maids, courtiers and soldiers she crossed hills and rivers, jungles and settlements. Sultan Khilji sent his men to burn the fields on their path, so they would have no food. To survive, Padmini and her soldiers began looting food and weapons, and attacking Khilji's men. For years these people were on the run. They intermingled amongst themselves and children were born, giving rise to Banjara, Moghiya, Kabutari, Nat, Kalandar, Bedia, Gadiya Lohar and other nomadic tribes/castes. Many were attacked by the British and became hardened rebels. Moving in guerrilla units, hiding in thick jungles, they began attacking British soldiers. The administration put its force behind the effort to capture and torture the guerrillas, and zamindars would tie captured rebels to horses' feet and lash the horses so that they trampled madly over the rebels. After the administration declared all these tribes and castes as 'criminal', large numbers were killed. Those who reached Bundelkhand appealed for shelter with Rani Lakshmi Bai, became her guards, soldiers and maids and helped her escape when attacked by the British. Many were caught by the British and forcibly sent off in ships to be drowned at sea. Yet there were rebels who broke the Sahabs' whips, snapped the gallow ropes.

2. Russell, R.V. and Lal, Hira, Tribes and Castes of Central Provinces of India, Vol 2, Rajdhani Book Depot, Delhi, 1975 (reprint; 1st printed in 1915).
3. Aggrawal, Anuja, *Kinship, Economy and Female Sexuality: A Case Study of Prostitution Among the Bedias*, PhD. thesis, Delhi University, 2002.
4. Khichdi is a food item prepared by mixing rice, lentils and spices. Various vegetables might also be added. It is often used to mean a muddle or a mess—as disparate items are mixed together.
5. Crooke, William, 1896, cited in Aggrawal, op cit: Crooke alluded to taboos on marriage between Bedia men and women. He noted that for Bedias 'in Farrukhabad… if a man marry a girl of the tribe, he is put out of the caste; and in Etawah, if a man marry a girl who has been a prostitute he is obliged to pay a fine.' He added that Bedia men 'take concubines from any fairly respectable class.' A woman would be kidnapped, then the marriage solemnised through a ceremony of presenting her with a suit of clothes and sharing a meal with her family.
6. Taleem means learning or education, while riyaz is used for disciplined practice of an art.
7. De Tassy, Garcin, *Muslim Festivals in India and Other Essays*, O.U.P., New Delhi, 1997 (tr and ed M. Waseem), O.U.P., New Delhi, 1997. Original work: Garcin de Tassy, *Memoire sur des particularites de la religion musulmane dans l'Inde, d'apres les ouvrages hindoustani* (in French), Paris, 1831. De Tassy's quotes above are from Valentia, *Voyages and Voyages de Valentia* [dates not mentioned]; Mir Kazim Ali Jawan, *Bara Masa*,1812; and Mir Shair Ali Afsos, *Araish-I Mahfil*, Calcutta, 1808.
8. There are other conjectural explanations accounting for the term 'Bedia'. It may be from 'beehar' harking back to the time when Bedias lived in thick jungles.
9. Quoted in Suresh Salil's article in the newspaper *Jansatta*, 9.9.1999, based on an interview with Gulab Bai.
10. Nautanki artiste Suraiya, who is Krishna Bai's niece, claimed

Krishna Bai came on the stage before Gulab. Siddheshwar Awasthi agreed this was possible. However there is no way of confirming the truth. I have chosen to go by the dominant version which everybody else holds – that is that Krishna came to the stage a short time after Gulab.

11. Hanne M. de Bruin, 'The Hybrid-Popular Theatre Movement and the Tamil Natakam Theatre' analyses these forms as developing in various part of South Asia during this period, and losing their dominant position with the advent of popular cinema.
12. Hansen, Kathryn, *Grounds for Play: The Nautanki: Theatre of North India,* Manohar, N. Delhi, 1993
13. Salil, *Jansatta,* op. cit.
14. Interview with Chinha Guru, Beeghapur, May 2003
15. Song in Gulab Bai's 33⅓ RPM record, EMI. The rest of the songs in this chapter are from the same record.
16. See Raheja, Gloria Goodwin and Gold, Ann Grodzins, *Listen to the Heron's Words,* OUP, 1996
17. According to Krishna Raghav, Kanpur's HMV dealer said, 'We got five records made. The first ghazal she sang was no. 93022, the second was 93023—*Banaras jai hai na . . .* [he reeled off the names of all eight records.] From the filmi line, Sunil Dutt stole two of our songs —*Moko peehar mein mat chhede* and *Nadi nare* . They gave Bai nothing, just stole her songs. We wanted to fight a court case, but Bai said "No, don't"'.
18. Interview with Chetan Bai, Delhi, 2003
19. Binda Prasad Nigam, Interview, Kanpur, 2003
20. The account of Gulab Bai's last days is based on interviews with Madhu and Asha, and Krishna Raghav's *Ek Thhee Gulab.*

Part III: Nautanki Today

1. Qurraitulain Hyder, translation and commentary, *The Nautch Girl* by Hasan Shah, Sterling, New Delhi, 1992

2. Raheja, Dinesh and Kothari, Jitendra, op. cit.
3. Interview with Asha, 2003: 'Shankar and Shambhu began singing and dancing as boys in Gulab's company. They were very poor and danced for just one paisa. For some time they and their father Chunni Lal lived in our house in Rail Bazaar. Later Shankar and Shambhu went to Bombay and became rich qawwali singers. They asked Amma to send me to Bombay to sing in their team but she didn't send me. Whenever they come to Kanpur to sing in a programme they make sure to visit us.'
4. *Indradhanush*, Volume 5 Issue 7, July 2004, Nehru Centre, Mumbai

References

Bibliography

1. Ahmad-ul-Umri, *The Lady of the Lotus*, tr from Persian by L.M. Crump, Rupa and Co., N. Delhi, 2000
2. Akbar, Khatija, *Madhubala–Her Life, Her Films*, UBS, N. Delhi, 1997
3. Appadorai, Arjun, Frank J. Korom, Margaret A. Mills, eds, *Gender, Genre, and Power in South Asian Expressive Traditions*, Motilal Banarsidass, Delhi, 1993
4. Awasthi, Suresh, *Performance Tradition in India*, National Book Trust, N. Delhi, 2001
5. Bahore, Ravindra Nath and Pandit, Vijay, eds, *Loknatya Nautanki–Kucch Prashna*, U.P. Sangeet Natak Akademi, Lucknow, 2000
6. Bharucha, Rustom, *The Politics of Cultural Practice–Thinking Through Theatre in an Age of Globalisation*, OUP, N. Delhi, 2001
7. Buck, C.H., *Faiths, Fairs and Festivals of India*, Rupa and Co, Delhi, 2002
8. Chaturvedi, Girish, *Tansen*, tr from Hindi by Sarala Jag Mohan, Roli, N. Delhi, 1996
9. Chakravarti, Uma, *Rewriting History–The Life and Times of Pandita Ramabai*, Kali for Women, N. Delhi, 1998
10. Dasi, Binodini, *My Story and My Life As An Actress*, ed and tr from Bengali by Rimli Bhattacharya, Kali for Women, N. Delhi, 1998
11. Devi, Savita and Chauhan, Vibha S., *Maa... Siddheshwari*, Roli, N. Delhi, 2000

12. De Tassy, Garcin, *Muslim Festivals in India and Other Essays*, tr from French and ed by M. Waseem, OUP, Delhi, 1997
13. Eaton, Richard M., *Essays on Islam and Indian History*, OUP, N. Delhi, 2000
14. Erdman, Joan L. with Zohra Segal, *Stages–The Art and Adventures of Zohra Segal*, Kali for Women, N. Delhi, 1997
15. Findly, Ellison Banks, *Nur Jahan–Empress of Mughal India*, OUP, N. Delhi, 2000
16. Gupta, Charu, *Sexuality, Obscenity, Community–Women, Muslims, and the Hindu Public in Colonial India*, Permanent Black, Delhi, 2001
17. Haider, Qurraitulain, *Chandni Begum*, tr Urdu to Hindi by Wahazuddin Alvi, Bharatiya Gyanpeeth, 2001,
18. Hansen, Kathryn, *Grounds for Play–The Nautanki Theatre of North India*, Manohar, 1993, Delhi
19. Kabir, Nasreen Munni, *Guru Dutt–A Life in Cinema*, OUP, N. Delhi, 1997
20. Kale, Kishore Shantabai, *Against All Odds*, tr from Marathi by Sandhya Pandey, Penguin, N. Delhi, 2000
21. Karanth, K. Shivarama, *The Woman of Basrur*, tr from Kannada by H.Y. Sharada Prasad, Ravi Dayal, Delhi, 1997
22. Kendal, Felicity, *White Cargo*, Penguin, N. Delhi, 1998
23. Kumar, Sukrita Paul, *Ismat–Her Life, Her Times*, Katha, N. Delhi, 2000
24. Lakshmi, C.S., *The Singer and the Song–Conversations with Women Musicians*, Kali for Women, 2000
25. Lakshmi, C.S., *Mirrors and Gestures: Conversations with Women Dancers*, Kali for Women, 2003
26. Mayaram, Shail, *Resisting Regimes–Myth, Memory and the Shaping of A Muslim Identity*, OUP, N. Delhi, 1997
27. Menon, Raghava R., *The Penguin Dictionary of Indian Classical Music*, Penguin, N. Delhi, 1995
28. Mukta, Parita, *Upholding the Common Life: the Community of Mirabai*, OUP, Delhi, 1994
29. Nadkarni, Mohan, *Bal Gandharva–The Nonpareil Thespian*, National Book Trust, N. Delhi, 1988

30. Narayan, Shovana, *Rhythmic Echoes and Reflections – Kathak*, Roli, N. Delhi, 1998
31. Parkes, Fanny, *Begums, Thugs and Englishmen–The Journals of Fanny Parkes*, selected and introduced by William Dalrymple, Penguin, N. Delhi, 2002
32. Pinto, Jerry, *Helen: The Life and Times of an H-Bomb*, Penguin, New Delhi, 2006
33. Poitevin, Guy, *The Voice and the Will–Subaltern Agency: Forms and Motives*, Manohar and Centre de Sciences Humaines, N. Delhi, 2002
34. Pukhraj, Malka, *Song Sung True–A Memoir*, tr from Urdu by Saleem Kidwai, Kali for Women, N. Delhi, 2003
34. Pushpa, Maitreyi, *Alma Kabutari*, Rajkamal, N. Delhi, 2000
36. Pushpa, Maitreyi, *Kahi Isuri Phag*, Rajkamal, N. Delhi, 2004
37. Racine, Josiane and Jean-Luc Racine, *Viramma: Life of a Dalit*, tr Will Hobson, Social Science Press, New Delhi, 2000
38. Raheja, Dinesh and Kothari, Jitendra, *100 Luminaries of Hindi Cinema*, India Book House, Bombay, 1996
39. Raheja, Gloria Goodwin, *Songs, Stories, Lives–Gendered Dialogues and Cultural Critique*, Kali for Women, N. Delhi, 2003
40. Raheja, Gloria Goodwin and Ann Grodzins Gold, *Listen to the Heron's Words–Reimagining Gender and Kinship in North India*, OUP, 1996
41. Rahman, Sukanya, *Dancing in the Family–An Unconventional Memoir of Three Women*, Harper Collins, N. Delhi, 2001
42. Ranade, Ashok Da., *Hindustani Music*, National Book Trust, N. Delhi, 1997
43. Saeed, Fauzia, *Kalank!–Red Light Ilakon ki Gopan Sanskriti* tr Urdu to Hindi by Hemant, Books for Change, N. Delhi, 2004
44. Sen, Geeti, ed, *Crossing Boundaries*, Orient Longman, Hyderabad, 1997
45. Sen, Geeti, *Feminine Fables - Imaging the Indian Woman in Painting, Photography and Cinema*, Mapin, Ahmedabad, 2002
46. Shah, Hasan, *The Nautch Girl–A Novel*, tr Urdu-Persian to English by Qurraitulain Hyder, Sterling, N. Delhi, 1992

47. Sobti, Krishna, *Dilo Daanish*, Rajkamal, N. Delhi, 1997
48. Spivak, Gayatri Chakravorty, *In Other Worlds–Essays In Cultural Politics*, Methuen, New York, 1987
49. Temple, R. C., *The Legends of the Panjab, Vols 1 and 2*, Intro by Kartar Singh Duggal, Rupa and Co., Delhi, 2002
50. Thapar, Romila, *Sakuntala–Texts, Readings, Histories*, Kali for Women, N. Delhi, 1999
51. Vaudeville, Charlotte, *A Weaver Named Kabir–Selected Verses, with A Detailed Biographical and Historical Introduction*, OUP, N. Delhi, 1993
52. Wenner, Dorothee, *Fearless Nadia*, Penguin, N. Delhi, 2005

Articles, Chapters, Theses

1. Aggrawal, Anuja, *Kinship, Economy and Famale Sexuality: A Case Study of Prostitution among the Bedias*, unpublished Ph.D. thesis, Dept of Sociology, Delhi University, 2002
2. Agnihotri, Anju, 'Dhrupad Dhamal ki Malika Asgari Bai se Mulakat', *Kala Vasudha*, Oct 2002-Mar 2003
3. Agrawal, Pratibha, 'Fida Hussain ki Parsi Rang-Yatra: Fida Hussain ki hee Zubaan Se', *Chhayanat*, Apr-Jun 2000
4. Bruin, Hanne M., 'The Hybrid-popular Theatre Movement and the Tamil Natakam Theatre', unpublished article, International Institute for Asian Studies, Leiden, the Netherlands
5. Dutt, Nirupama 'Nautanki ki Bai', *Indian Express*, 8.7.1999
6. Hansen, Kathryn, 'Stri Bhumika: Female Impersonators and Actresses on the Parsi Stage', *Economic and Political Weekly*, 29.8.1998
7. *Indradhanush*, Volume 5 Issue 7, July 2004, Nehru Centre, Mumbai
8. Jain, Shanti, 'Tu Nandlal Sada Man Kapati', *U.P. Dalit Sahitya Visheshank*, Sept-Oct 2002
9. Mehrotra, Deepti Priya, 'Can Umed Khan Be Meera Bai?', *Women's Feature Service*, 1997
10. Mehrotra, Deepti Priya, 'Journeys With Khayal', unpublished Alaripu report, 1997

11. Mishra, Sheokesh, 'The Tragedy in the Script', *India Today*, 13.10.2003
12. Narain, Uma, 'Resurrecting the Mother in "Mata Hidimba", *Economic and Political Weekly*, 26.4.2003
13. Narayan, Badri, 'Heroes, Histories and Booklets', *Economic and Political Weekly*, 13.10.2001
14. Pandey, Mrinal, 'Women in Indian Theatre: From Bharat Muni and Bharat Vani to Bharat that is India Today", in Karuna Chanana, ed, *Socialisation, Education and Women*, Orient Longman, New Delhi, 1981
15. Pandit, Vijay, 'Gunda Pada Hai Mere Peechhe Hero Honda Lekar urf Kaise Bachegi Nautanki', *Madai*, 2000
16. Pandit, Vijay, 'Loknatya Nautanki aur Bharatiya Svadheenta Andolan', unpublished article, 2003
17. Raghav, Krishna, 'Ek Thhee Gulab', *Rang Prasang*, Jan-June 2000, pp 19–42
18. Rao, Vidya, 'On Thumri', in Nivedita Menon, ed, *Gender and Politics in India*, OUP, N. Delhi, 1999
19. Rege, Sharmila, 'Conceptualising Popular Culture—Lavani and Powda in Maharashtra', *Economic and Political Weekly*, 16.2.2002
20. Salil, Suresh, 'Gulab Bai', *Jansatta*, 9-9-1990
21. Sen, Sibu, 'The Show is Over, The Show Must Go On', *Hindu*, 9.10.1992
22. Swann, Darius L. 1990, 'Introduction to the Folk-Popular Traditions' in Richmond, Farley P., Darius L. Swann and Phillip B. Zarilli, eds, *Indian Theatre: Traditions of Performance*, Honolulu: University of Hawaii Press, 1990, pp. 239–247

Nautanki Script Books (all published by Shrikrishna Khattri Pustakalaya)

1. *Aankh ka Jadu urf Nakli Sadhu*, 1989 (79th reprint)
2. *Akbar Kunwar*, 1989 (19th reprint)

3. *Alam Ara*, 1989 (34th reprint)
4. *Alha Manaua urf Gajmotin Sati*, 1996 (60th reprint)
5. *Amarsingh Rathore urf Hindu Musalman ka Yarana*, 1995 (60th reprint)
6. *Bahadur Ladki urf Aurat ka Pyar*, 1998 (64th reprint)
7. *Bansuri Vali*, 1996 (60th reprint)
8. *Bauna Chor ka Byah*, 2003 (2nd reprint)
9. *Bhakt Prahlad*, 1997 (61st reprint)
10. *Bichitra Dhokhebaaj*, 1990 (29th reprint)
11. *Daku Hasina*, 1997 (63rd reprint)
12. *Dhool ka Phool urf Mohabbat ki Bhool*, 1996 (61st reprint)
13. *Dhruv Charitra*, 1997 (61st reprint)
14. *Dost Dushman*, 1996 (61st reprint)
15. *Garib ki Duniya*, 1995 (60th reprint)
16. *Gulbadan urf Jannat ki Shaadi*, 1997 (61st reprint)
17. *Laila Majnu, 1998 (60th reprint)*
18. *Laakhan ka Gauna*, 2002
19. *Madau ki Ladai*, 1996 (61st reprint)
20. *Mohabbat ki Putli*, 1995 (60th reprint)
21. *Mughal-e-Azam*, 1989 (61st reprint)
22. *Pati Bhakt*, 1994 (60th reprint)
23. *Puranmal*, 1996 (61st reprint)
24. *Raja Harishchandra*, 1998 (63rd reprint)
25. *Roop Basant*, 1996 (61st reprint)
26. *Satyavadi Harishchandra*, 1995 (64th reprint)
27. *Shankargarh Sangram*, 1996 (61st reprint)
28. *Shanki Lakad-hara*, 1995 (64th reprint)
29. *Shravan Kumar*, 1996 (61st reprint)
30. *Shrimati Manjari*, 1996 (60th reprint)
31. *Singaldvip ki Ladai*, 2003 (65th reprint)
32. *Sultana Daku*, 1995 (62nd reprint)
33. *Triya Charitra*, 1989
34. *Veer Abhimanyu*, 1996 (52nd reprint)
35. *Veer Vikramaditya*, 2003 (48th reprint)

Nautanki Drama Performances

1. *Teen Betiyan urf Dehleez ke Paar*, by the Great Gulab Theatre Company and Alaripu, 1997, Garadiyapurva, Kanpur and some other venues in and around Kanpur
2. *Akhtari Bai*, dance-drama by Rita Ganguli, staged at India Habitat Centre, 2002
3. *Amar Singh Rathore*, staged at Chamber Theatre, Triveni Kala Sangam, New Delhi, 2003

Records, Cassettes, Audio-visuals, Films and Posters

1. *Gulab Bai*, Long Play 33⅓ R.P.M. Gramophone Record, Gulab Bai songs, the Gramophone Company of India Ltd, one of the EMI group of companies, Dum Dum
2. Recorded interview with Gulab Bai, cassette no. 476, Uttar Pradesh Sangeet Natak Akademi, Lucknow
3. Audio-visual recording of *Dahiwali*, by Great Gulab Theatre Company, Sangeet Natak Akademi, New Delhi
4. Recorded interview with Rashid Khan Warsi, cassette no. 476, Uttar Pradesh Sangeet Natak Akademi, Lucknow
5. Audio-visual recording of *Bahadur Ladki urf Aurat ka Pyar*, AIR-Doordarshan, New Delhi
6. Gramophone record, *Amar Singh Rathore*, Sangeet Natak Akademi, New Delhi
7. Gramophone record, *Indarharan*, Sangeet Natak Akademi, New Delhi
8. *Teesri Kasam*, film by Raj Kapoor 1966
9. *Umrao Jaan*, film by Muzaffar Ali
10. Poster advertising 'Nautanki' by Dreamgirl Shilpa, 2003, Mumbai

Material from the Internet

1. Advertisement for *Ajuba Dance and Drama Company*, Centre for South Asia, University of Wisconsin-Madison
2. 'Nautanki 2003', *The Mirror Has Two Hands,* Society of Indian Scholars, National University of Singapore
3. *Indradhanush—the Rainbow of Indian Folk Arts*, Nehru Centre Auditorium, Mumbai